Escaping Perfect

Escaping Perfect

EMMA HARRISON

Simon Pulse
New York London Toronto Sydney New Delhi

This book is a work of fiction. Any references to historical events, real people, or real places are used fictitiously. Other names, characters, places, and events are products of the author's imagination, and any resemblance to actual events or places or persons, living or dead, is entirely coincidental.

SIMON PULSE
An imprint of Simon & Schuster Children's Publishing Division
1230 Avenue of the Americas, New York, New York 10020
First Simon Pulse hardcover edition March 2016

Jacket designed by Karina Granda
Interior designed by Tom Daly
The text of this book was set in Adobe Caslon Pro.
Manufactured in the United States of America
2 4 6 8 10 9 7 5 3 1
Library of Congress Cataloging-in-Publication Data
Harrison, Emma.
Escaping perfect / by Emma Harrison. — First Simon Pulse hardcover edition.
pages cm
Summary: To escape her extremely sheltered life, eighteen-year-old Cecilia grabs a chance to strike out on her own in Sweetbriar, Tennessee, where she is transformed by her first job, apartment, and love but always waits for her mother, a U.S. Senator, to find her.
[1. Runaways—Fiction. 2. Identity—Fiction. 3. Dating (Social customs)—Fiction. 4. Family problems—Fiction. 5. Tennessee—Fiction.] I. Title.
PZ7.H2485Esc 2016
[Fic]—dc23
2015001539
ISBN 978-1-4814-4212-1 (hc)
ISBN 978-1-4814-4214-5 (eBook)

For Mama Bean

Chapter One

"Senator Montgomery! Senator Montgomery! Roll down the window! Just for a second! Senator Montgomery!"

There was a bang and a shout—some photog getting so close to the limo that he tripped and slammed his camera into the side of the car—and so the most hellish part of my day from hell truly began.

The rest of the paparazzi crowded around the limousine's tinted windows as it eased through the wrought-iron gates of the South Palm Memorial Cemetery. They couldn't see me or my mom and dad, would only go home with pictures of their own cameras' reflections. But that didn't stop them. Nothing ever stopped them. Some people made a living just by selling whatever pictures they could get of our family. And now the one unfamous person in my world had died, and of course the photographers were still here, clamoring for shots of the living.

Sometimes I really wished their cameras would spontaneously combust in their faces. But only when I was feeling truly pissed at the world. Like now.

"Five minutes, Cecilia," my mother said tersely, glancing up from her tablet to check her Cartier watch. "We have to get this show on the road. I have a briefing at three."

I felt my father's body go rigid, even with him sitting clear on the other side of the limo.

It's Gigi's funeral, I thought bitterly. *You couldn't take one day off?*

What I said was, "Yes, ma'am."

Outside the windows, rows of white and gray headstones stretched into the distance for what seemed like miles. It was all so anonymous. My grandmother didn't belong here, camouflaged by the dreary sameness. She belonged someplace special.

My mom's eyes narrowed. "Don't take that tone with your mother."

The great Rebecca Montgomery, aka dear old Mom, loved to refer to herself in the third person. Ever since I was a toddler, it was:

Look, Cecilia, Mommy's on TV!

Mommy will only be gone for three weeks, but don't worry. Miss Jessica will take care of you!

No, no! Mommy can't hug you right now. This suit is couture.

Yeah. The word "maternal" was not in her vocabulary.

"It's not as if I can take the time off right now," she added, reading my mind. "Not when there's so much work to do."

Of course there was. It was an election year. Nothing was more all-consuming for my mother than an election year.

She huffed out a breath and placed the tablet aside, opening a compact to check her perfectly bobbed chestnut-brown hair.

"I still don't understand why we had to fly all the way down here to this godforsaken swamp for her funeral when we have a perfectly beautiful burial plot back in Beacon Hill."

"Because my mother lived *here*," my father said, still staring out the window. "She wanted to be buried *here*. You never gave her anything she wanted in life, Rebecca; you'd think you could at least give her this."

"Oh. So I see everyone's ganging up on me today." My mother clicked the compact closed and shoved it back into her black Birkin bag. She had a right to be surprised. My father, a high-powered defense attorney for Boston's wealthiest residents, usually saved all argumentative tones for the courtroom. I hardly ever heard him raise his voice or even snipe at my mom, unless it was from behind very firmly closed doors. "It wasn't entirely my fault that Maura and I didn't get along. She did play a hand in it, you know."

"But she's still Dad's mom," I said quietly. "And my grandmother. And we're never going to see her again."

You could at least pretend to be sad.

My mother sighed her impatient sigh. "Cecilia . . ."

"Mom, please," I said, my voice shaky. "Could you maybe not be a bitch right now? Just for today?"

My left cheek exploded in pain. I didn't even see my mother move until she was settling back into her seat across from mine, tucking the hand that had just slapped me into her purse.

My left eye prickled over with purple and gray spots. I brought my quaking fingers to my cheek.

"Was that really necessary?" my father asked.

I blinked, surprised he'd even bothered. He'd never said anything to her the many other times she'd smacked me.

"Stay out of it," she growled at him.

My father clenched his jaw and looked out the window. Mother tugged down on her suit jacket and glared at me. "How dare you?"

It had been a long time since she'd hit me. Possibly because I had hardly seen her for more than an hour or two here and there over the past two years. Maybe I hadn't had time to piss her off enough. But now? On the day we were burying my grandmother?

"Gigi was my best friend," I muttered to the door, turning the stinging side of my face away from her. "Just leave me alone."

"What was that? If you're going to speak, at least enunciate," my mother said.

I sat up straight, trying very hard not to tremble. "I said, Gigi was my best friend. And she was more like a mother to me than you've *ever* been."

My mom made an indignant noise at the back of her throat. "I should throw you right out of this car, young lady."

"Like you'd ever do that," I shot back. "You'd rather die than let me see the light of day."

I hadn't even been allowed to go out for my eighteenth birthday last month. Instead my mother—or rather, her assistant, Tash—had sent me a gift at boarding school, but she hadn't otherwise acknowledged it. No call, no text, no e-mail. Just a hand-delivered box from Tiffany containing an ugly ladybug pendant I immediately donated to my graduating class's silent charity auction.

I crossed my arms and sat back, but the huge bun her stylist had fashioned out of my mane of curls held my skull away from the headrest at an uncomfortable angle. My irritation spiked. Even though I was sitting here declaring my ability to be my own person, I'd spent the entire day letting her order me around as always.

I said the Kenneth Cole, Cecilia, not the Calvin Klein.

Take off that god-awful lip color. Did you pick that yourself? When was the last time we had your eyes checked?

And then, when she'd seen my hair hanging loose around my shoulders: *I'll have Felicia come take care of you next. How you deal with all that hair, I have no idea.*

And what had I said all morning long? "Yes, ma'am."

Sometimes I really loathed myself. I should have asked her how she dealt with having a stick up her butt all the time.

Of course, my hair wasn't the only thing about me that my mother couldn't wrap her brain around, but it wasn't surprising, considering her hair had always been tame and shiny and cut above the chin. I had inherited her skinny bones and angular face, and my dad's extreme height and dark curly hair—though he kept his almost entirely shaved. My skin color was all my own, somewhere between his dark chocolate and her milky white. I pushed my butt all the way back so I could straighten my posture, barely containing the urge to rip out the three hundred bobby pins stabbing me in the skull.

"Please, Cecilia," my mother said with a derisive chuckle.

"If you want us to treat you like an adult, you should stop moping like a child."

My face burned.

"We're here," my father said gruffly. "Five minutes, Cecilia."

Of course he was agreeing with her timeline. He always agreed with everything she said. Which is how I'd ended up with her last name instead of his. But I felt suddenly too exhausted to argue anymore.

The mound of dirt and the casket on its metal lift were situated about three rows in from the car. My grandmother's grave site sat beneath the shade of a huge weeping willow. She would have loved it, and the thought brought fresh tears to my eyes.

I stepped shakily out of the car. It was stiflingly hot and humid.

My mother's security team sat on alert in the Town Car behind ours along with Tim "the Tank" Thompson, the former pro wrestler who had followed me around for the past ten years. I sensed their eyes on me as I slipped my sunglasses on and walked over to the grave site, alone, feeling oddly exposed without Tim there as my shadow. But he'd been told, I was sure, that I was to have these five minutes.

Because my mother refused to let anyone ever get a glimpse of me, I would not be allowed out of the limo during the actual service and burial later. Ever since I was eight years old and a man named Scott Smith had attempted to kidnap me for ransom, my mother had kept me on a short leash. Well, more like locked up in a cage and transported from place to place only by heavily armed professionals.

It was why I had spent the past ten years cloistered behind the brick walls of the Worthington School, where no camera phones were allowed and every student signed a confidentiality clause. Why I'd never seen the inside of a movie theater or a Starbucks or a commercial airport. Why I'd spent every summer trapped in our house on Martha's Vineyard with a team of tennis coaches, academic tutors, and etiquette experts grooming me for the day I'd emerge from the suffocating cocoon in which I'd spent most of my life.

Suffocating like the starched jacket of the black suit I'd been forced to wear, which now itched at the back of my neck under the glare of the sun as I approached the grave. The length of the pencil skirt—just above the knee—clamped my legs together and made my steps small and awkward in my black kitten heels. I finally came up alongside the white coffin and lost my breath, imagining Gigi inside. Instead I trained my eyes on the sky as blue as cornflower and dotted with white clouds. I wanted to say the right thing. Tell her how much she'd meant to me. But she knew all that. And the first words that came spilling out of my mouth weren't so much a grateful homage as a selfish plea.

"How am I supposed to do this?" I asked, my voice cracking. Sudden, hot tears streamed from the corners of my eyes. "How am I supposed to do this without you?"

It was all I could think to say. Then I bowed my head forward, covered my face with my hands, and wept.

An hour later, it was all over. At least a hundred friends and family members stood alongside her grave while the pastor spoke and my father and his sister cried and my mother's lip wobbled dramatically.

Our driver stood under the shade of a palm tree alongside the car, which was parked at the front of a winding line of limos and Town Cars awaiting their passengers. He watched the proceedings while I stared through the window, open half a centimeter so that I might catch a stray word. My face and eyes were dry, my skin itching from the tears I'd shed earlier. And the longer I watched, the angrier I felt.

The whole thing was a sham. My parents hadn't even told my grandmother's real friends where she was being buried. This was not about her. It was about my mother. The senator. The glamorous Senator Montgomery, fourth child of Jack and Marianne Montgomery and niece of former vice president Frederick Montgomery. Currently, my mother was the highest-profile Montgomery in the country with her ascension to the US Senate, and she had no intention of stopping there. She had turned my grandmother's funeral into a networking party.

Finally the flowers were strewn, the dirt was tossed, and those in attendance were saying their good-byes. I sat up straighter as my parents approached the waiting cars, my father supporting my mother as if she were the one suffering.

I steeled myself for round two, but my parents and their entourage of bodyguards slipped between parked cars and walked up a slight incline on the other side of the roadway. I had to turn around and crane my neck to see where they were going. The driver moved away from the car to join the rest of the security team. They stopped at a spot atop a grassy knoll near the brick fence that surrounded the cemetery grounds. I saw Tim find a position midway up the hill. My father stood just behind my mother's right shoulder. Always, always, he stood behind her.

"We'd like to thank you all for coming and showing your respect for my husband's late mother, *our* late mother, really," my mom began, her hair shimmering in the sun. "One of the great matriarchs of our family."

Bile. I tasted actual bile. Matriarch? *Our* mother? My mother had treated Gigi like crap. Any overtures from my father's mother were swept under the rug. Any offers of advice or assistance were scoffed at. How dare she get up there and act like Gigi had meant something to her?

"Maura also meant a good deal to our daughter, Cecilia," my mother continued, gazing down at the car. "The two of them had a special relationship, and for that we will always be grateful."

My fingernails dug into the flesh of my palms. I was sweating under my arms and along my upper lip. She was such a liar. Such a fraud. And I hated her. I hated what she'd done to my life. I'd never had a boyfriend or even a real friend. Never been allowed to invite anyone to my house, go to a regular party or out to a concert. I was hardly even a functioning human being.

Heat crept up my neck as my heart pounded out of control. I unbuttoned the suit jacket and yanked the tight sleeves from my arms, straining my shoulder muscles in the process. It didn't help. I couldn't breathe. I needed air. I had to get out of there. I had to.

My hand fumbled for the door handle, but then I froze. If just one member of the paparazzi happened to turn their head, they would be on me like starving crows on roadkill. I wouldn't get two feet from the car before the security detail easily caught up with me and tossed me back inside.

My eyes darted around the confines of the limo as my pulse raced and raced and raced. Suddenly I felt a cool breeze on my ankles and realized that the air-conditioning was blowing. The car was running. I turned and glanced at the ignition. There dangled the keys.

Without thinking, I got on my knees and shoved myself through the open window that divided the driver's seat from the rest of the car. Within seconds I was behind the wheel—thank God the Tank convinced my mom that my learning to drive was necessary for my safety. The crowd was at least six or seven cars behind me to the left, eyes and lenses riveted on the senator. There was nothing in front of me but open road.

I clicked the car into drive, put my hands on the wheel, and pressed my foot down on the gas pedal.

I had been on the road for fifteen minutes when my phone began to ring, but I refused to look at the screen. I gripped the steering wheel with slick fingers, hardly able to take a full breath. But even in all my panic and elation and terror and sadness, my logical side was still functioning, and it was telling me that the cops were going to be on me in about thirteen seconds. A scrawny black girl behind the wheel of a stretch limo with livery plates? *That* was something people were going to notice.

I had to get off this highway. But where the hell was I supposed to go?

I had barely asked myself the question when a sign appeared before me. An actual sign for Everglades National Park. Gigi used to take me there every December 26 for a picnic at a secluded spot near the water. No one would ever look for me there, and there were enough trees to hide the limo, even if my mother somehow got NASA to train a satellite on the area. Which she could totally do.

I just had to find the right turnoff once I got inside the park area. Then maybe I could stop for a while, give myself some time to think, figure out what I was going to do next. I eased the limo off the road.

A few drivers peered curiously out at me as they blew by in the other direction. I noticed that the driver had left his black hat on the passenger seat, and I jammed it down on top of my hair. Not the greatest disguise in the world, but better than nothing.

More signs pointed off to various sections of the park. Fishing piers, wildlife preserves, designated water sports areas. Finally, I found what I was looking for: an old, chipped sign that read PICNIC GROUNDS with a red sticker slapped across it—CLOSED. I ignored that, just like my grandmother always had. I almost laughed, remembering how her irreverence had stressed me out, how I'd spend the first half hour of any picnic worried that we were going to get caught. Never the rule breaker, and now I was breaking every rule in the book.

As soon as I turned onto the packed dirt road, the trees and undergrowth bent in around me. High above, the canopy of leaves blocked out the sun, and long green grasses swished against the sides of the car. I eased my foot off the gas and realized that my ankle hurt from being in the same tense position for so long. Finally I found myself able to breathe. Able to think.

What the hell was I doing?

Did I really think that this stunt would prove anything? That I could escape my mother? No, in fact, I didn't. When I'd crawled through that window, I hadn't been thinking at all. I'd been working on instinct, hopped up on emotion. I had wanted to get away, plain and simple. I'd seen my chance and I'd taken it.

The question was, what to do now? I took a deep breath and considered my situation. I had a ton of cash in my backpack—the bag I never left home without—from the tutoring services I offered at school. Okay, the flat-out writing-papers-for-other-kids business I'd been lucratively running behind Tim's back for the past five years. Most of the money was hidden under a floorboard in my room back home in Boston, where I made deposits every break, but I'd brought my latest haul—about two thousand dollars—with me, in case the school did one of its random sweeps while I was away at the funeral. If I could just get somewhere, somewhere off the grid, maybe I could really and truly be free.

I came to the end of the road and hit the brakes. The car stopped soundlessly. Fingers trembling, I shoved the gearshift into park. Before me was the bog where Gigi and I had picnicked just this past December. Where we'd tossed out a couple of lines and sat munching on cold fried chicken, not catching anything and not caring. I'd leaned my head against her shoulder and we'd daydreamed about going to Europe together. We'd talked about how once I turned eighteen, I could do anything I wanted, I could escape, and she'd be here to do it with me.

Except that she wasn't. Thanks to one tiny blood clot, she was gone.

I leaned back in the seat and cried. I cried in total earnest and abandon in a way I hadn't since Tash had called me to tell me Gigi had passed. For the first time in forever, I was truly and completely alone, no bodyguard hovering, no driver or personal assistant or tutor listening in. I cried with everything I had in me.

And by the time I stopped, I had a plan. By the time I stopped, I knew I wasn't ever going back.

Chapter Two

Lia Washington. My name is Lia Washington. Hi! I'm Lia Washington.

The fingers on my left hand twitched atop my knee the following morning as I sat on the edge of my seat on the half-empty bus. It was an old habit from when I played the violin as a kid. I used to stay up nights, fingering scales and concertos under the covers, hearing the notes inside my head. I hadn't touched a violin in four years, but my fingers still remembered everything, and considering my current freak-out level, they were twitching like crazy.

It took some concentration, but I stilled them. *Lia Washington,* I thought calmly. *That's my name.* I'd chosen my grandmother's maiden name, and I knew she'd approve.

Outside the window, the green hills of Tennessee rolled

by; horses raced across an open field in the distance. It was all so peaceful, a serious contrast to the pounding of my pulse. I couldn't believe I was here. I couldn't believe I was doing this. I'd daydreamed about this moment my entire life—the day I would finally break free. When I was nine, I'd envisioned a distant foreign princess cousin swooping in to bring me back to her castle. Around age thirteen, I'd devised a plan to break out of Worthington and hire someone off Craigslist to pick me up and race me across the country to California, where I'd spill my secrets to a filmmaker, become an instant millionaire, and file for emancipated-minor status. Of course, I'd never truly believed any of those plans were plausible. And now, here I was. Without a plan. And it had somehow worked.

For now, anyway. How long would it be before my parents or their security team or the FBI found me? What would they do to me when they did?

My fingers were twitching again, and now they started to shake. I had to get a grip. I reached up to crack the window and let the scent of fresh, wet earth fill my lungs. For half a second the panicked rate of my heart slowed.

You're doing the right thing. For the first time in your entire life, you're free.

"Lia Washington," I whispered, trying to make them sound like words I'd said every day, forever. "I'm Lia Washington."

The bus's brakes squealed, and I almost threw myself into the aisle, ready to run. But when I looked back, there were no police cars, no black vans bearing down on the bus. We'd simply come to a stop sign.

"Pull it together, Cecilia," I muttered under my breath, sitting back again. I wasn't even going to make it one day if I was this on edge.

But I couldn't stop thinking about it. What was my mother doing right now? My father? Had they found the limo at the bottom of the bog yet? My crushed and drowned cell phone? Did they realize I'd run away, or did they think I'd been kidnapped again?

My mother was probably frantic, trying to deal with the press and figure out what her official statement would be. And Dad . . . well, I'd be surprised if he even noticed I was gone.

A lump welled in my throat, but I swallowed it down. I'd long since adjusted to the fact that my family didn't actually care about me as a person, didn't care to know who I really was or love me for it. There was no reason for me to get all sentimental about it now, when I didn't have to think about it anymore. In fact, if everything went as planned, I'd never have to think about it again.

We hit a bump in the road, and when I looked up, I was

staring at the big, white sign with its scrolling green letters—WELCOME TO SWEETBRIAR, TENNESSEE, POP. 5698—as it slipped by the window. My exhausted heart fluttered with excitement. Make that 5699.

I sat forward as, within seconds, the buildings of downtown rushed by. This was it. I was home.

I had only been to Sweetbriar once before, when I was six years old and Gigi had brought me here to visit with her best friend, Daria, and her grandson Jasper, who was two years older than me. It had only been for a couple of days, but the place had made an impression, and everything was exactly as I remembered it. The clapboard storefronts. The fat, pink blooms on the magnolia trees bobbing in the light breeze, casting shade over the brick-lined sidewalks. I gripped the back of the seat in front of me, scanning the stores for Daria's place. I hoped it was still here. Please, please let it still be here.

Daria had a salon on Main with an apartment above where she and Jasper lived. It had been the home base for the best two days of my life. Gigi and Daria had taken the two of us kids to a park nearby, where we'd been allowed to climb trees and jump from monkey bars and eat peanut butter sandwiches without first making use of the hazmat kit my mom always kept in her bag.

I had never felt so free.

The bus screeched to a stop at a small bus shelter—a pretty white structure with a green shingled roof—and I held my breath until the noise died down. Then, shouldering my battered backpack, I shakily made my way down the aisle and out into the sunshine, into my new life.

I froze.

Up until this very moment, my goal had been to get to Sweetbriar and find a job and a place to stay. But now that I was here, staring at Main Street, the panicked questions I'd been trying to ignore crashed to the front of my mind, demanding to be heard.

What if I couldn't find a job that didn't require me to share a social security number or a valid ID? The ones I had belonged to the daughter of the senator from the great state of Massachusetts. The second somebody typed my digits into a computer, I was toast. How long would my two thousand dollars last me? Truth be told, I had no clue what rent or food or anything else cost. Would it last me a month, a week, a day? My palms started to sweat in the awful way they did back at school every time someone had knocked on my dorm-room door. How could I have ever thought this was going to work?

"Hiya!"

I flinched and turned around, instinctively tugging my hood forward to hide more of my face. I was greeted by the wide, toothy smile of a bottle-ginger grandma in a floral dress and cowboy boots, pushing a stroller as she walked by.

"Welcome to Sweetbriar, hon!" she said with a nod.

In my entire life no stranger had ever said hello to me out of nowhere, possibly because I had never been allowed to encounter actual strangers. Even though I didn't answer, she kept right on smiling and walking, her stride wide and purposeful. I glanced into the stroller and found a little pink pig in a bow tie staring up at me. I swear it scoffed when it caught my eye.

A door across the street opened, releasing a burst of piano music as two girls my age spilled out in full-on cotillion dresses, looking back over their shoulders like they were being chased. They ducked into Hadley's Drugs next door, giggling, just as a pack of guys chugged by in an old red pickup, two of them hanging in the back, singing at the top of their lungs to the country music that blared from inside.

Clearly, the people-watching in this town was going to be distraction enough.

I took a deep breath and let it out.

"It's okay," I told myself, trying as hard as I could to believe it. "Everything's going to be okay."

Slowly I let the hood fall off my hair, looked both ways, then crossed the street. Daria's was somewhere on the far side of Main, facing the park. I wasn't sure whether I'd even go in. If Daria recognized me, the jig would be up before it even started. But I wanted to know it was there—that she was there. As a safety net, I guess. I needed to know that if I screwed it all up, I'd have somewhere to turn.

"Morning!"

A middle-aged man with a black beard to his navel tipped his cowboy hat at me. I managed a small smile back. His eyes flicked over my outfit, and I self-consciously tugged up the zipper on my hoodie, hoping he hadn't noticed the swipe of blood on the white shirt underneath. After I'd used that rock to weigh down the gas pedal and put the car in drive, it had moved a lot faster than I'd thought it would, and I'd scraped my stomach pretty badly trying to get out before it submerged itself in the water. At present I was sporting a mud-stained black skirt and blood-spattered white shirt and the blue Hilfiger hoodie I kept in my bag. I'd be lucky if I wasn't run off the street. Or arrested.

Keeping my head down, I shakily tucked my hair behind my ears. Clothes. I was definitely going to need some clothes. Where was a Target or a Walmart when you needed it? But I shouldn't have been surprised. Sweetbriar wasn't the big-box-chain type of place.

Suddenly a girl on a bike came careening around the

corner and almost mowed me down. She had a guitar strapped to her back and black-painted fingernails, and she wore a white football helmet instead of a bicycle version. I yelped and jumped backward, colliding with the window of Hadley's.

"Sorry, miss!" the kid shouted as she tore down the street.

I covered my eyes with one hand. I couldn't do this. I couldn't. How could I ever have thought I could? Thanks to my effing mother, I was a total basket case. *Maybe* if she hadn't hidden me away in a maximum-security private school for the past ten years I would be able to, I don't know, walk down a damn street in broad daylight without having a panic attack. God, I hated her. I hated her for turning me into this skittish loner freak with few friends and no life and no future.

Trembling from head to toe, I tried to look around, tried to focus, but everything seemed blurry. I needed to calm down. I needed to get a grip, and fast.

"You okay, miss?"

I let out a yelp and staggered back a step or two. A dark-skinned man wearing a crisp white apron over a bright-orange button-down leaned out the door of Hadley's.

"I'm sorry. Didn't mean to spook ya," he said, holding up a steadying hand. "Why don't you come inside for a second? You look like you could use a sit-down."

Through the plate-glass window I saw the cotillion girls sitting at an old-school ice cream counter, perched on vinyl stools as they ate from silver dishes. Even in the midst of my nervous breakdown, my stomach grumbled. The only thing I'd had all day was the granola bar I'd bought from a vending machine at the bus's last pit stop. I was about to take him up on the offer—maybe food would help chill me out—when something caught my eye, and my heart dropped to the sidewalk.

On the ground outside the drugstore was a stack of newspapers held down by a half a brick. Peeking out from underneath the end of that brick was a curly brown pigtail held by a big red bow. I recognized that bow.

Holding my breath, I crouched to the ground and picked up the brick. There was my smiling eight-year-old face, big gap where my two front teeth should have been, my plaid pinafore tight over my starched white shirt as I posed in front of the standard school-pic backdrop of faux bookcases. My skin looked darker, and with the grainy print my dark green eyes appeared brown somehow, but it was me. The headline read: KIDNAPPED! DAUGHTER OF AMERICA'S FAMILY PLUCKED FROM GRANDMOTHER'S FUNERAL.

Well. At least they didn't think I'd run away. Although why that should make me feel better, I had no idea. Maybe because my default setting was to avoid defying my mother at all costs. But this way they weren't looking for a runaway. They were looking for a criminal, maybe waiting for a ransom note. Somehow I felt like this was a positive development. My fingers itched to grab the paper and read the whole article. Had they found the car? My phone? Did they have any supposed leads? But the man from Hadley's was watching me closely, and I couldn't seem to make myself move.

If I held this picture of eight-year-old me too close to my face, would he recognize me? Would anyone?

I let the brick fall over my huge smile and stood up again, finding my hazy reflection in the store window. For the first time ever, I was grateful for the strict rule against public use of cell phones at my school, in place to prevent photos of the children of dignitaries and billionaires and (rumored) drug lords that went there from getting out. There was always a slim possibility that someone had snuck a shot of me somewhere, but not that I knew of. And if this was the only photo the press had—the last school picture taken before my attempted kidnapping—there had to be a reason. If my mom wanted them to have a new picture, they would have one.

But how much did I still resemble that girl on the front page? Would anyone look at tall, skinny Lia Washington and see little, pudgy Cecilia Montgomery?

The breeze shifted and tugged a stray curl across my face. I reached up and pulled it taut. My hair. I loved my hair. Always had. But it was my only defining trait that hadn't changed. If I wanted to be inconspicuous, I was going to need a makeover.

The man tsked quietly. "Such a shame, that story. Like that family hasn't been through enough? And that girl . . . to survive one kidnapping only for this to happen."

The kidnapping. Whenever someone mentioned it, which was rare—since the topic was verboten in my family—the same set of images flashed through my mind. My mother shaking hands with the crowd at the local spring festival. The shimmery red fish in their tiny spherical bowls that had enticed me to wander off. The dirty fingernails of the man whose hand had come down over my mouth. The white van with the dented side he'd dragged me toward. That van still appeared in my nightmares, because even then—even as a naïve, coddled eight-year-old—I instinctively knew that if we made it to that van, I was dead.

The whole thing had lasted ninety seconds, but it had defined the rest of my life. Inside the apartment of Scott Smith, my would-be kidnapper, they'd found a room he'd prepared for me, a video camera, and various drafts of his ransom demands. He'd been stalking us for weeks, just waiting for his opportunity. It was because of Scott Smith that I was enrolled at the Worthington School that fall. Because of him that my mother turned warden on me.

"Miss? You're shakin'." The man reached for my arm, ostensibly to help me inside, but I flinched away.

"No!" I blurted, which made his eyes widen. "I mean . . . I'm sorry. No, I'm . . . I'm fine."

Though, if his expression was any indication, I looked anything *but* fine. I flipped my hood up again, ducking my head. "Is Daria's Salon still . . . here somewhere?"

"Sure." His brow furrowed as he pointed. "Just across Peach Street and five doors down."

Relief rushed through me.

"Thank you," I said, suddenly remembering my manners.

He nodded, and I speed-walked away on weakened knees, crossing Peach without even bothering to check for cars. I did, however, notice the huge, colorful message spray-painted on the brick wall on the far side of Peach—the outer wall of a shop called the Book Nook. Scrawled against a purple background in bright pink and yellow letters were the words IF YOU LIVED HERE, YOU'D BE HOME NOW.

I felt like the wall was speaking directly to me. I *was* home. I was. I just had to make sure I didn't get caught.

Daria had changed her formerly purple awning to a

bright aqua one, but otherwise everything looked the same—the white iron benches outside, the curved front windows, the big pink shears painted on the door. Would it be better if she was working right now, or if she wasn't? I realized it was semi-insane, walking into the business establishment of the one person in town who might recognize me, but I needed to see her. Seeing her would make me feel closer to Gigi, and right now, I needed Gigi more than anything.

If she recognized me, I'd just have to beg her not to send me home. Since she was Gigi's best friend and all, I had a feeling that doing my parents a favor wouldn't be high on her priority list.

I was a few steps away from the salon when I heard a shout; then someone bolted out of an alleyway. I didn't even have time to react before his shoulder slammed right into my side.

"Hey! Watch where you're—"

He stopped midsentence, holding on to my arm with one hand and the handle of a black guitar case with the other. His blond hair stuck straight out on both sides like he'd just woken up, and his square jaw was dotted with light stubble. The snap-front brown-and-white cowboy shirt he was wearing was tucked in on one side only, and the top button on his jeans was undone. His blue eyes caught mine, and for a split second neither of us breathed.

"Hey," he said, his original accusation forgotten. "Look at you."

It was odd, as greetings went, but then he flashed a smile and my heart turned to goo. This guy was trouble. With a smile like that, he couldn't not be trouble. Unfortunately, my heart didn't care. And neither did my skin, from the way it was tingling. When he released my shoulder, I could still feel his grip, like his fingers had burned my skin.

He glanced over his shoulder, up the alleyway, then at me. Right. My turn to speak.

"I'm . . . I—"

"Oh, hey. You dropped this." He stooped to pick up my faded gray Red Sox cap. The plastic clasp had been fastened around my bag strap but must have come undone. "Boston, huh? You're a long way from home."

My cheeks warmed. The twang. What was it about the twang that made my pulse flutter? Also, I'd forgotten I had that hat. I should probably get rid of it, since it tied me to Boston and I had to pretend to be from . . . somewhere else.

"Hey, asshole! You forgot this!"

A beefy man leaned out of a third-floor window into the alley and tossed a well-worn black cowboy hat down to us like a Frisbee. The cowboy clutching my baseball cap made a grab for it, but it landed at my feet. I picked it up.

"Thanks, Petey!" the cowboy shouted.

"Stay the hell away from my girlfriend!" Petey replied.

Then said girlfriend leaned out the window, a flowered robe hanging half off her shoulder, her black hair a tangled mess.

"Will do!" the guy said, lifting my cap like a wave.

I must have seemed shocked, because he looked sheepishly at the toes of his cowboy boots. "Long story," he said. "So . . . trade?"

He held out my baseball cap. I pretended to ponder it, but then made the exchange. He palmed the hat and placed it on his head, adjusting the position.

"Here. Allow me."

Before I could react, he'd nudged the hood off my hair with a gentle touch, grabbed my hat from my hands, and tugged it down over my forehead. Then he whistled.

"Girl, that is some head of hair," he said, backing away toward a classic white convertible parked at the curb. "Whatever you do, don't ever change that hair."

He placed the guitar on the passenger seat, then touched the brim of his hat with a nod. "Nice to meet you, Red Sox."

"You, too, home-wrecker," I replied, finally finding my voice, the effort of which made me blush—hard.

His grin widened; then he swung himself into the driver's seat and took off. Halfway down the block, his radio blared on, blasting country music loud enough to entertain the entire town.

Damn.

Who. The hell. Was that?

Slowly I turned toward Daria's place, my adrenaline from earlier totally sapped. I reached back and ran a hand down my hair, feeling its familiar softness under my fingertips. What were the chances of bumping into a guy who said he loved my hair two seconds before I was about to cut it? Was it a sign that I shouldn't?

A chorus of shouts erupted from above the alleyway—Petey and his girl getting into it, I supposed. Just like that I flashed back to reality. I didn't even know the guy's name, and obviously he was a shameless player with a flirt addiction. This was my life I was trying to start here. I had to stay focused.

I strode across the street and shoved my way inside Daria's. The acrid scent of bleach mixed with nose-itching aerosol hairspray hit me square in the senses.

Daria Case looked up from the roots she was checking. She'd put on about ten pounds, but otherwise the folds of her face, the particular salt-and-pepper of her hair, and the gold bracelets on her arms were exactly as I remembered them. Suddenly I felt like Gigi was about to walk in from the back room, and I almost laughed and cried at the same time.

"Hi there!" Daria said brightly. "What can I do for you today, sweet pea?"

I smiled. "Sweet pea" had been my grandmother's nickname for me. I took Daria's use of it as a sign. There was no recognition behind her eyes, so I knew I was truly safe. I tugged my cap off, shaking my hair out over my shoulders.

"Cut it all off, please," I said. "And dye it. Blond."

Chapter Three

"I'd love the help, believe me. But I'm not really supposed to make decisions without checking with my dad first."

Wow. That sounded familiar.

The girl behind the counter at the Little Tree Diner—Fiona, if her name tag was to be trusted—looked like she'd just been through finals. Twice. Her stringy blond hair fell out of what might once have been a neat bun but now looked more like something dug out of a bath drain. She had purple splotches under her eyes, her skin was dry, and her gaze darted around the busy room like she was waiting for it to explode.

"Well . . . is your dad coming in soon?" I asked.

"Not until tonight."

"Miss?" someone shouted. "Miss! I need more butter!"

"Miss? This burger is undercooked."

"I ordered chicken parm, not chicken piccata."

"Fiona? A little help over here?" a busboy asked.

Fiona's small shoulders slumped. "Can you start right now?"

"You're serious?" I asked.

"I mean, I can't guarantee you'll get a full-time position, but we're understaffed today . . . clearly," she replied, wiping her hands on her black waist-apron. "Jason, can you please get the butter and fix those mixed-up orders while I talk to . . ."

She looked at me for a name.

"Lia," I said. "Lia Washington."

It sounded perfectly natural rolling off my tongue. I'm sure my proud smile confused her.

"Nice to meet you, Lia. I'm Fiona Taylor," she replied.

Jason scurried off to do as she'd asked, and Fiona started bussing.

"I've got one girl who called in sick, one who helpfully texted an hour ago to tell me she landed a contract in Nashville and isn't coming back, and my dumbass brother is forty-five minutes late," she explained. "I'll pay you out of my own wages if I have to."

She looked up at me and her skin went blotchy. "Sorry. I don't usually swear."

Had she sworn? I hadn't noticed. I was too busy hoping my butt off that this would turn into a real job somehow. "Oh, it's okay. Don't worry about it."

"Can you wait tables?" she asked. "Do you have any experience?"

"Yes!" I said. "I waited tables at my school back . . . at school."

Terrified that I'd almost blurted out a biographical detail, I looked away and reached up to tuck my hair behind my ear. Except my hair wasn't there anymore. This Lia Washington person—her background, her look, her life—was going to take some getting used to. I caught my reflection in the foggy mirrored wall behind the counter. My hair was all but shaved in the back and around my ears. Daria had kept it slightly longer on top, so that a few stray curls fell over my forehead, but those curls were now blond. I looked nothing like myself. But damn. It turned out I had some serious cheekbones. At least that's what Daria had told me.

I'd also stepped into Daria's bathroom and popped out my contacts, replacing them with my rectangular tortoiseshell glasses. The more disguise, the better. I felt like

I looked older—more sophisticated—this way. I wondered what that cowboy from the alley would think if he saw me now. Not that it mattered. Was that really how you wanted to meet someone? When he was busy crawling out some other girl's window? I shouldn't have been thinking about romance anyway. I had enough on my plate. Like securing a job and a home and making my new identity stick.

"You sure? 'Cause we get pretty busy around here," Fiona said, walking along behind the counter with the bussing bin, tossing used plates and cups in at random. "You gotta be quick on your feet."

"Pretty busy" was an understatement. We were standing smack-dab in the middle of the lunch rush, and every booth, table, and stool in the small L-shaped restaurant was taken. There were kids on their lunch break from school, a pack of guys probably from the nearby college taking up two eight-tops near the back, and some business lunches, too. Not that I was surprised. If the scent of the burgers and the thickness of the shakes were any indication, this place deserved its popularity.

"I can do it, I swear," I said as I kept pace with her across the counter.

One of the more random and controversial policies at the Worthington School was that each semester every student had to hold down a different campus job. The kids of the very wealthy and very connected would take on blue-collar tasks like sweeping the gym and cutting the lawns and, yes, waiting tables at the school café. Parents were always up in arms about it, and a lot of students complained, but I secretly liked it. It was nice to get out of my single room and be around other people, to be active. And waiting tables had been my favorite. Aside from my few casual friends, I barely ever interacted with my fellow students unless they were paying me to do their work—about the only thing I'd ever done wrong until yesterday. At the café I'd had a couple of actual conversations about things unrelated to school. Music, movies, books, life. It was like Mardi Gras. As if I'd ever experienced Mardi Gras.

"All right, then. You can stash your stuff in the back, wash your hands, and grab an apron. I'll give you a four-hour trial, and if you pass, you can meet my dad, Hal. He's the owner."

"Cool. Thank you for the opportunity."

I barely kept a straight face. It was all I could do to stop myself from turning a cartwheel in the middle of the diner. Fiona's bin was overflowing by now, and at the end of the counter were three half-full glasses of soda.

"Here. I'll get those," I offered, giddy. I was employed!

I wasn't going to go broke! I could buy clothes! Maybe I'd even get my ears pierced so I could wear dangling earrings and my neck wouldn't feel so naked without my hair brushing against it. Pierced ears. My mom would die.

I pressed the three glasses between my fingers, holding them the way I'd done a million times at the café and, yes, showing off a bit. When I turned around to head for the kitchen, the front door opened, and a guy with dark hair wearing some kind of sports uniform caked in sweat came flying through.

"Sorry, I'm late, Fi!" he said with a grin, planting a kiss on the top of her head. "But we won!"

"I'm so happy," Fiona said flatly. "Now go wash up before I murder you."

He laughed, a carefree, booming sound that resounded inside my chest, and then he looked me up and down. This guy was undeniably handsome in a compact, muscular, boyish sort of way. He was maybe two inches shorter than me, but the sheer energy coming off of him made him feel a foot taller.

"How's it going? Duncan Taylor. I'm Fiona's cooler twin."

He stretched a hand out to me, but mine were currently full. Still, I made some sort of move. I don't know if it was a nod or a curtsy or somewhere in between, but my backpack slid heavily off my shoulder and yanked down on my elbow, sending me sideways. I let out a curse as all three glasses slid from my grasp. One hit the floor and smashed into a million pieces, showering the legs of the patrons at a nearby table. The other two fell into the lap of a girl who screeched so sharply I was shocked she didn't shatter even more glass.

The diner went silent. The girl, who was Asian and about my age, with perfectly olive skin and long black hair that skimmed her tiny butt, looked up at me, her chest heaving. She plucked the two glasses out of her lap with her fingertips and deposited them on her table. The soda had puddled in the folds of her white sundress along with a few ice cubes. A constellation of brown spots decorated her chest. Her almost black eyes were homicidal.

Duncan spluttered a laugh.

"What the *hell*?" the girl spat.

Her three friends, who had gone unscathed, seemed frozen in terror.

"I'm so sorry!" I blurted. "My backpack fell . . . and I . . . I'm so—"

"Do you even work here?" she shouted, her arms out at her sides, palms up, as if waiting for someone to come towel her off. "Duncan!" she cried accusingly.

"Sorry. Sorry, Shelby." He reached over the counter to

grab a towel for her, struggling to keep from cracking up all over again.

I looked hesitantly over my shoulder at Fiona, expecting her to throw me out like a stray dog off the street. Four seconds into my four-hour trial and I was done.

But instead Fiona pressed her lips together and lifted her chin at Shelby. It took some obvious effort, like me talking back to my mother had, and I felt oddly proud of her, considering we'd just met.

"Yes. She does." Her eyes fixed on me. "Lia, would you please run to the back and get a mop and dustpan? And you can change into a Little Tree souvenir T-shirt, too. They're on the shelf in the staff room. We all wear 'em."

Swallowing hard, I grabbed my backpack and ran, shooting Fiona a grateful glance.

"What about me?" I heard the girl wail as I rounded the counter toward the kitchen door.

"Well, Shelby," Fiona said, sounding tired, "I suggest you go home and get yourself changed. But don't forget to pay at the register on your way out."

My four-hour trial turned into an eight-hour shift. At ten p.m., when Fiona and Duncan's father finally arrived, bringing a new team of waitresses with him, the three of us were sitting at the end of the counter slumped over sweating glasses of sweet tea.

"So, Lia, where're you from?" Duncan asked.

"Florida," I replied automatically. It was, after all, where Lia Washington had been born. Sort of.

"So . . . this place is open till midnight every night?" I asked, changing the subject.

At the moment there were only three tables with patrons, and they all had their food. I knew that I should get up and make sure they had everything they needed, but I'd barely slept in the last day, and every muscle in my body ached. Plus it was slowly settling in that I'd taken a job when I had no clue how much it paid, that I had no place to sleep tonight, and that the only thing I'd eaten since that awful granola bar was a half a burger I'd scarfed during my fifteen-minute dinner break.

"Yep," Fiona said. She brought her tea to her lips but couldn't seem to catch the straw, chasing it around with her mouth popping like a guppy's. She finally gave up, put the glass down again, and placed her cheek on her arm. "And as the new girl, you're probably going to get the worst shifts, I'm sorry to tell you."

"Isn't my sister a big ol' ray of sunshine?" Duncan joked, patting her on the back.

"'S okay," I said with a yawn. "I can handle it."

Keeping busy would also probably be a good thing. It would prevent me from constantly wondering what the hell I was doing and whether I was completely selfish and insane, which was what had happened every time I'd stopped to breathe this afternoon.

"So, you're Lia Washington!" Hal Taylor burst out of the kitchen with so much energy my tired brain almost whimpered. He was thin and wiry, with defined arms and what looked like a naked-lady tattoo half peeking out from beneath his T-shirt sleeve. He was bald everywhere but around his ears, where a perfect ring of short white hair circled from one side of his head to the other. His blue eyes crinkled when he smiled, and he was tan. Very tan. "Tell me why I should hire you."

I opened my mouth to speak, but Fiona beat me to it. "Because she saved me today, Dad. Honestly. Please, hire her now before she has a chance to think better of it and run."

Hal laughed, his head jerking back, and crossed his arms over his chest. He had the same room-filling laugh as Duncan. "Think better of it? Who wouldn't want to work here?"

"Oh, I don't know. Maybe the three people who didn't bother to show up today?" Duncan joked.

"Nature of the business, son! People come and people go," Hal replied, squeezing Duncan's shoulder. "We pool tips here," he said to me. "That cool with you?"

"Definitely." My mouth went dry as I tried to figure out how to broach the subject of my lack of ID.

"And if you don't mind, I'll pay ya in cash. At least for now," Hal continued. "I don't usually put the new kids on the books unless I know for sure they're staying on for at least six months. Can you guarantee that?"

I stared, dumbly, unable to believe my luck. He had just given me an out. "Um . . . no. Not exactly."

"She's a drifter," Duncan joked, winking at me as he popped a sugar cube from the bowl into his mouth. "An outlaw."

I smiled. He got up and sauntered around the end of the counter to join his dad on the other side.

"Good. It's all settled, then." Hal turned and slapped his hand down on the Formica as he looked at Fiona. "Get her on the schedule. She can have that good-for-nothing Jennifer's shifts."

Fiona slid off her stool. "Oh, please. You loved Jennifer."

"I did, and when she becomes a big star, I'm gonna say 'I knew her when,'" Hal said without missing a beat as he organized the glassware behind the counter.

"Who's Jennifer?" I asked.

"The one who's down in Nashville," Fiona replied. She gestured over her shoulder with her thumb, in what I guessed was a northwesterly direction.

"Jenny's in Nashville?" Duncan asked, his eyebrows raised.

Fiona nodded. "She got a gig singing backup for Patty Parkman."

"No way!" I said. "Good for her."

The door behind me opened, and Fiona's posture instantly straightened.

"Good for who, what?"

My heart twirled inside my chest. I knew that voice. Slowly I turned around, and there he was, my home-wrecker cowboy. He'd changed into a blue plaid button-down over distressed jeans, and this time the shirt was tucked behind a serious silver belt buckle. His blond hair was clean and pushed back from his face, accentuating the ridiculous cheekbones, square jaw, and blue, blue eyes. He gave me a quick glance but didn't seem to recognize me at all. Meanwhile, I was sitting there practically gaping. I turned around again, mortified, my back to the door.

"Jennifer Kay. She's backing up Patty Parkman now," Fiona said, sweeping her stray hairs behind her ears.

"Wow. How'd she land that gig?" he asked.

For the first time all day Duncan's expression darkened. "Why? Looking for a way to grab onto her coattails?"

The cowboy shot him an irritated look. Fiona and I glanced at each other, and instantly I knew—there was some kind of history between these guys.

"Well, Jasper Case! As I live and breathe," Hal interjected, like he was greeting a major celebrity, but with a touch of sarcasm. "To what do we owe the honor of this visit?"

I almost fell off the stool. "You're Jasper Case?"

Jasper smiled at me. That smile. Obviously. Obviously it was Jasper. How had I not realized it before? The eyes, the hair, the teasing personality. Of course, the last time I'd seen him he'd been pulling my pigtails and stuffing a wriggling worm down the front of my dress, but still. It was clearly the same boy.

"You heard of me?" he asked.

Duncan scoffed, wiping out a glass with serious vigor.

"What? No . . . I . . ." I paused and took a breath. "I got my hair cut at your grandmother's place earlier," I improvised. "I think she mentioned you."

Jasper's eyes narrowed, and he took a half-step back, staring at my head. "Red Sox?"

I reached up and self-consciously touched my neck, which was burning. "Yeah, it's me. Home-wrecker," I added for good measure.

He leaned away and looked me up and down. "I didn't recognize you," he said. "But I like it. It's very you."

"You don't even know me," I said, sliding off the stool to do one last check on my tables. I had this sense that it would be a good idea to put some distance between me and Jasper Case. Not because I thought he'd ever realize who I really was, but because my body was reacting to being near him in ways I didn't know how to handle.

"Fair enough." He chuckled. "But I still like it."

I turned away before he could see the huge smile that lit my face.

"So Jasper, are you gonna order something, or did you just come in here to flirt with my waitresses?" Hal asked, rolling his shoulders back.

"Take a guess," Duncan muttered under his breath as he dropped the clean glass onto the shelf with a clatter.

"Duncan! Shut *up*," Fiona said through her teeth.

"I'll take a fried chicken basket to go, and throw some of those delicious tomatoes of yours in there too," Jasper said. "They got the best fried green tomatoes on the planet," he told me, coming up behind me and leaning in like he was sharing state secrets. "And here. Flyers for tonight's open mic."

When I turned around, I found myself face-to-face with a bright green flyer. It advertised open-mic night at the Mixer Bar and Grill, starting at midnight. Jasper lowered it to reveal that damn smile.

"My new band's playing our premier performance. You should come."

I plucked the flyer from his hand and moved past him to the counter. He handed out more to the couples sitting at my booth. "Are you going?" I asked Fiona.

She looked from the flyer to me to Jasper. "I don't know. I'm kinda tired."

"Come on, Fi," Jasper said, grabbing her around the waist and twirling her toward the window. "We even got a new song we're gonna try out. You've gotta be there."

By the time he released her, Fiona was breathless. She also had more of a spark in her eye than she'd had all day, which made her instantly prettier.

"I'll go if you'll go," she said to me tentatively.

"I'll go if you have some clothes I can borrow," I replied, looking down at my once-crisp, now-ketchup-mottled Little Tree Diner T-shirt. "And possibly a shower."

Jasper clapped his hands and rubbed them together. "Now we're talking."

I blushed, and Fiona shoved Jasper's shoulder from behind.

"Duncan?" Jasper said genially.

"I wouldn't go if you paid me," Duncan replied. Then he shot me a look I couldn't quite pin down, turned around, and disappeared into the kitchen.

"What flew up his butt tonight?" Jasper asked, making Fiona laugh.

"Of course you can come back to our place for a shower. I don't know how well my clothes'll fit you, but we'll give it a try," she said to me. "I may even have an idea of an apartment for you."

"Awesome."

Walking into the Little Tree Diner was the best decision I'd made all day. Maybe ever, considering I hadn't been making decisions on my own for very long.

I picked up the water pitcher and reached over the booth to refill some glasses. Jasper stood back, and I could see his reflection in the window as he blatantly checked me out from behind. God. If he could think I was attractive after a whole day on the road, no sleep, and eight hours slinging burgers, then something was clearly wrong with him.

"So you'll be there, Red Sox?" Jasper asked.

"I'll be there," I said.

"Good. 'Cause my new goal in life is to earn a standing ovation outta you," he said.

I turned around and looked him in the eye. Very brazen of normally reserved little old me. But maybe I wasn't the old me anymore. "Good luck with that," I said.

As I walked away, he whistled like he was impressed, and I just about died. Suddenly I wasn't that tired. In fact, I wasn't tired at all.

Chapter Four

After a free dinner of sliced steak and fried green tomatoes—they were as good as Jasper had promised—I went to Hadley's, which thankfully stayed open until eleven p.m., and scored a shower cap and some of the foaming apricot scrub I loved so much. Then Fiona took me home and showed her pity by letting me shower first. Nothing had ever felt so good as the warm water hitting my skin and washing off the grime. Good-bye, sticky Everglades pollen; so long, dried blood; sayonara, bus exhaust; hardly knew ye, ketchup stuck up in my arm hairs.

Fiona and Duncan lived with their father and mother in a big, beautiful home near the edge of town, where everything was antique but impeccably preserved. In Fiona's room was a huge canopy bed with about a zillion pillows that had made me almost sick for sleep, but I'd powered through. The thought of seeing Jasper again, of hearing him sing and play guitar, had a lot to do with it.

Now, an hour later, I was freshly scrubbed and wearing a knee-skimming floral skirt and white T-shirt—borrowed from Fiona—and my black heels, since my feet turned out to be two sizes bigger than hers. I felt almost normal as we walked the surprisingly busy streets of Sweetbriar. All around us cars edged into parking spots, crowds of people chatted and laughed, couples ducked into alcoves to steal kisses. I felt like I was back in busy, touristy Boston instead of moseying the streets of a small southern town. Of course, the most I'd ever walked the streets of Boston was from a car into a building, and even then I'd been constantly surrounded by guards. Just being able to breathe, look around, not worry about someone trying to snap my picture was beyond freeing.

"This place is a scene," I commented, as we slid around a crowd of teenagers smoking cigarettes in the center of the sidewalk.

"It is every Thursday through Sunday," Fiona replied, her hands shoved deep in the pockets of her denim jacket. She'd put on a striped sundress and cowboy boots; her blond hair fanned out over her shoulders. With a little mascara and a swipe of blush she'd become startlingly pretty in a doe-eyed, pixieish kind of way. "They say our population doubles on big bar nights."

I believed it. When we got to the Mixer, the line to get in looped down the block and around the corner, but Fiona walked right up to the surly-looking man at the door. It wasn't until that moment that I realized he was probably checking IDs. Instantly, I began to sweat. This night was going to be over before it began.

"Hey, Felix," she said. "This is Lia."

"Ladies." He gave me a nod and stood aside to let us through the door.

The people at the front of the line groaned in protest, but their gripes were instantly drowned out by the noise inside the bar.

"You know him?" I shouted to be heard.

"I know everyone in this town." Fiona made this declaration wearily, as if it was not something she was proud of.

Inside, the Mixer was almost impossibly dark, aside from the huge glowing beacon that was the stage at the top of the room. On it were two girls in ripped jeans, one playing a violin, the other strumming a guitar and crooning into the mic. There were about twenty round two-top tables in front of the stage, each one currently crowded by four or five people, and the bars at either side of the room were stacked three partiers deep.

My palms began to prickle. This was a crowd. An uncontrolled, unsupervised crowd. And I had no bodyguard. I had never been in a situation like this. Not once in my entire life. What if someone recognized me? What if someone tried to hurt me, or worse, kidnap me again? I felt an almost unbearable need to get back outside. To be alone—my natural state of being.

This was what you wanted, a little voice inside my head chided. *You going to chicken out now?*

Fiona surged ahead. I took a deep, steadying breath and gripped the back of her jacket to keep from getting separated. I kept my head down, waiting for my eyes to adjust, trying to calm the erratic beating of my heart. No one here knew me. No one here was looking for me. I was Lia Washington. Unfamous, uninteresting Lia Washington. I breathed in and out deliberately, just as I'd been taught in meditation, and gradually unclenched.

Where was Fiona going? She just kept walking, snaking around the chairs and bodies like she had a destination in mind, even though there were clearly no seats left in the entire place. Finally she stopped at a table front and center and proved me wrong, falling into an empty chair.

"Hey, Britta."

A broad-shouldered Asian girl with a couple dozen tiny

ponytails sticking out in all directions from her head looked up from her laptop. She wore a black T-shirt that read I CAN BEAT UP YOUR HONOR STUDENT over a pair of plaid shorts, torn purple tights, and knee-high black boots.

"Way to be late. Do you know how many times I've had to say 'these seats are taken'?"

"Sorry. My fault," I said, taking the other empty chair. "I hadn't showered in a while, and I think I stayed in there a little too long."

The girl looked at me and pushed her black-framed glasses up on her nose. Only they weren't glasses, because there was no glass in them. She had Band-Aids in a rainbow of colors around her fingers.

"You're pretty," she said, like an accusation. Then she went right back to typing.

I looked at Fiona, confused. "Britta both tells it likes it is and saves most of her words for her music review blog," Fiona explained, nodding at the computer. "I'll bet you ten dollars she's ripping these poor girls to shreds right now."

"Give her ten dollars," Britta said, her fingers never slowing.

I laughed as the girls finished up their song. There was a mild smattering of applause from around the room, and then a gangly black kid in a white cowboy hat too big for his head took the stage.

"That was Danny and Delia! Let's hear it!" he shouted.

The crowd cheered again, but this time with even less enthusiasm.

"All right, all right," the MC said cheerily, not seeming to notice. "Next up we have the Case Files!"

The bar filled with hoots and cheers and hollers as Jasper bounded onto the stage with a gleaming black guitar, followed by two other guys with guitars and one drumstick-twirling girl. They all wore some combination of distressed jeans and artfully wrinkled T-shirts, and each sported a small, distinguishing accessory—a sparkly green scarf for the drummer, a slew of rope bracelets for guitarist number one, a silver nose ring and eyeliner for guitarist number two. But not Jasper. Jasper looked every bit the cowboy in his pressed snap-front shirt, gleaming belt buckle, and black hat. My heart caught at the mere sight of him. He gazed past us, over our heads, out at the crowd, and I somehow felt disappointed that he hadn't psychically known I was there, down front, and caught my eye right away.

Honestly, there was something wrong with me. There were probably a dozen other girls in this bar he really did know. Maybe a dozen girls in this bar he'd even hooked up with. I had no idea. What I did know was that he hadn't played a note yet and I was thinking like a groupie idiot.

"The Case Files?" Britta scoffed and shook her head at her computer screen. "Worst name he's come up with yet."

Her fingers flew furiously.

"So, Fiona, what's the deal between your brother and Jasper?" I asked, keeping one eye on him as I spoke to her.

Britta made a startling bleating sound that might have been a laugh or a hiccup. "Got a few hours?"

"They just . . . don't get along," Fiona said, adjusting herself on her chair. "It's a long story."

"Understatement!" Britta sang.

Up on the stage Jasper leaned in to the mic. "Evening, everyone! We're the Case Files."

Then he turned around and counted the rhythm. "One, two, three, four!"

The music began, a harmonious, upbeat strum of guitars, and I tore my eyes off Jasper, deciding to change the subject. "Worst name yet?" I asked.

"This is Jasper's third band in two years," Fiona replied, nodding along to the beat. "The first one was In Case of Emergency, and he had a keyboardist. The second was the Black Case, which included a brass section. He told me now he's trying to pare things down."

Wow. Talk about an ego. Naming every one of his bands after himself? Not that I was surprised. Boy was full of himself when he was eight years old, and that was before the testosterone and the cheekbones and what I was betting were some pretty serious abs under all those silver snaps.

The thought had barely formed in my mind when Jasper looked down at us midstrum and winked. I blushed as at least twenty girls in the room turned to stare me down.

Britta groaned. "Lord, you'd think he was still channeling JT."

"JT?" I asked.

"Justin Timberlake," she clarified. "He had this whole phase in middle school."

I snorted a laugh. *That* I would have liked to see.

"So, Lia, Britta's looking for a roommate. She used to live with Jennifer. You guys should talk," Fiona said.

"Oh, yeah?" I said hopefully. "Where do you live?"

As if it mattered. I'd take a mattress in the back of someone's pickup right now.

"Apartment above Hadley's." For the first time her fingers stopped moving, and she really looked at me. "Two bedrooms, one bathroom, unreliable water heater. Rent is six fifty a month, but I pay three fifty for the bigger room. You have a job?"

"Yep."

"You smoke?"

"Nope."

"You like boy bands? Because I can't live with someone who likes boy bands."

"Um, no."

"Okay, then. You're in," she said. "Jen left all the furniture, but she took the sheets. You'll need sheets."

"Oh my gosh, thank you," I said. "You have no idea—"

"Shh!" She held up a hand, a Buzz Lightyear Band-Aid glowing at me in the dark. "He's coming to the bridge."

We looked up at Jasper. The music slowed. He closed his eyes as he got into the emotion of the song, letting his guitar hang as the drummer pulled back and the other two guitarists strummed quietly.

Man. Jasper was Hot with a capital *H.*

"So, Lia, why'd you leave Florida?" Fiona asked.

It was amazing how fast my throat went dry. I coughed into my hand and couldn't seem to stop.

"Are you okay? Is she okay?" Britta asked, looking at Fiona.

"Sorry," I croaked. "Tickle in my throat."

"I'll get you a drink." Fiona started to get up, but I grabbed her arm.

"No. I'll go." I was desperate to avoid their questions. I cleared my throat half a dozen times as I stood. "Will they serve me here?" I tried to focus through teary eyes. "I'd love to get us some drinks to celebrate our new living arrangement."

As long as they were cheap drinks. And not very high proof. I'd only been drunk once in my life, when my classmate Trevor Thurmonson had smuggled vodka into his dorm room in shampoo bottles. After downing almost an entire Frederic Fekkai bottle myself, I'd spent half the night puking, the other half begging the Tank not to tell my mom, and I still tasted soap whenever I felt even slightly nauseous.

"Oh, they'll serve anyone," Britta said. "But I only drink water and one hundred percent fruit juice."

"Would you mind getting me a beer?" Fiona asked.

"I'm on it," I said, with one last cough into my fist. Beer and water I could handle, both financially and gastrointestinally.

As I stood up, the song finally came to a close. Half the crowd was on its feet, and everyone was whistling and applauding. A crowd of girls in tight little dresses shouted Jasper's name and held out Sharpies and autograph books, like he was some kind of country god and not just participating in an open mic night where literally anyone could perform. The band started to walk offstage as I headed for the bar.

"Well, look-a here!" Jasper shouted into the mic. "I got the standing O I was hoping for."

He gestured in my direction, and the spotlight swung

around to blind me. My heart hit the trashed wood floor.

"Actually, no. I was just going to the bar," I said. "Sorry to disappoint."

The people at the nearest tables—the ones who could hear me—laughed. Jasper's smile faltered for half a second, but then the MC came out again and whispered something in Jasper's ear. Jasper's grin widened.

"Well, well. Guess what, folks?" he drawled into the mic. "Ryan here's just informed me that we've come to my favorite part of the evening."

There were cheers all around, and I felt a slight tingle of apprehension. Probably because Jasper was giving me this totally focused, *you are so going down* kinda look.

"That's right!" Ryan shouted, taking the mic back from Jasper. "It's time for . . . the Hidden Talent Showcase!" More screams and cheers. Jasper jumped down from the stage and took my hand. Which, yes, gave me goose bumps. "And it looks like we have our first volunteer!"

"Here we go, Red Sox!" Jasper said, tugging me toward the stairs.

My stomach was in my shoes. "What? No! I can't go up there!" I staggered along behind him, trying to pull away, but he held my hand tight. "Jasper! I can't!"

"Yes, you can, Red Sox," he said, guiding me in front of

him and placing his hands on my hips now. He maneuvered me up the stairs until I was finally standing on the stage, albeit the very edge of it. I looked out at the audience—more people than I'd ever seen in one place in my life—and my pulse palpitated. There were camera phones everywhere. Suddenly I felt faint. I was about to just jump and run and hop on the next bus to wherever, when Jasper leaned in from behind, his lips oh-so-close to my ear. "Come on, Red Sox. I'm sure you're talented in a lot of ways."

As soon as my entire body was done responding to *that*, it hit me. I'd escaped so I could live a life. I'd escaped so I could have experiences. Experiences like this one. If I wanted to live, it was time to start living.

But still. I couldn't let anyone get a good picture of my face. I turned around and plucked the black cowboy hat from Jasper's head. He reached up to pat down his sweaty blond hair as I placed the hat on my head and brought the brim down low.

"Well," I told him. "You're right about that."

I walked across the stage to where Danny and Delia were hanging out in the wings. "Any chance I can borrow that for a sec?" I said, gesturing at the violin. "Danny?" I ventured.

Her blue eyes widened in surprise, but she shrugged. "Sure, darlin'. You do your thing."

"Thank you. I think I will."

Then I walked back to center stage and over to the mic. "I'm Lia Washington," I said. My voice reverberated throughout the room. "And I guess this is my hidden talent." I ducked my chin as best as I could and started to play.

My song of choice was Dolly Parton's "Jolene," which was one of Gigi's favorites. The second I started playing, I forgot all about the crowd, about the camera phones, even about Jasper. All I could think about was Gigi and the music. Damn, I had missed playing the violin. Why had I ever given it up? Oh, right. Because my mother had decided my time would be better spent learning Mandarin.

Wrong again, Mom.

When the last strains of the song faded into nothing, I hazarded a glance at Fiona and Britta's table. Fiona was on her feet cheering, as were a lot of other people. Ryan came over and took the mic, giving me a wide smile.

"You, my friend, can come back anytime!" Then he looked at the crowd. "Lia Washington, everybody!"

I lifted one hand, my chest inflating with pride and adrenaline and sheer joy. Then I returned Danny or Delia's violin to her, and jogged back over to Jasper and placed his hat back on his head. He tipped it back, and my heart caught. His eyes were filled with this sort of awed admiration. No one had ever looked at me like that before.

"Holy fiddle, girl. That was intense!"

I raised a shoulder, tilting my head. "Sorry you didn't get to humiliate me."

"I wasn't trying to humiliate you!" he said, following me as I hoofed it down the stairs.

"Yeah, yeah," I called back. "You keep telling yourself that."

His guitar still hung around his neck, which made it difficult for him to navigate the crowd on his way to the end of the bar. A few people stopped him to congratulate him, and a few stopped me to congratulate me, which made it slow going. Ryan, meanwhile, had picked another unwitting volunteer, who was now onstage showing everyone his double-jointed arm moves.

"You have this way of putting me in my place," Jasper said as we finally reached our destination.

"Sorry," I said, leaning into the bar. "You just bring something out of me."

Which was true. I wasn't usually quick with the one-liners, but somehow that was different around Jasper.

"Something nasty, I guess," he said, but he was still grinning. He swung his guitar behind him so he could hook his thumbs into his front pockets.

I smirked back, my pulse thrumming in my wrists. "I guess."

I signaled for the bartender, but he was too busy with the hundred other people he was serving.

"You ain't never gonna get his attention," Jasper said.

"You do know that's not proper English, right?" I said, then blushed. Jasper looked me up and down, his eyes narrowed.

"How about you and me head over to this place I know that's not so packed?" he said. "I'd like to know everything about you, Red Sox."

He almost had me what with all the music and the smiling and the hotness, but that last notion stopped my blood cold. He couldn't know everything about me. Not until I figured out who Lia Washington was. And clearly, as evidenced by my coughing fit back at the table, I didn't even know where Lia Washington was *from.* And even when I figured out a backstory for myself, everything I said to him—to anyone—would be a lie.

"I'll pass," I said, swallowing down my disappointment. My stomach was tied in knots, tightened by uncertainty. I knew that walking away from my old life meant leaving my identity behind, but I'd never really thought about what it would be like to create a fictitious one—to have to lie every moment of every hour of every day.

"You're kidding," he replied.

"Hey, bartender!" I shouted at the top of my lungs. It

felt good to shout. Miracle of miracles, he looked over. "Two beers in the bottle and an ice water."

I pulled out some cash and looked at Jasper, trying to collect myself. I didn't want him to see how rattled I was. "People don't say no to you very often, do they?"

He leaned in to the bar on one elbow. "What is this 'no' word of which you speak?"

I smiled, and the bartender dropped two sweating bottles of beer and a glass of water in front of me.

"That'll be fifteen," he said.

I tossed him the money—plus tip—and picked up the drinks.

"I liked your song," I said to Jasper, turning away.

"Well. That's something to build on," he replied.

"We'll see."

As I sauntered away, I felt giddy and high, but it didn't last. Halfway across the room, my guilt, my doubt, and my fear had snuffed it out. All I'd wanted was a new life. *My* life. But how could I ever really have that when I was always second-guessing what to say? When I couldn't let anyone get near me for fear I'd slip up? When I didn't even know who the hell I was supposed to be?

What if I'd made a huge, horrible, irreversible mistake?

Chapter Five

The hazy, early morning light was coming from the wrong side of the bed, and when I stretched out my legs, my toes caught on something hard. I sat up and blinked, pushing my hair back from my face. Except there was no hair to push. That was when it all came rushing back to me. I opened my eyes and winced against the sunlight. East-facing windows with no curtains. Awesome.

Then I looked around the bare room and smiled. There was a three-drawer dresser with a missing handle and a water-ringed top. The small green table next to the bed was round and metal and slightly rusted, as if it had once been used as outdoor furniture. The door to the closet was an old shower curtain with a painting of Johnny Cash midcroon, and the bed beneath me was bare—it was the hard, rolled edge of the mattress that my foot had hit when I woke up. I had slept under an old Mickey Mouse blanket of Britta's that had covered all of me only if I curled up in a ball. Over my head a ceiling fan creaked lazily, bleating out a constant waltzlike rhythm.

But it was mine, all mine. *Mine-all-mine. Mine-all-mine,* I thought to the beat.

I flopped back on the bed, covered my face with the balled-up blanket, and squealed into it. Yes, there were still ten million things to figure out, but for the moment I decided to revel in the fact that I was free. I was finally, finally free.

After a few indulgent minutes of lazing around in the bloodied shirt I'd put back on before bed, I realized I was too excited to sleep in. Plus I had made a date to go shopping for new clothes with Fiona at ten. I pushed myself up and stretched, then dropped to the floor to start my usual morning routine—fifteen minutes of meditation, followed by a full twenty minutes of tai chi. (Friday was a tai chi day. The other six days of the week I alternated between tae kwon do and karate.) Sitting with legs crossed on the hard floor, I closed my eyes and tried to clear my mind, but it was next to impossible. Too much had happened in the past couple of days. The funeral, the paparazzi, my mom's speech, my escape, a new haircut, a new identity, a new job, Fiona and Duncan and Britta and Jasper. Jasper, Jasper, Jasper.

Just thinking about the way he'd looked at me last night made me itch for a cold shower.

There was a clatter out in the common area, and I heard Britta curse under her breath. My eyes flew open. Why was she up so early? And what was she doing out there? For the first time in my life I had a roommate, and I had no clue what I was supposed to do. If I opened the door, would she think she'd woken me up? Did she want to be alone? Or would it be rude if I didn't say good morning?

I sat there, frozen by indecision, until a flash of indignation shoved me to my feet. I was not totally socially incompetent. I was just going to go out there and say hi. This was my life now. I had to take part in it.

My hand was on the doorknob when I realized I was wearing nothing but my underwear and a white button-down that looked like it had been lifted from a crime scene. I quickly changed back into Fiona's clothes and walked out. Britta was in the small, open kitchen area, dumping coffee into an ancient-looking coffeemaker. She wore unflattering khakis and a white polo shirt, her hair pulled back in a conservative bun. Gone were the fake glasses, the dark lipstick, and the Band-Aids. For a second I wasn't even entirely sure it was her.

"Um, hey," I said.

She looked over at me. "Coffee?"

"Sure."

I slowly padded toward the kitchen, taking in the rest of the apartment, which I hadn't seen much of in the pitch-black exhaustion of last night. The living room was actually quite large, with high ceilings and three long windows looking out over Main Street. Each of these was hung with a sheer, red, flowered curtain drawn aside to let in the light. There were two mismatched couches—one brown plaid, the other white with pink stripes—and a large-screen TV that was so new and sleek it looked out of place with the thrown-together décor. There was some workout gear piled in the corner: a BOSU, several hand weights, a couple of kettlebells, and a yoga mat, all of it collecting dust. Along the far wall—the one that backed what I assumed was Britta's bedroom on the other side of the apartment—were five huge bookcases all packed to the gills with books. More piles of books were stacked in front of them, some listing precariously.

"Wow. You must really like to read," I said.

"I have a book blog too," Britta said, yawning. She stood with one hand on either side of the coffeemaker's base, as if holding on to it was keeping her upright, and stared at the dripping brown liquid.

"Yeah? What kinds of books?" I asked.

"Mystery, mostly."

She didn't elaborate. Fiona was right: Britta was a girl of few words. I clicked my teeth together, feeling awkward as the coffeemaker's burbling peppered the silence. I slid onto a stool at the kitchen table, which was covered by magazines—everything from the *Atlantic*—which was one of my mother's favorites—to *Entertainment Weekly*, *Travel and Leisure*, *Rolling Stone*, *Food Network*, *Star*, *US Weekly*, *InStyle*, *Every Day with Rachael Ray*, *O*, *Fitness*, *Lucky*, and on and on. It looked like Britta subscribed to every periodical still being printed in the USA.

"What's with all the magazines?" I asked finally.

"I like to read." She poured two mugs of coffee and brought them over to the table, finding a square inch in front of me, where she placed mine. Then she went back for milk and sugar and perched them atop one of the piles, covering Jennifer Lopez's sultrily smiling face.

It wouldn't be long before the weekly tabloids started running stories about me. What if my mom finally did release a new photo? How long would it take for Britta to realize she was living with the supposedly kidnapped daughter of the Montgomery family?

The next swallow of coffee felt like a baseball going down my throat.

Britta took a last slug of her coffee, then dumped the mug in the sink. "I'm out."

"Where're you going?" I asked.

"Work. I'm at the coffee shop on Braxton in the mornings and the Book Nook in the afternoons." She grabbed a set of keys out of a small drawer and tossed them on the counter. "Big one's for downstairs. Smaller one's for this door. Have fun shopping with Fiona."

"Thanks!" I said.

With that, she let herself out, slamming the door behind her. I took a deep breath and a sip of my coffee. A laugh sounded from somewhere below the legs of my chosen stool. Shoppers at Hadley's Drugs just downstairs. Part of me wanted to crawl back into bed—such as it was—and hide. The very idea of going out into the world, of constructing a life or even a day for myself, suddenly felt exhausting. I even got up and walked back to my room, but one look at the bare mattress and a couple of nebulous stains I hadn't noticed before passing out on top of them the night before knocked some sense back into me.

I needed clothes. And clearly, I needed sheets. And also? I could not prove my mother right. I could make it on my own. I could, and I would. I turned around and headed for the shower.

Chapter Six

The sun was warm on my face as Fiona and I walked up Main Street together later that morning. As we crossed Peach, I noticed that the wall on the far side of the street had changed. IF YOU LIVED HERE, YOU'D BE HOME NOW had been painted over by a new message, this one in black, white, and teal.

THE BEGINNING IS ALWAYS TODAY.

Okay. This wall was really speaking to me. I was so startled I sort of slid off the curb.

"You okay?" Fiona asked.

"Yeah. It's just . . . that wall. It said something different yesterday."

"Oh, that. Yeah. It says something different every morning."

"Someone paints over it every night?" I asked.

Fiona shrugged, like I was asking whether or not the sun came up each morning. I stepped around the waist-high shelves of PREVIOUSLY LOVED BOOKS outside the Book Nook's front door.

"Who?" I asked.

"No one knows. Benedict McCann—he owns the Book Nook—once had a security camera installed, and the person stopped painting it, but then everyone in town got upset." She gave me a wry look. "Apparently the good people of Sweetbriar wanted their daily dose of inspiration back, so Ben took the camera down and the painting was back the next day."

"But couldn't you just camp out on the corner and wait to see who it is?" I asked.

"Duncan and his friends tried once, but the guy—or girl—didn't show," Fiona told me. "Now people just avoid that area between, like, midnight and five a.m. It's a pretty quiet corner anyway, so it's not hard."

"Wow. That's actually kind of cool," I mused.

"I guess," Fiona said. She seemed bored.

"You don't think so?" I asked.

"No. It's not that. It's just . . . I'm so over this town," Fiona told me, plucking a white bloom from a flowerpot in front of

Daria's. "I can't wait to get to the University of Tennessee in the fall."

An image of my Harvard acceptance letter popped into my mind. It was the only school I'd been allowed to apply to—the only future my mother would allow for me. Never even asked what I wanted. I cleared my throat. None of that mattered anymore.

"But this town is beautiful! And the people are so nice," I said, feeling oddly offended. Of all the places in the world, I'd chosen to come here.

Fiona sighed. "I guess. If you haven't lived here your entire life. Those of us who have generally want out. That's actually how Britta and I met. When she was a senior and I was a freshman, she started a club called the Wanderlust Society, for anyone who wanted to see the world. The school made her change it to the International Travel Club to attract more students, but it didn't matter. It ended up just being me and her, sitting around and researching all the places we want to go. That's why Britta works so many jobs. She's saving to go to Europe."

In the park that bordered the far side of the street, a group of young moms moved through yoga poses in a circle while a full zydeco band—washboard player and all—jammed nearby.

"See what I mean? The town runs a class called Yoga 'n' Zydeco. Like, what?" Fiona said.

"But where else are you going to get yoga and zydeco?" I pointed out.

"Exactly!" she cried, as if I was agreeing with her. "Also, it's not '*and* Zydeco,' it's ''*n*' Zydeco.' The people over at town hall are very particular about the ''*n*','" she added, rolling her eyes.

"I'll try to remember that," I said, and laughed.

"Do," she said with a twinkle in her eye. "'Cause they'll run you right outta town."

Fiona paused next to a small shop with three dress forms in the window, each one wearing a wildly different outfit—one preppy, one hippie, one biker chic.

"This is Second Chances—my favorite store. Britta's mom owns it, which unfortunately means Britta's sister works here," she said wryly. "But the clothes are worth the torture."

"Britta has a sister?" I asked as Fiona started to open the door.

"Yeah. You met her yesterday. Remember Shelby?"

My jaw dropped. "Shelby and Britta are sisters?"

"Believe me, they're just as surprised about it as you are," Fiona said.

Inside, the store was small and cozy and smelled like lavender and cinnamon toast. Racks of clothing lined the walls, and the shelves above them were stuffed with hats and bags. A glass counter near the back corner displayed trays of glittering rhinestone costume jewelry and pegs holding belts and more handbags hung behind the counter. Shelby was at the register with her back to us, wearing a yellow sundress, her straight black hair hanging down her back in a perfect blunt cut.

My mother and her stylist would have loved this girl.

When she turned around, she was smiling, but as soon as she saw us, she stopped.

"Can I *help* you?" she said, in a tone that made it clear she thought both of us were beyond help of any kind.

"We can take care of ourselves," Fiona replied.

Shelby was opening her mouth for a comeback when the curtains behind her snapped sideways and out walked a tall woman with olive skin and curly black hair, wearing a green and black halter dress and big gold jewelry. She took one look at me and her jaw dropped.

"As I live and breathe! It's *you*!"

I felt as if the floor had just crumbled beneath me, and my vision tilted sideways. This was it. I was done.

"It's who?" Shelby asked snidely, looking me up and down.

"The fiddle player from last night!" The woman stepped forward and took both my hands in hers. "Girl, you know how to play!"

"Doesn't she?" Fiona said.

I pulled in a breath and the world straightened out again. Okay. I was okay. She didn't actually recognize me. But my blood still hammered in my ears, as if it hadn't gotten the memo yet. I took another deliberate breath, then another, knowing it was my turn to say something, but unable to get myself together enough to do it.

I swear my life had just flashed before my eyes.

"Do I even want to know what you're talking about?" Shelby asked impatiently.

"This girl right here played a mean 'Jolene' last night at the Mixer," the woman said, releasing me. "You shoulda been up there in your own right, not just as part of Ryan Fitzsimmons's silly hidden-talents thing."

"Thank you," I said finally.

"Awesome. So glad to know my mother's hanging out at bars again," Shelby groused, closing a jewelry cabinet with a bang.

"Woman's gotta meet a good man somewhere," her mother singsonged.

"You met a good man already," Shelby said irritably.

"Yes, and your daddy *was* a good man all the way up until the day he walked out on us." Shelby's mother said this like she was reading the weather out of the newspaper. No big thing. But Shelby's face darkened.

"Mother!" she whined, looking at me. Then she turned on her heel and shoved her way into the back room.

"So sorry about that," the woman said to me, turning to pick up a tray full of muffins. "My daughter just can't seem to accept the fact that her daddy's not coming back. Muffin?"

I hadn't eaten yet, and my stomach growled at the sight of the big, crumb-topped muffins. I was never allowed to eat anything with that much refined sugar in it. Ever. Even on birthdays we always had sugar-free frozen yogurt or pies baked by my mom's health-guru personal chef. At school, Tank kept a watchful eye on my diet and reported back to my mom. Buzzkill.

"Thank you."

I cracked a tiny bit off the top and placed it on my tongue. It was so delicious I had to concentrate to keep from shoving the whole thing in my mouth.

"I'm Tammy Tanaka," Shelby's mom said, replacing the tray. "And you are Lia Washington, as I recall."

"Yeah. Yep. That's me," I replied, stupidly. "I love your store."

"Well, thank you," Tammy said. "What are you looking for, Fiddler? Something to wear for your Opry debut?"

"Fiddler?" Fiona said. "That's what you're going with?"

"I give everyone nicknames," Tammy explained. "Britta's

is Brainiac, for obvious reasons. Shelby's is Binky, because she sucked on a pacifier till she was about six years old."

"Mo-*om!*" Shelby griped from behind the curtain.

Fiona and I stifled laughs.

"I'd give you one that comes from your name, like Fifi over here, but Lia's already sort of a nickname, right?" She narrowed her eyes. "That short for anything?"

I almost choked on a muffin crumb. "Nope. Just Lia. You can call me Fiddler, if you want. And I'm looking for everything. Whole new wardrobe," I said, trying to distract her.

It worked. Tammy grinned and rubbed her hands together, her gold bracelets clinking. "Well, then. *This* is gonna be fun."

Half an hour later I was standing inside a small dressing room, checking out one of my new outfits—low-slung jeans, a studded belt, black vintage Converse, and a white T-shirt with a blown-out stencil of the Eiffel Tower on the front, plus a gold chain with a little bird pendant on it, the wings spread out like it was taking flight. Tammy had seen me admiring it and had thrown it in for free. It was pretty and delicate and seemed symbolic of my new situation. I was still getting used to the sight of myself in glasses again, but generally? I looked frickin' awesome. My mother would have retched if she could have seen me.

"The beginning is always today," I whispered.

Outside my little fashion cocoon, Fiona and Tammy were chatting, while Shelby continued to hide somewhere on the premises. I was just loading up my arms with the two other pairs of jeans, three summer dresses, one long gray skirt, two sweaters, and stack of T-shirts I'd picked out, when I heard the front door open. Heavy footsteps tromped in and I froze, imagining FBI, CIA, some kind of acronym in sunglasses and a gray suit. Until I heard Jasper's voice. And then my wrists began to hum.

"Good mornin', Miss T.," he said, and I imagined him touching the brim of his cowboy hat. "Fiona."

"Hello, Jax . . . Fitz," Tammy said. "To what do we owe the pleasure?"

"Just stopping by to check in about my plans with . . . hey! Who's trying on clothes?"

I glanced in the mirror. Did I look okay? What if the shirt was all wrong?

"It's Lia. She's giving herself a makeover."

"Like Lia really needs a makeover."

"Jasper, don't—"

Suddenly the curtain was jammed aside, and there stood Jasper. He wasn't wearing his cowboy hat after all, and his blond hair fell adorably over his forehead. His smile slowly turned into a frown.

"Shucks. I was hoping to find you at least half indecent," he said, blue eyes merry.

I tried hard not to blush, but it didn't work. Then the curtains to the back room opened, and Shelby stepped out, her slim arms crossed over her chest. "Real nice," she said, scowling at Jasper.

He gave her a look I couldn't decipher, and they stared each other down. Weird. Awkward. Unsettling.

"Sorry to disappoint," I told him, suddenly just wanting out of the line of fire.

Jasper turned to let me pass as I made my way to the counter with my new clothes.

"You could never disappoint, no matter how much clothing you do or don't have on," Jasper said.

Fiona stared at me as I pretended to not be affected by him. I was certain I was failing miserably. Shelby, meanwhile, walked over to a stack of jeans and started to unfold and refold them, snapping each pair as loudly as possible. The tension was thick enough to gnaw on.

Oh, God. Shelby and Jasper weren't, like . . .

"Speaking of little to no clothing, I hope you bought yourself a bathing suit," Ryan Fitzsimmons said, thankfully obliterating a highly disturbing image that was trying to form itself inside my mind. Without the spotlight on him, he looked entirely different. He was a little skinnier than I'd realized last night, his skin darker and his smile blinding. But the energy was the same. He looked like he was set to pop at any moment, like he was the kind of guy who was up for anything. "Mischievous" was the word that came to mind.

"I don't sell secondhand bathing suits, Fitz. It's unsanitary," Tammy said, shuddering as she began placing my things in a paper bag.

"Why would she need a bathing suit, exactly?" Fiona asked. Then she took one look at Ryan's face, and hers flooded with understanding. "Oh, crap! It's Fun Run tonight!"

"You know it, baby!" Ryan said, pointing at her with both index fingers. "And this one's gonna be epic."

"Although I think the bathing suit is strictly optional, no?" Jasper said, leaning one hip against the counter as he looked me up and down. "And I mean that in the best possible sense."

Shelby snapped another pair of jeans. I tried to ignore her.

"What the heck is Fun Run?" I asked.

"It's this thing Ryan's crazy brother came up with a few years ago, and now that he's off at college, Ryan has kept it going," Fiona explained.

"Um, excuse me, it's just this *awesome* thing my brother

came up with a few years ago." Ryan turned to me, rubbing his palms together, his knees slightly bent like he was about to catch a baseball. "On the first Friday of every month, we do a Fun Run. Every citizen of Sweetbriar between the ages of sixteen and twenty-five gets a text, from *moi.*" He paused to put his hand on his chest and bat his eyelashes. "The text tells them where to meet up and when. You have twenty minutes to get to the spot with the proper gear, or you have to work the party instead of enjoying it. And let me tell ya, we do enjoy our Fun Runs."

I glanced at Fiona. She nodded grudgingly. "They are pretty cool."

"So tonight's Fun Run requires a bathing suit?" I asked.

Jasper raised his hands. "I still say strictly optional."

Snap! went Shelby's jeans.

"Jax, don't be corrupting our Fiddler here. She just got to town," Tammy admonished.

I smiled. Her protectiveness felt oddly gratifying. And this Fun Run thing had gotten my adrenaline racing. It sounded like an adventure. Like just the kind of thing Cecilia Montgomery was never allowed to do, which meant that Lia Washington was all over it.

"Thanks so much, Tammy. For everything."

"Anytime, Fiddler," she replied. "And if you decide you

want those boots you've been eyeing, come on back and make me an offer."

"Bet on it."

I paid her for the clothes and slid the heavy bag from the counter. Along with my change, Tammy handed me a gold chain with a pretty bird pendant on it, wings spread out like it was taking flight. She must have seen me admiring it earlier.

"Gift with purchase," she said with a wink and a look that told me not to argue.

"Thanks," I replied.

Shelby stared me down so hard on my way out I almost flinched.

"Where you two off to in such a hurry?" Jasper asked. "I just got here."

"Well, apparently I have to go find myself a bathing suit," I told him.

"I suggest a halter style!" Tammy called after us. "It will totally flatter your figure!"

"Thank you!" I laughed as I followed Fiona out the door and on to the sidewalk. "She is awesome. How in the world did she produce Shelby?"

Fiona shook her head, eyebrows raised. "One of the many mysteries of nature."

"Hey, Red Sox!" We turned to find Jasper holding open

the door, giving me a teasing grin. "You need any second opinions on those bathing suits, you give me a holler and I'll come running."

I just about melted into the sidewalk. Luckily, before I could blurt out what was sure to be an incoherent response, Shelby appeared behind him.

"Are you coming back in, or are you just going to stand there wasting all the air-conditioning?"

Jasper laughed and gave us a little salute. "Ladies."

He went back inside, letting the door swing shut behind them. I caught one glimpse of Shelby's scowl before Fiona started up the sidewalk.

"Ryan seems nice," I said, trying to get my mind off Jasper. And Shelby. And the potential of Jasper and Shelby.

"He is. He's harmless," Fiona replied. "Those two have been friends practically since birth. Started out as day-care buddies, and now they're each other's wingmen whenever they go out."

Of course. It would come back to picking up girls.

"Is Jasper always that much of a flirt?" I asked.

"That's Jasper for you," she said, looking at the ground as she walked. She was pink around her ears, and her posture had slumped. "Don't know why he does it in front of Shelby, though. It's like he's trying to make trouble for himself."

Oh, for the love of . . . so it *was* true!

"Are he and Shelby, like—"

"Oh, right." Fiona looked up and smirked. "For a second I forgot you aren't from around here. Allow me to fill you in on the on-again-off-again saga that is the Jasper and Shelby story."

The saga of Jasper and Shelby? Ugh. This was a story I definitely didn't want to hear. But then . . . if he could go for a girl like her, it was just one more reason to write him off. I needed to stop thinking about that smile, stop seeing him up on stage with that guitar, stop fantasizing about what he looked like under those infuriatingly sexy cowboy shirts. Maybe imagining him with the awful Shelby was exactly the remedy I needed to get Jasper out of my system.

Resolved, I gave Fiona the nod. "Tell me every gory detail."

Chapter Seven

Jay's Pizzeria and Italian Ristorante, Home of the South's Best Pie, was all chrome and glass and lit by red and green fluorescent lights up front, with a candlelit restaurant in the back. The plan was for me to pick up the pizza and garlic knots that Britta, Fiona, and I had ordered for our postwork snack and bring them back to the apartment to await this Fun Run text, but I had other things on my mind. Namely, money math. After the shopping spree at Second Chances and splurging on sheets, bras, underwear, and the requisite Fun Run bathing suit at the Target three towns over, to which Fiona had kindly driven me, I had just over a thousand dollars left, three hundred of which would have to go to rent on July first. Plus Britta had just informed me that we were supposed to split the cable bill, which was another twenty-five bucks a month. It looked like I was going to be living lean until my first paycheck, whenever that came, and I'd yet to buy shampoo, soap, or any sort of food to tide me over.

A tiny knot of dread coiled inside my gut as I pulled out a few bills to pay for the food. I'd never had to worry about where breakfast, lunch, or dinner was going to come from, let alone any of the other necessities of life. What if my mother was right? What if I couldn't hack it out here on my own?

As if my own thoughts had conjured her, Senator Montgomery herself suddenly appeared on the small flat-screen TV that hung behind the counter, walking briskly up the steps of our Boston brownstone above the flashing words BREAKING NEWS. My fingers curled tight around the money in my hand as my throat went completely dry. The blood rushed so loud and hard through my ears, it took me a minute to tune in to what the voice-over was saying.

". . . still no leads on the whereabouts of her daughter, Cecilia Montgomery. Sources close to the family say that the FBI has recovered a set of suspicious fingerprints from inside the limousine in which Miss Montgomery was waiting when she was taken." This statement came over video of the water-logged limo being towed out of the bog where I'd left it.

Then the feed cut to my mom standing behind a podium

with about a dozen microphones attached. The shock of seeing her looking out at me was so severe I had to turn my back to the television.

"If anyone has any information as to the whereabouts of my daughter, please call the FBI's tip line," the senator said.

"So far, no ransom demands have been received. It seems all the family can do is wait and hope," the voice-over finished. "For channel four, this is Lacie May."

I let out a breath and tears stung my eyes. What the hell was wrong with me? I didn't give a crap what my mother was thinking or feeling or doing, any more than she'd ever cared about me. She was probably loving every minute of this, being in the spotlight, having a constant platform to discuss her agenda. If anything, I'd done her a favor.

A loud laugh caught my attention, and I turned around again. The TV was playing a commercial for window cleaner. Following the greeter down the center aisle of the restaurant was Shelby Tanaka, and Jasper Case had his hand on the small of her back. She laughed again as they settled into a cozy table in the back corner, their faces lit by the dim flicker of a single candle.

Great. That was exactly what I needed to see right now.

"Yeah, you don't want to get mixed up in the middle of all that."

I jumped at the sound of a voice at my shoulder. It was just Duncan, Fiona's brother, looking freshly showered with his dark hair wet and tossed back from his face. He wore a heather gray T-shirt, which showed off his pectorals quite nicely, and black athletic shorts that exposed his tanned, muscled calves. With his shoulders back and broad and his chin slightly raised, he gave off the air of a born athlete and someone who was completely comfortable in his own skin. But it was his smile that really caught the eye—big, and uninhibited.

"In the middle of all what?" I asked.

He chucked his chin toward Shelby and Jasper's corner. "That. Those two. They pretend like they're so fine being friends, but no one really believes it. It's a long story."

I looked back over at the couple and saw them leaning across the table to whisper. Then Jasper cracked up laughing, and my heart about died. There was no way Shelby Tanaka was in the least bit funny. It just wasn't possible.

"Yeah . . . Fiona told me some of it," I said. "Whatever. It's not like I care."

Duncan laughed. "Yeah, right." He shook his head as he twirled his keys once around his finger, then caught them in his palm. "Why do all the coolest girls always fall for Jasper Case?"

I caught his eye and blushed. Was he calling me cool? But wait, was he also saying he thought I'd already fallen for the town player?

"Order for Lia?"

I opened my mouth to reply to Duncan, but he gave me a quizzical look that stopped me cold.

"Order for Lia?" someone called out again.

"Um . . . that's you, right?" Duncan asked.

My heart lurched like I'd just been caught cheating. Crap. Yes. That was me. "I'm Lia!" I said, possibly a tad too loudly, considering the guy behind the counter was standing two feet away.

"All righty, then," he said pleasantly. "One pie with pepperoni and two orders of garlic knots."

I paid the man and waited for my change, which, I was disappointed to see, was not as much as I'd hoped for.

"You're eating with my sister," Duncan said with a sage nod. "Word to the wise: If you want one of those knots, I'd eat it now."

I laughed, trying to swallow back the nervousness left over from my moment of total oblivion. Rule number one when assuming a new identity: Answer to your own name.

"What're you guys up to?" Duncan asked.

I picked up the pizza box, the bag of garlic knots balanced

on top. "We were just going to eat and wait for this Fun Run thing to happen. Me, Fiona, and Britta."

"Ah, Fun Run. It's amazing how this place just sucks you right in, isn't it?" he said with a smile.

"You don't hate it here like your sister does?" I asked.

"Hate it? Please. I'm never leaving this place. Hell, one day I'm gonna run for mayor."

He was just about to push open the door for me when his phone beeped. In fact, several phones in the restaurant beeped. I glanced over my shoulder and saw Jasper and Shelby checking theirs. Duncan pulled his out of his pocket.

"Is that it?" I asked.

"Yep! We have twenty minutes to get to Little Lake with our bathing suits."

Jasper and Shelby had already jumped up from their table and were rushing our way, giggling like little kids. The sight of his hands on her waist as he steered her toward the door—much as he'd done with me at the Mixer last night—hurt my heart more than I'd ever admit.

"Do you have to go home and change?" I asked.

"Nope. I have a suit in my car," Duncan said, bouncing on the balls of his feet. "You?"

I reached up and tugged the bow at the back of my halter-top one-piece out from under my collar with my thumb. "Someone tells me to be ready, I'm ready."

Shelby shot us an irritated look as she and Jasper blew by. Jasper cleared his throat and ducked his head. Somehow I wanted to throttle them both.

"I like it," Duncan said, focused on me and only me. He offered me his free hand. "Fun Run, here we come!"

I hesitated just half a second before balancing my pizza and garlic knots on one hand and taking his with the other. "Let's do this thing."

Little Lake was exactly that—a pretty body of water that was somewhat larger than a pond and was so hemmed in by trees they seemed to be growing out of the water. By the time Duncan and I got there, him bumping the wheels of his VW over the dirt-and-rock parking area, there were already dozens of people milling around in bathing suits and shorts, drinking from red plastic cups and unloading food from their trucks and cars. On the skinny, rocky beach, a huge fire raged inside an open barbecue pit, where a beefy man in a chef's hat was throwing ribs on the grill. I heard a shriek and a splash and looked across the water. In the center of the lake were three huge bouncy houses with mesh walls and winding water slides. On the far side of the lake the sun was just starting to dip below the horizon, sending bursts of purple, yellow, and orange light through the leaves in a blinding show.

"This," I said, taking a breath, "is awesome."

"Welcome to Fun Run!" Duncan rubbed his hands together as he moseyed into the crowd, slapping a hand here and giving a hug there. He seemed to know everyone, and everyone seemed to be happy to see him.

"Wow. You really are going to be mayor one day," I said as we reached the water's edge.

Duncan laughed. "Hope you'll vote for me."

"I will." *If I'm still here,* I added silently.

Cars continued to pour into the lot behind us. Suddenly there was a loud peal of feedback. Ryan climbed up on the tailgate of a red pickup and lifted a megaphone to his face.

"Let the countdown begin!" he shouted. "Ten! Nine! Eight!"

"What's the countdown for?" I asked.

"The twenty-minute rule," Duncan explained, taking two cups of beer from a passing tray and handing me one. "If you're not here within the twenty minutes, you're put to work."

"Seven! Six! Five!"

"I thought that was a joke."

Duncan took a sip and shook his head. "Nope."

"Four! Three! Two! One!"

Everyone raised their cups and cheered as a few breathless stragglers raced to the beach. I saw Fiona and Britta among them. Britta bent over at the waist to suck in air.

"Sorry, ladies!" Ryan said, jumping down in front of them. "You're on keg duty for the next hour."

"Oh, man!" Fiona wailed. "We were, like, two seconds late!"

Ryan shrugged and moved off to make other assignments. Just then Britta looked up and spotted me. "You!" she cried.

"What?" I asked.

"You're *here*?" Fiona groused. "We were late because we were waiting for you."

My heart sank. "What? Why?"

"It's my fault, guys," Duncan said, stepping in. "We bumped into each other at Jay's, so when the text came in, I drove her."

"Duncan! You could have texted," Britta muttered. She took out her iPhone and checked it, as if expecting to find that she'd missed his text.

"Sorry, guys," he said knocking Britta's arm with his. "It's just an hour."

"Are y'all ready to swim?"

Jasper appeared as if from nowhere and pulled his T-shirt off over his head. The sudden sight of all that skin and all those abs knocked the wind right out of me. I took a step back and my foot came down on Duncan's toes.

"Ow! Okay! Okay! Maimed for life," Duncan cried, lifting his foot up.

Jasper just grinned at me. Shelby was nowhere in sight. "Like what you see?"

"Um . . . no," I said. "I just . . . no."

His smile only widened. He tossed his T-shirt toward a backpack he'd dumped on the beach and clapped his hands. "You guys wanna race to the rafts?"

"We have to work," Fiona groused.

"Oh. Bummer. D.? Red Sox?" Jasper asked.

"I think I'll sit this one out," Duncan said drily, turning away to take another sip of beer.

"Red Sox?" Jasper said again, raising his eyebrows adorably. "You swim?"

"Of course I swim," I said, hoping the waning light hid my lingering blush. I was a pretty strong swimmer, in fact, having been trained in the choppy ocean off Martha's Vineyard. I was pretty sure I could make it to the bouncy-house rafts in two minutes flat.

"So let's go! Strip down! Let's see this new bathing suit of yours!"

All four of them were eyeing me, waiting to see how I'd respond to the challenge. I handed Britta my beer and then very quickly and self-consciously took off my glasses, dropped my shorts and pulled off my T-shirt. The air was warm, but I still shivered standing there in nothing but my black bathing suit. Hardly anyone had ever seen me in a bathing suit before.

Jasper whistled. Duncan stared. All I could think about was getting in the water and letting it close over me.

"Ready-set-go!" I said quickly, like a little cheating kid, and tore off toward the water.

"Hey! No fair!" Jasper whined, equally like a little kid.

I was laughing as we plunged into the water.

"This is the life." I sighed, leaning back on the bobbing deck that was attached to one of the inflatable rafts.

"You said it," Jasper replied.

It took all my willpower not to run my eyes over his half-naked body for the fiftieth time that night, but I took a tiny peek. Just the way his shoulder muscles tapered into his arm gave me shivers.

"You like what you see, you can always make an offer," Jasper drawled lazily, closing his eyes.

I clamped my jaw shut and tried not to laugh. For two blissful hours Jasper Case had never left my side. It might have been the sky full of stars overhead, the giddiness of being free enough to swim under said stars, or the incredible cut of his wet muscles as they shone in the moonlight, but I couldn't seem to make myself care about anything else. Shelby had been MIA all night, so I didn't have to think about her, and Britta and Fiona had thawed once their keg shift was over and they'd been allowed to swim out. Duncan had spent most of the night playing basketball in a floating hoop with a bunch of friends.

"Dude!" Someone slapped the side of the raft, and I sat up so fast I almost fell off. It was Ryan. He smiled up at me, his legs treading water beneath us. "A bunch of us are swimming over to the other side to go skinny-dipping. You in?"

A thrill of the forbidden went right through me. Last year, after the junior-senior dance, a bunch of kids had snuck out of the dorms to go skinny-dipping in the school's Olympic-size pool. I had told my friends I'd meet them in the lobby, just wanting to do something—*anything*—remotely wild. I'd been hoping against hope that the Tank would sleep through me sneaking past his room, but when I opened the door at one a.m., he'd been standing right in front of it in a full suit, staring me down. Apparently he'd heard about it through the bodyguard grapevine. Some of the other kids' handlers were letting them go. But an employee of Rebecca Montgomery's? No way.

"Please. Not a chance," Jasper said, sliding into the water. "This girl has 'puritan' written all over her."

"I'm in!" I said.

Jasper's jaw slackened. He reached out to hold on to the raft for support. "That worked faster than I thought it would."

"I'm not in because of your lame attempt at reverse psychology," I said, splashing him in the face. "I'm in because I'm doing this thing where I'm trying stuff I've never tried before."

"Well." Jasper's eyes went smoldering. "That sounds promising."

I splashed him again and started to swim, following a handful of people who were headed to the far side of the lake. A couple dozen yards from the water's edge, when I could just feel my toes sliding against the slippery bottom, everyone stopped. I glanced around at the half-dozen strange faces and started to question my sanity. I didn't know any of these people. Was I really going to get naked with them?

Jasper and Ryan finally caught up. Ryan swam into the center of the circle, and within seconds his bathing suit was thrust in the air. All the girls cheered.

I started to hyperventilate. Slowly I eased back from the crowd, back toward the rafts, but then I bumped into something. Or, rather, someone.

"Are you okay, Red Sox?"

His voice was a low rumble in my ear. When I turned around, he was clutching his bathing suit in one hand. I yelped and pushed back.

"Oh, wow. You really never have done this before." Jasper glanced around. "Here. Come with me."

"What? Where?" I asked. With all the gasping for air, I wasn't sure how much longer I could tread water.

"Over here where you can stand. Before you have a heart attack."

He grabbed my hand and tugged me behind one of the trees, its branches stretching up from beneath the shallow water. When I put my feet down, I felt them scrape something solid. Tree roots.

"You okay?" Jasper asked. His hand was on my shoulder, but he was keeping a respectful distance. "Look me in the eye and breathe."

I did as I was told. After a few deep, meditation-style breaths, I forgot that he was naked under the water. All I saw were his blue eyes.

"You really don't have to skinny-dip. It's lame anyway," Jasper said.

He let his hand trail down my arm, and my skin shivered. Behind him I heard a whoop and a laugh, but I couldn't see anyone else beyond the tree's thick leaves. The bouncy-house rafts shuddered and shimmied, the peals of laughter seeming very far away.

If I was ever going to do this, the time was now.

"One sec," I said. Then I sank beneath the water's surface.

Just do it. Just do it do it do it. You're Lia Washington now. You can do anything.

My hands shook as I lifted the bathing suit strap over my head, then shoved the whole thing down. Water rushed in over my bare skin, tickling me all over. It was insane how removing that one skinny layer of fabric made me feel light as air—both brave and silly all at once. The suit was right around my knees when my lungs began to scream for air. This was it. I kicked the thing free, grabbed it up in one hand, and broke the surface, gasping.

When I rubbed the water from my eyes, Jasper was open-mouthed.

"Are you?"

"Yep!" I replied with a grin.

"No way," he said, and laughed.

"Yeah way." I was laughing too. Our mutual nakedness was making us giddy.

"No *way*!"

"*Yeah* way!"

All at once it hit me. This intense moment of déjà vu. Me standing with my hands on my hips in the park at the center of Sweetbriar, trying to make Jasper believe I could climb this big old oak I had no business trying to climb. Our exchange back then had been exactly the same. All the way up until I'd tried to climb it, gotten to the first limb, and then cried until Gigi got me down.

I looked at Jasper now, and my heart thunked. His expression mirrored mine. Then his gaze traveled over the tree next to us, and my toes curled into the thick bark beneath me. *Oh no, oh no, oh no. Please don't. Please don't remember me.*

A sudden splash startled me, and suddenly Shelby came swimming around the outermost branches of the tree. Her shoulders were bare too, and her hair was slicked back from her angular face, making her look like she was ready for the cover of *Sports Illustrated.*

"Thought I'd find you over here!" she said, swimming right up to Jasper, and she slung one arm around his neck in a familiar way that must have brought all sorts of naked body parts into contact with one another. Her eyes sliced right through me. "You can go now."

"Shelby!" Jasper said, then looked at me. "You don't have to—"

"Yeah, I really do," I said.

He called something after me, but between the swimming and the humiliation and the residual panic, his words were entirely lost.

Chapter Eight

The next morning, Britta was gone before I woke up, and I was feeling antsy. My meditation and tae kwon do exercises calmed me slightly, but not for very long. Jasper had almost recognized me. I was sure of it. Or maybe he had and I just didn't know about it yet. And also? I had skinny-dipped. *Skinny-dipped!* I had been naked inches away from a very hot, also very naked *guy*.

Yeah, there was no relaxing for me.

I had a shift at the diner starting at noon, and I needed to show up if I wanted to pay my rent and not end up sleeping on the street. But until then I had to get out of the house. I showered and dressed quickly, grabbed my backpack, and headed out. The morning sky was overcast, bathing the town in its dim, gray light. I looked around as if the world might drop a new adventure at my feet, but the town was extremely lazy this morning. Aside from a couple of kids flipping their skateboards in the park, there was nothing going on.

At a loss, I turned toward Peach Street to see what message the mysterious midnight painter had in store for me today. I paused at the sight of the green and blue lettering.

DO SOMETHING TODAY THAT YOUR FUTURE SELF WILL THANK YOU FOR.

Huh. Interesting. But what? And what could I do today that my future self would thank me for . . . for free? My stomach grumbled, and I decided to go to Second Chances. Maybe Tammy would have some more of those muffins to give away—and some suggestions for what to do around here. And if not, maybe I could just hang out with her.

When I shoved open the door of the shop, it was Shelby behind the counter again, this time in a light pink sundress with a shimmering cherry print. Her lips puckered at the sight of me. I wasn't exactly thrilled to see her, either. What was the deal with her and Jasper? If they weren't currently together, why was she so obsessively possessive of him? And worse, why did he let her act that way?

"What do *you* want?" she snapped.

I decided to play it cool. Act like last night hadn't affected me. The last thing I wanted was for this girl to think she had something over me.

"Is your mother around?" I asked.

Her eyes narrowed. "Why?"

"I . . ." I couldn't exactly say I'd been hoping her mommy would feed me, so I gestured toward a line of footwear against the wall. "She told me to come back and make an offer on those boots."

Shelby sashayed out from behind the counter and crouched, the skirt of her dress fluttering artfully to the floor around her. "Which ones? These?"

"The black ones with the steel toes," I said.

With a smirk I couldn't guess the meaning of, Shelby plucked the cowboy boots from the floor and whacked me in the chest with them. "They're yours. Just stay the hell away from Jasper."

With a flip of her hair she returned to the counter, forcing me to grab the boots before they could hit the floor.

"I'm sorry . . . what?"

"Back off," she said, her hands flat on the glass countertop. "He's mine."

I laughed. "Okay, first of all, I've talked to the guy exactly four times. And second, I hate to tell you this, but the first time I met him he was crawling out of some random girl's window."

Shelby's perfect skin flushed, but she didn't break eye contact. "I'm aware of Jasper's extracurricular activities." She took out a black velvet tray full of glittering bracelets and began to carefully rearrange them. The overhead lights were reflected in the perfect cherry-red lacquer on her nails. "We're on a break right now while I allow him to sow his wild oats."

It didn't look much like a break last night, I thought.

"Really? And it doesn't bother you?" I asked, genuinely curious.

"Oh, believe me. I'm sowing a few of my own as well," Shelby said, though she seemed so tightly-wound I could hardly believe it. "But Jasper and I?" Here, she looked up and folded her hands primly on the counter. "We're meant to be. We will be together in the end. So don't waste your time."

"Well, thank you for your concern about my precious time, but I can take care of myself."

With that I walked out, feeling shaken, but also a little bit proud as I turned up Main Street. I'd never been in a fight with a mean girl before. I felt like I'd just survived some sort of milestone or pledging ritual. It wasn't until I was half a block away that I realized I was still clutching the boots and that I hadn't paid for them. God, I wished I'd tossed some money on the counter and said something about not taking charity. Why was this only coming to me now and not when I'd had the opportunity to pull it off? I'd have to go back and pay Tammy for them later.

The scent of frying bacon made my stomach grumble, and I realized I was closing in on the diner. I was just wondering if Hal offered an employee discount on food (it was free when I was on shift) when a sleek black Town Car pulled around the corner of the park onto Main Street. My pulse began to thrum in my ears as the car ever so slowly trawled its way toward my corner. I couldn't see who was behind the wheel, but it was completely out of place among the pickup trucks and minivans that populated Sweetbriar. I knew I should run, that I should duck inside the closest shop and hide, but I couldn't seem to make myself move. And besides, whoever was inside that car had already seen me. I was standing out in the middle of the open air like a sitting duck.

The car drew closer, and I knew in my heart of hearts that it was going to stop at the curb in front of me. That the driver would get out and open the rear door, and out would step my mother, the red soles of her Louboutin heels crunching against the pavement.

Well. It was fun while it lasted.

I held my breath, but the car kept right on driving. Maybe Gigi was smiling down on me and had momentarily distracted whoever was in the car so they'd turn away before they could catch me. Or maybe it was just some livery driver lost on his way to the airport. Whatever the reason for this stroke of luck, I turned on my heels and ran straight to the diner. When the door closed behind me, I waited to feel safe, to feel like everything was going to be fine. But that feeling never came.

I reached up to touch the flying-bird pendant that hung against my collarbone. Why did I suddenly feel as if there was a ticking clock on my newfound freedom?

"We have to take this girl water-skiing at Lake Pleasant, ASAP," Duncan said, reaching around me with a plate of fries that night. His torso leaned against my back as his arm brushed mine, and I got the distinct feeling that he lingered there a second longer than was strictly necessary.

Was Duncan interested in me? He wasn't unattractive. And he'd be a much safer bet than the possibly taken, definitely playing Jasper.

Not that I was looking for romance anyway. Romance was not my focus. Living was my focus. Trying new things, experiencing life. At least until the Wicked Witch of the Senate descended on Sweetbriar with her flying FBI agents. Ever since my close encounter with the black sedan earlier this morning, I couldn't stop thinking about it. To my lifelong East Coast–dwelling mother, Sweetbriar was the serious middle of nowhere, but what if she did, somehow, find me? I had to live each second as if it were my last. Which was all the more reason I was loving the current trajectory of our conversation.

"Do you water-ski?" Fiona asked, sliding a bottle of ketchup toward me.

"Never have," I said. "But I'm in."

"That's my girl." Duncan squeezed my shoulder, then doused half the fries in ketchup. Outside the plate-glass windows rain was falling at a steady pace, and it had been for the last few hours. A baseball game was playing on the flat-screen TV that hung in the corner, the volume muted, and the atmosphere inside the diner was equally hushed. It was after eight o'clock now, post–dinner rush and pre–late-night snack binge, so the diner was mostly empty. A family of four with two well-behaved little kids occupied a table near the door, and a teenage couple sat on the same side of one of the two-top booths, making out between sips of their sodas. Other than that, the three of us, Hal, and the two chefs in back were alone.

"What else do you need to do to call yourself a true Sweetbriaran?" Fiona mused, leaning sideways against the counter while Duncan and I munched on our fries. It was all I could do not to shovel them into my mouth by the handful.

Aside from a quick bowl of cereal right before my shift, I hadn't eaten all day.

"I like Sweetbriarite better," Duncan said.

I narrowed my eyes thoughtfully. "It does have a ring."

"Race bikes down the Brookline hill," Duncan said, snapping his fingers.

"Yeah, if you're twelve," Fiona chided. "Oh! You have to try the dim sum at Jimmy's." She leaned toward me to whisper, "Best food in town."

"Don't let Dad hear you say that," Duncan chided. "What else do we do for fun around here? You could come to one of my soccer matches."

"He's only saying that because he wants to show off," Fiona told me. "He does this spin-kick move that makes all the girls swoon. In his opinion."

Duncan's face fell. "Hey! Way to be supportive, Fi."

"Just trying to look out for my new friend here."

"Well, I appreciate that," I said, popping a fry into my mouth. "But I think I should be able to survive the sight of a soccer kick without fainting dead away. No matter how glorious it is."

Duncan lifted a finger as if he was about to make a very important point, but he was cut off when his father walked out of the kitchen carrying two large paper to-go bags.

"Lia, your shift's almost up. You mind delivering this over to Daria Case's house? Apparently Jasper's band got hungry mid–jam session." His tone was slightly sarcastic, as it was whenever he spoke about Jasper.

There was a distinct shift in Duncan's posture, his expression darkening.

"Daria's house? I thought she lived over the salon."

The three of them looked at me kind of funny. "Daria hasn't lived up there in years. She's got a house over on Greenwood," Hal said.

"Oh." Crap. There went my stupid mouth again. "I . . . uh . . . I guess I just assumed . . ." I grabbed the bags from Hal. "Yes, I can bring them. No problem."

Anything to get out of here right now.

Besides, the thought of seeing Jasper was definitely intriguing. I'd promised myself I'd stay away from him, and I had also been warned in no uncertain terms to stay away from him, but I needed to know if he'd remembered me last night. And also, okay, I *wanted* to see him.

So much for romance not being my focus.

"I'll do it, Dad," Duncan said, eyeing me as I untied my apron. "She doesn't even have a car."

"It's a short walk," Hal said. He tore a page off one of the order pads and scratched out directions on the back before handing it to me. "She can take one of the umbrellas from the lost and found."

"Yeah, but—"

"It's fine," I told them both. "I could use the fresh air."

Hal passed me an umbrella and I headed for the door, cradling the bags. Duncan looked so forlorn, I felt a small twinge of guilt. It was nice to be noticed by someone like him. It was nice to be noticed by anyone. And I felt like I was squashing his hopes under the heels of my new black boots.

"I do appreciate the chivalry, though," I told him.

Duncan grunted. "You just remember that when you're in the presence of the great Jasper Case."

Aside from a few porch lights, the house at 221 Greenwood Lane was dark, but the detached garage was ablaze with light. Rain battered the umbrella over my head as I shifted the straw handles on the bags inside my palm. The bags were heavy, and the straps had been cutting into my flesh throughout the walk. It was a warm night, even with the rain, and a trickle of sweat wove down my spine. In fact, I felt clammy all over and wished like anything I had looked in the mirror for wayward swipes of chocolate or ketchup on my person before trekking out to see Jasper. Which was probably why I didn't notice the lack of music until I was almost right outside the garage's side door. That's when a cymbal crashed and almost scared the life out of me.

"What the f—"

"You know, I'd heard you were a controlling jackass, but I chose not to believe it," someone shouted. "Bad on me."

"Benny," a girl's voice said in a conciliatory tone.

"Well, excuse me for trying to get our name out there!" Jasper's voice. "I was just hoping to get us some exposure!"

"That's all well and good, but you can't just go around booking gigs without runnin''em by us!" the first voice shouted again. "My baby girl's birthday party is that day, and there's no way I'm missin' it. Cheryl'll kick my ass to the curb if I do."

Silence.

"So?"

"So . . . what?" Jasper asked.

"Are you gonna get us out of it or what?"

"I can't! If I cancel now, they're never gonna ask me—us—to play there again!"

"God. You are so transparent." The girl's voice cut in now. "It's all about you, isn't it? Always has been, always will be. I'm outta here."

The door shoved all the way open, and I jumped. The girl—the drummer—stood there for a second, as surprised as I was, then shook her head and stormed off to a big, fairly badass motorcycle parked nearby. As she pulled her helmet on and started the engine—a roar that I actually felt inside my chest—the other two band members walked out. Neither of them acknowledged me. They simply flipped their hoods up over their heads, trundled over to an old Buick, got in, and peeled out.

There was another crash from inside the garage as I slowly approached the door. Jasper was sitting on a worn-out old couch with his head in his hands, his chest heaving. The two high hats from the drum set had been toppled over, and one of them was rolling across the floor.

"Um . . . hi," I said quietly.

There was hope in his eyes as he stood up, and I can't say I wasn't disappointed when it died on the spot. Maybe he thought I was the drummer returning to give him a second chance.

"Oh. Hey."

I stepped inside warily, lowering the umbrella and shaking it out over the asphalt floor of the garage. My palms screamed mercy when I shifted one bag to the other hand and held them both up by my fingers.

"Guess you won't be needing all this food, then."

He exhaled shortly, hands on his hips as he angled away from me. "Nope. Guess not."

I wished he would look at me directly so I could see whether there was any recognition or suspicion in his eyes. But then I gave myself a mental smack. Clearly, Jasper was upset. Right now was not about me.

"What happened?" I asked.

"Oh, nothing. Just lost another band. This one's a new record." He groaned, his back to me now, and tipped his head back with his hands over his face. "We were only together for a month and had exactly one gig."

I put the food bags down and moved tentatively into the room, stepping over thick black cords and skirting a huge amp balanced on top of a wooden platform. "What was the longest?"

He turned to face me. My heart gave a little lurch. But there was no hint of recognition or suspicion there. He hadn't figured out who I was. I let out a breath of relief, and he dropped down again onto the beat-up couch.

"The second one. We were together a whole nine months before it imploded." He shook his head ruefully, letting his hands fall between his knees. The pose made him look vulnerable. I found myself standing right across from him now, not knowing what to say. This was the first conversation we'd ever had that wasn't based on flirtatious banter. "You know, sometimes I honestly think I was not meant to be around people."

My heart squeezed. That was something I'd thought about myself a million times over. When I was little, right after the attempted kidnapping, I'd been so cloistered I hardly ever saw anyone other than my tutor and my bodyguards. Then, when my parents enrolled me at the Worthington School, I had no clue how to relate to kids my own age. I was so nervous that whenever someone talked to me, I froze up, and eventually they stopped trying. Sure, over the last couple of years I'd made a few casual friends, but no one I felt a real connection with. I was never sure how much I was supposed to reveal or what kinds of questions were okay to ask, and in the back of my mind I was always thinking that if I screwed up, they'd just stop trying again. So mostly I agreed with everyone and everything out loud, even when I didn't inside my head.

No wonder I ran away. It was easier to steal a car than to really have it out with anyone, especially my mom. Of course, none of this had anything to do with Jasper's current situation.

"Have you ever thought about going solo?" I suggested. "Then you won't *have* to deal with people."

Jasper laughed and leaned back on the couch. I walked around a pile of magazines and newspapers to join him, and he looked me up and down as I sat. We were separated by the length of a couch cushion, but I still felt a sizzle between us, simply from sharing the same furniture.

"Like it's that easy."

"Why not? Is there really that much difference between being a solo act and fronting a band?" I asked. "You could do some gigs completely solo—just you and your guitar—or you could hire backup players, right? For when you absolutely need a drummer."

With a smirk Jasper lifted one leg onto the couch so he could face me. "Or you could play with me."

"Jasper," I said, exasperated. There he went again, making everything an innuendo. "Don't—"

"No! I'm serious! You have some real talent."

Oh. Oops. I averted my eyes, embarrassed.

"Well, thank you, but I don't even own a violin anymore," I said.

"What? That's crazy! How can you possibly squander a talent like that? You can't—"

"And besides," I interjected, "we're talking about you right now."

Jasper let out a sigh. "Okay, fine. But if I had backup musicians, I'd still have to figure out a way to pay them. And besides . . ."

He picked at a loose string on the cushion between us.

His fingers were so close to my leg now, I imagined I could feel the heat coming off them.

"Besides what?" I asked.

"Besides, if he goes out on his own, there's no one to blame when things go south." We both looked up as Daria walked into the room, carrying a brown bag with the word JIMMY'S emblazoned across it and grease stains near the bottom. She was wearing a big pink rain jacket and a matching rain hat with a black flower attached to it. "Isn't that right, baby?"

Jasper and I both stood up. "Lia, I believe you've met my grandmother, Daria?" Jasper said formally.

"Yes. It's good to see you again," I said, my palms prickling with sweat. Every time I saw her, I was overwhelmed by memories of Gigi.

"You too, sweet pea." She gave me an appraising flick of a glance before her eyes rested on mine. My heart skipped a startled beat. She knew. She *knew*. "Care to stay for dinner? It looks like we have more food than we can handle."

Okay, maybe not. Maybe I was just being paranoid. Still, I knew I shouldn't stay. So far I didn't have the greatest track record for keeping my mouth shut. If I said the wrong thing in front of Daria, this was all over.

"Thank you, but I really have to get going," I said, looking at Jasper.

Are you crazy? my heart asked as I moved toward the door, pounding like mad. *You can't leave now. Look at him! You were just having your first meaningful conversation. Don't bail on him now! Don't—*

"Wait up, Lia," Jasper called, stopping both my feet and the insane ramblings of my heart. He jogged across the room. "I'll walk you home."

Chapter Nine

"What are you thinking about right now?" Jasper asked.

For the first time since we'd left his house, I stopped staring at my feet. That was when I realized we weren't walking back to town the same way I'd come. Jasper had led me away from his grandmother's house to the north instead of the south. He was purposely taking a longer route. Daria lived on a quaint street lined with deep front porches and flowering hedges. Droplets of water glistened on the petals of pink and white blooms, shimmering under the streetlights, and the whole world seemed hushed. Somewhere in the distance I could hear car tires *shoosh*ing over damp streets, but the soothing noise only served to make me feel more alone. Alone with Jasper.

I took a deep, soothing breath. A smattering of stars peeked out from between two wispy clouds. If Gigi were looking down on me, she'd want me to live in the moment. I resolved to try, but I also knew that I couldn't tell Jasper what I'd actually been thinking about. Namely his naked body in the lake last night.

"Do you live there? With your grandmother?" I asked.

"No." He laughed. "Not anymore. I have a little apartment on the other side of town."

"But you grew up with her?" I already knew this to be true, of course, but he didn't know that I knew.

"Yep," he replied. "My dad split before I was born, and my mom died when I was two. I don't even remember her."

The lump that seemed to be ever so fond of my throat these days reappeared with a vengeance.

"I'm so sorry. I didn't know." Gigi had never told me anything about Jasper's parents when I was little, and at six years old I'd never thought to ask.

"How could you?" Jasper said with a shrug.

"What was it like, growing up with Daria? She seems like she knows you pretty well."

"Oh, yeah? Why? Because of that comment she made about me blaming other people for my failures? That was nice of her." There was an edge to his voice, but then he laughed, running his hand along the back of his neck. "Growing up with Daria was . . . growing up with Daria. She was the only parent I ever really knew. I went through a kind of asshole phase when I was thirteen, but she nipped that right in the bud."

"An asshole phase?" I asked with a laugh.

"Yeah, you know, smoking cigarettes, tearing up the town with these losers, vandalism. All standard lashing-out-because-I don't-have-a-father crap. At least that's what the guidance counselor at school reckoned."

It was interesting, how he talked about it so casually. Clearly it had affected him, but he wasn't letting it affect him now.

"Anyway, after that she told me I had to get involved in something at school. Didn't care what. Just wanted me to focus on somethin'. You know, care about somethin'. A lot of kids around here were forced into football by their parents or had to be on the farm every day after school, but she let me find what I loved, which was cool."

"And you found music," I said.

Jasper smiled. "I found music."

"I miss the violin sometimes," I mused. "I miss how I could get so lost in it."

"Why'd you quit?" Jasper asked.

I couldn't exactly answer that question honestly, could I? Not without him thinking I was half cracked. I was just trying to cobble together a response when suddenly Jasper's hand shot out and stopped my forward progress. I was so surprised I almost yelped.

"Sorry. Puddle."

Sure enough, I'd been about to step in a deep lake left behind by the storm.

"Well, thank you, kind sir," I joked, batting my eyelashes like a cartoon character.

"Just tryin' to be a gentleman," he replied. "Or don't they have those where you come from?"

"None like you," I said.

We shared a smile. A long, languid smile. A light breeze tickled the hair across Jasper's forehead, and I realized I could have stayed there all night. For the first time in a long time, my mind was quiet. The ticking clock had faded to a slight background noise. But then a motorcycle revved nearby, and we kept walking, stepping wide around the puddle.

"What about you? What was your home life like back in Florida?"

Great. An even more difficult question to answer. I pressed my lips together. Time to feed him a few more lies with a dash of semitruths. This part of my new life I really hated.

"Well . . . my dad was okay," I said. "He used to take me to movies and baseball games—stuff like that—when he could." Which was technically true . . . but it had been a long time ago. So long that I barely remembered it now. Just stray images. A box of dropped popcorn, a big foam hand, my dad's smile backlit by glowing neon advertisements. "He's a big Red Sox fan, which is why I have the hat. But we'd go see the Rays play."

"I was wondering about that," Jasper said, easily accepting the lie. "And your mom?"

My fingers curled into fists. "I don't like to talk about my mom." Also truth.

"Oh. Sorry. I just figured—"

His phone beeped, and he paused to pull it from his back pocket. "Saved by the tone," he joked, holding it up.

I laughed, but inside I was cursing myself. What the hell was wrong with me? Here we were, out for a romantic walk that he had suggested, and I couldn't be lighthearted for five minutes in a row. When I turned back again, Jasper quickly hid the screen behind a cupped palm. The tops of my cheeks burned. He was texting a girl. Of course he was.

"Who's that?" I asked.

"Just an e-mail blast about this acoustic showcase coming up in a few days in Nashville. They're holding last-minute auditions in a coupla days."

"You should do it!" I exclaimed, possibly a bit too heartened by the fact that it wasn't actually a girl. "It's your chance to go solo!"

"Yeah? I don't know." Jasper looked doubtful and adorably hopeful at the same time. "I don't have a lot of time to practice . . ."

"So? Sing whatever song you know the best," I suggested. "You have to do it. You'll be great!"

"Maybe." Jasper pocketed his phone as we turned up one of the side streets toward Main. "What makes you so confident?"

"I'm not. I just want to see you fall on your face," I joked.

Jasper laughed, and the sound sent my hopeless heart racing. "Thanks a lot."

"No, but seriously, why not try?"

"You mean like last night? Trying stuff you've never tried before?" he asked with a twist of a smile.

I blushed like crazy but refused to look away. "You've played in front of crowds before."

He lifted a shoulder and looked around. "Yeah, I mean . . . crowds around here, sure. Here I know everyone.

But Nashville? With actual record people there?"

"Omigosh, you're scared," I said, surprised.

He blinked, hurt.

"No, no! I don't mean it like that!" I said, gamely grabbing his arm. "I just mean, I didn't think you were scared of anything."

"Yeah, well, I guess I'm not like you," he said, and kept walking.

Huh? He thought *I* was brave? I was stunned frozen for so long I had to jog to catch up. "What does that mean?"

Jasper paused and threw his arms wide. "It means you don't seem to be scared of anything!" he exclaimed. "It's one of the things I like most about you. Even though it also kind of makes me crazy."

Just *one* of the things? Wow.

"I don't follow."

"You show up here out of nowhere and make friends and get a job and start a whole new life. You don't even blink in the face of Hidden Talent Showcase or skinny-dipping or *anything*. And you've put me in my place more times than I can count."

Huh. I really had done all those things, hadn't I? I chewed on my lip, trying not to smile.

"So tell me, Lia Washington, what exactly *are* you afraid of?" he asked.

Everything, I thought. *Life. My family. You.*

We stepped out under the brighter streetlights of Main Street, and I felt a shiver as he looked me in the eye. I realized, suddenly, that I could tell him the truth. That it might be the first real truth I shared with him since we'd remet. The idea, while terrifying, was also tantalizing.

"Honestly?" I said. "Being here right now scares me a little."

Jasper's eyes searched mine. He took a step closer to me, ran his hand down my arm from my shoulder to my fingers, and took them lightly in his. His hands were large and rough and calloused, but his touch was gentle.

"You've got nothing to be scared of here," he told me.

My eyelids fluttered. Suddenly I saw the wall of the Book Nook in my mind's eye. Maybe this was the something I'd do today that my future self would thank me for. The idea almost made me giggle as Jasper shifted his weight, leaning in ever so slightly to—

"Jasper Case! There you are! I've been waiting on you for fifteen minutes!"

I staggered back so quickly and blindly that my skull collided with a lamppost. Standing in front of a set of stairs leading up to a glass doorway was a short, curvy brunette with the shiniest lips I'd ever seen. She had taken a defensive stance, hip out, arms across her chest, as she stared the both of us down.

"Oh, hey there, Charlene!" Jasper said, recovering himself. "I'm so sorry. I thought we said nine thirty!" It was pretty clear from his face that he had no recollection of making any plans with her at all, but luckily for him, I seemed to be the only one who noticed.

"We *said* nine," Charlene replied, shifting her weight so that the other hip cocked. "Were you about to kiss her?"

Oh, God, now I really was going to die. Jasper's jaw hung slightly open as if he didn't know how to answer that question. I might have found it funny in any circumstance other than this one. Because yes, he had been about to kiss me, and even though this particular moment was completely humiliating, I still kind of wished she'd turn around so he could do it. Something was seriously wrong with me.

"Um, no," I said, stepping sideways down the walkway. "He most definitely was not."

"Lia, hang on. At least let me walk you the rest of the way to your place."

I glanced up at the apartment building where Charlene had been waiting. Was this her apartment, or his? Had he actually asked a girl to come get him at his place and then forgotten he was supposed to be there? I wasn't sure whether to be flattered that I was the one who'd made him forget, or completely appalled that he could ever do such a thing.

"No. I'm good. It's only a couple blocks." I turned on my heel and stormed off. "You two have fun!" I shouted back over my shoulder.

"Oh, don't worry! We will!" Charlene yelled back.

It was all I could do not to scream in disappointed, heart-broken fury as I speed-walked the rest of the way home.

By the time I shoved my new key in the lock, my whole body was vibrating with rage. I wasn't sure who I was angrier at, myself or Jasper. I mean, obviously I had no claim on him. We'd just met. He'd probably made that date days ago, and it wasn't like he had any sort of responsibility toward me. I wasn't even sure if he remotely liked me. He did flirt with any person in possession of double X chromosomes. What made me think I might be special? It was all my fault, really, getting my hopes up, letting my guard down, allowing myself to be vulnerable.

But then he was the one who was going in for the kiss when his date for the night was standing not ten feet behind him.

I finally managed to get the door open and stormed inside, slamming it for all it was worth.

"Damn. Way to make an entrance."

Britta sat on the brown couch, reaching down to lace up a pair of purple knee-high boots over her signature fishnets. Fiona sipped a beer at the small kitchen island. The pile of magazines and newspapers had grown, and the one on top had a giant picture of six-year-old yours truly emblazoned across the cover, this one from the riding camp I'd attended until I was eight. Until everything changed.

MONTGOMERY FAMILY HEIR STILL MISSING!

Awesome.

"You okay?" Fiona asked. "You look a little Mentos-in-a-soda-bottle over there."

"I'm fine. Great!" I exclaimed, tossing my keys onto the counter. They slid off the glossy cover of an *US Weekly* and hit the floor with a clatter. I stared at them for a second and briefly considered picking them up and flinging them across the room. Instead I took in one breath for nine counts, then breathed out for the same, a tried-and-true calming technique. "What're you two up to?" I asked brightly.

"We're going to Ruckus to see the Firebrand Three," Britta said, like I was supposed to know who that was.

"The Firebrand Three?" I asked.

Britta stared at me. "They're this totally up-and-coming band, like, seconds from scoring a serious record deal." The "duh" was implied.

“They’re really awesome live,” Fiona said. “Plus their music is totally danceable. Right, Brit?”

“If you like to dance.” Britta shrugged her shoulders into a slouchy knit bolero and pushed her faux glasses up on her nose. “You wanna come?”

“Yeah. Yes! I am one hundred percent in. Just let me change my clothes.” I grabbed my keys and strode into my room, which gave me the gratifying opportunity to slam another door.

“Just make it quick! They go on in half an hour!” Fiona shouted after me.

I pushed aside the curtain that hid my closet. Quick was not going to be a problem, considering my lack of choices. I stripped out of my clothes and boots, ripped down one of the sundresses I’d bought at Second Chances—a blue one with white flowers embroidered along the hem of the skirt—and pulled it on over my head. Then I yanked the black cowboy boots I’d yet to pay for back onto my feet. Folding some of my cash into the dress’s side pocket, I grabbed my keys and walked out again, headed for the bathroom. Fiona and Britta kept a good distance as they watched me tromp across the living room, as if they really were worried I was about to blow. After a quick swipe of deodorant and a splash of water on my face, I put my glasses back on and I was ready.

"You good?" Britta asked when I walked out of the bathroom five minutes later.

"Oh yeah," I said, flipping my keys once around my finger before dropping them in the second pocket. "This girl is ready to party."

And put Jasper Case entirely out of my mind.

"This place is freaking amazing!" I shouted, waving my hands over my head on the dance floor.

Ruckus was like no place I'd ever been before. It was huge—about three times the size of the Mixer—and had three separate, raised dance floors. The one in the center was a circle made of wood planks where only line dancing was allowed, while the two flanking it, closer to the stage, were a couple of black lacquer free-for-alls. Along the walls were battered wooden benches, on top of which a throng of girls and guys danced like no one was watching. The Firebrand Three was bringing the house down, and I'd never danced so hard or so long in my life.

In fact, to be quite honest, I couldn't remember the last time I had danced at all, at least not outside the confines of my tiny dorm room, listening to music on my iPod so as not to disturb the serious studiers in the rooms around mine.

"Told you they were awesome!" Fiona shouted back,

her skirt flaring out around her as she twirled.

Somewhere up near the stage, Britta took notes on the band in a tiny notebook, since there were no tables to speak of. I was kind of in awe of her work ethic. How could she be surrounded by so much fun-having and not feel the need to let her freak flag fly?

Fiona suddenly grabbed my arms, her fingers around my elbows. Sweat beaded her upper lip and forehead, and her hair had come loose from its carefully woven side braid. "I need a break," she gasped. "Let's go get a drink!"

"Works for me!"

We jumped down from the platform on which we'd been dancing and, holding hands, wove our way through the crowd to the spot where Britta was standing. She stared up at the band with a thoughtful expression, so close to the stage she could probably count their nose hairs.

"Brit! Could you go up and get us a couple beers?" Fiona asked her, screaming in her ear to be heard over the music.

Britta nodded and lifted a finger in a *be right back* gesture. Being twenty-one made Britta's job much easier, since so many music venues were bars, and a lot of them didn't allow patrons under twenty-one through the door. This one did, but they'd immediately cuffed me and Fiona with bright pink armbands, proclaiming to the world our inability to legally drink.

Luckily, we had Britta. I was already two beers in and feeling a buzz. Which was nice, because while it didn't completely erase all thoughts of Jasper from my mind, it did take the sting off. Between the dancing and the drinking and the girl bonding I was starting to feel as if everything might be okay. As if Jasper Case and what he did with his evenings didn't matter.

I lifted Fiona's hand and twirled her once under my arm, laughing like I was just so carefree. She lost her balance, forcing me to catch her, and when I looked up, the buzz was gone.

Because Jasper Case was here. And so was his date, Charlene. One of her legs was between his, and their groins were smashed up against each other as they grinded for all they were worth. As I watched, dumbfounded and sick, he trailed his hand down her back—the very hand that had held mine just a couple of hours ago—and cupped her very ample and perky ass.

"Ugh. Charlene Carson? Seriously?" Fiona said, making a disgusted face.

What would Shelby think of that*?* I wondered.

"Here."

Britta returned and shoved a bottle of beer at each of us. Fiona and I clinked the long necks of our bottles, then chugged. The beer went down the wrong way, and I leaned forward, gagging foam and ale out all over my boots.

"Are you okay?" Fiona asked.

"Fine!" I shouted back, coughing. I wiped beer off my face with the back of my hand and noticed a few drops down the front of my dress. My mother would have been disgusted if she'd seen me like this, but I couldn't have cared less.

Everyone else in this town was sowing their wild oats. It was about time I started sowing mine.

My head was on fire, but my palms were cold and clammy. Streamers of colorful light whipped past my vision, dizzying me. I was trying to get to the bathroom, but the floor seemed to be moving. Every time I put my foot down, I stepped on someone else's. I'd never been cursed out so violently in my life by that many people in succession.

Actually, I'd never been cursed out, period. I was having a lot of new life experiences lately.

"How much further?" I asked Fiona.

But my words ran together, and it came out more like "Homfutter?"

"We're here," she said, supporting half my weight as we staggered sideways.

She shoved open the door with one hand and dragged me past the mirrors, where I caught the grossed-out expressions on the reflections of maybe two dozen girls. Then we were inside a tiny stall, and I saw the grit mashed into the space between the tiles and a dead fly with its legs up in the corner and the brown rim around the water inside the toilet and that was it.

I threw up.

My hands gripped the ring of the somewhat slimy bowl, and my knees hit the floor with a crack. Fiona put her hand on my forehead, supporting my head as the heaves racked my body. Finally, I spat, closed my eyes, and flushed.

"Are you okay?" Fiona asked.

My butt hit the floor as I pushed my glasses up on my nose with the side of my hand. "'M glad you're here. It's much nicer puking with you than it is with the Tank."

I leaned the side of my face against the cool wall of the stall and closed my eyes. I remembered Tim hovering over me that time I was sick with the stomach bug that had ravaged my entire school, and the private nurse my mom had hired taking my pulse while I shook in bed. My mother had never in her life been there when I was sick. Never held my hand or read me stories or taken my temperature. Nope. No motherly love for me. Instead I got a retired pro-wrestler bodyguard and a nurse with a puggle nose and a severe attitude problem.

"The Tank?" Fiona asked with a giggle. She was a tad drunk herself, but clearly not as drunk as me. "What's that?"

"Just this guy who used to watch me," I said, adjusting my skirt and pressing my face tighter against the wall. The wall held me up. The wall was my friend. "It's a whole big thing."

"What? You mean like a stalker?" Fiona asked, suddenly shrill. "Did you have to get, like, a restraining order?"

My eyes popped open, and pain stabbed my skull. Damn it. What had I just said? I tried to remember the words that had, but seconds ago, spewed from my mouth and in what order, but trying to remember only made the pain worse.

"Can you just go?" I said to Fiona, waving my hands at her.

"What? No. I'm not gonna leave you in here without—"

"Go!" I shouted now, shoving myself up as best I could. "Please! Get out, Fiona. I need to be alone."

I needed to figure out exactly what I'd told her and how to explain it later when I was sober. If I was ever sober again.

"Fine. But I'll be right outside." Fiona opened the door, which was next to impossible with both of us in there, and slipped out.

As soon as she was gone, I slammed the bowl closed and

somehow half crawled, half hoisted myself up onto it. Sitting now, I put my head between my knees and groaned.

"Hey! Are you ever coming out of there?" someone shouted, banging on the door.

"One second!" I muttered.

I took a deep breath and blew it out. Then another. Then another. The insides of my nostrils prickled with the pungent odors of ammonia and pee. My head pounded along with the beat of the dance music vibrating the walls all around me. The band had signed off more than an hour ago and we'd been dancing to music spun by a DJ ever since. Britta had kept the beers flowing, and I'd just kept handing over the dollar bills until I was cleaned out. Cleaned out and potentially screwed.

Had any of the news outlets mentioned Tim's name? Or worse, had he actually been interviewed? If Fiona saw a news story connecting Tim "the Tank" Thompson to Cecilia Montgomery, she would definitely put it all together and realize who I really was.

Why couldn't I seem to keep my big mouth shut?

Someone smacked the door with her palm, and I was so startled that another spew of barf came up inside my mouth. With a grimace, I swallowed it—ugh. But I really didn't want to put my head near that toilet again. I stood up and slowly, shakily opened the door. A broad girl with a flat face and a ton of eye makeup stared me down.

"Some of us have gotta pee!" she announced. Then she basically shoved me out of the way and slammed the door in my face.

I made my way to the sinks and splashed some cold water on my cheeks, then staggered out the door. I saw Fiona, but she was looking the other way, which was lucky. I didn't want to deal with her and her follow-up questions right now. Blindly, I turned around and saw a big red EXIT sign at the end of the hall. I made my way to it and pushed out into the alleyway, taking a big gulp of the warm, humid air outside.

The pungent scent of rotting garbage hit me like a brick wall and almost made me heave again. I turned and pressed my hands and forehead into the concrete side of the building, breathing through my mouth. After a minute my stomach seemed stable. I carefully stepped out onto the busy street where the front door of Ruckus was situated. We'd walked here, so I knew I could make it home, if I could only remember the way.

After a few minutes of extreme concentration, I was about 90 percent certain that I wanted to make a left, so I did. Ignoring the laughter and catcalls of my fellow late-night partiers, I walked very slowly until I found myself on

Main Street, where I turned around and slammed right into Duncan Taylor.

"Lia!" he blurted, sounding almost frightened. "What are you doing here?"

"Duncan!" I cried out. And then I burped.

Duncan's eyes closed as his head reeled back. "Damn. You smell like a brewery." He locked his arm around me tight and quickly turned me entirely around, which made my head spin in an unfortunate way.

"Where're we going?"

And then I saw where we were—across the street from the Book Nook, and the wall was painted black. No message. Where was the new message? And wait, if the new message wasn't up yet, then where was the painter?

"Home! I'm taking you home," Duncan said.

Then he pulled me forward so quickly my head snapped around, and I almost tripped on a slab of uneven sidewalk.

"Do we have to go so fast?" I asked, my skull pounding.

"No. Sorry. No. Of course not," Duncan said. "I guess I just want to get you there before you barf on my new kicks."

"Already did that," I told him, puffing out my cheeks. "Barfed, I mean. Not on your new kicks."

Before long we arrived at Hadley's, where I extricated myself from Duncan's arms, dropped down on the bench outside the drugstore's front windows, and leaned my head back against the glass.

"You okay?" Duncan asked.

I groaned.

"So . . . that's a no, then."

I just waved at him, unable to answer. Okay. This was not good. This was not the person I wanted to be. A girl who went out and got herself sloppy drunk all because the guy she liked had taken some other girl out dancing. That wasn't me. It wasn't Cecilia Montgomery, mature, intelligent, sophisticated daughter of America's sweetheart senator, and it certainly wasn't Lia Washington, the independent girl who'd left behind a crappy family to strike out on her own. I didn't need a guy, damn it. What I needed was a life. And this was no way to live one.

"Well, I'm not leaving until I at least get you to your door, so . . ."

I groaned again, hating that he was here to witness me in my ignominious state.

"Duncan, you are *such* a good guy," I said.

As I lifted my head to look at him, a flash of headlights nearly blinded me. I raised my hand and my heart gave a lurch. It was the Town Car again, making its way slowly toward me around the park. Whoever was driving the car wasn't close enough yet to see me, and with a burst of sudden adrenaline I dove off the bench and down the alleyway that led to the drugstore's back door.

"Lia? Hey! Wait up!" Duncan shouted.

I was just ducking around the corner to safety when the car eased by, and I could swear I saw a curious face staring out at me from the passenger-side window. Then Duncan appeared in front of me, cutting off my view, and the car was gone.

"What just happened?" Duncan asked.

"Nothing. I just really need to go to bed. Like now."

Pulse skipping erratically, hands slick with a new supply of sweat, I fumbled my keys out of my pocket and they dropped to the ground.

"I've got it," Duncan said.

He grabbed the keys and walked me over to the door, which he kindly unlocked for me.

"Thank you, Duncan," I said, turning away. "Let's forget this ever happened."

"Will do," Duncan said. "Are you sure you'll be okay?" He glanced toward the stairs. "Maybe I should—"

"No. I'll be fine. I really just want to be alone right now," I told him. All I could think about was getting upstairs and hiding under the covers. "But thanks again."

And then I let the door slam in his face. I'd just have to hope he'd forgive me tomorrow. The door locked automatically behind me, and I ran up the steps as fast as I could and let myself into the apartment. Everything was dark, but the moon shining through the window cast a glowing beam directly on my smiling six-year-old face atop the pile of newspapers and magazines.

"Screw you!" I shouted into the silence, not even sure who I was shouting at. My mom? The reporters? My first-grade self?

I grabbed the paper, tore off the front page, and balled it up as I tromped over to my bedroom. Tears shaking from my eyes, I hastily shredded the picture into a million tiny, sweat-soaked pieces and let them rain all over my bedroom floor. Little bits of me fluttered everywhere: the corner of my smile, a bit of a nostril, a slice of eye white staring up at me, shattered.

When I was done, I thought I'd feel better, but I didn't. My mouth was dry, my head throbbed, and my heart bounced around like a jackrabbit, trying to break my ribs. I curled up in a ball on my bed, drawing the covers around me, but no matter what I did, I couldn't make myself feel safe.

My friends were asking questions, a dark car was stalking me, and before long the headline would read MONTGOMERY

HEIR FOUND! And then there was Jasper and Charlene.

How could he touch her like that, after the way we'd talked? After the way he'd touched me?

Somehow that mental picture was worse than everything else combined.

Chapter Ten

Through a thick haze of sleep I became dimly aware of an insistent pounding. I pried my eyes open and was instantly blinded by sunlight. When I lifted my head, pain radiated out from the center of my brain into every inch of my skull. My clothes and sheets were soaked with sweat, which was unsurprising since it was about ten thousand degrees inside my room. I had passed out without turning on the ceiling fan or opening any windows, and the sun was high in the sky. What time was it, anyway? Where the hell was Britta?

The pounding started again, and suddenly my heart caught up with the rest of me and started freaking out. I leaped to the window and looked down at the street, expecting to see the mysterious Town Car parked in front of my building, but it was nowhere in sight. I did, however, see Jasper's Jeep.

"Lia! Are you alive in there?"

Jasper. Damn. I turned around and ran for my closet, ripping out a T-shirt at random, along with a pair of jeans.

"Just a second!" I shouted as I tripped blearily toward the bathroom, shoving my glasses on, my head throbbing with every step. The clock on the microwave read 1:15.

One look at myself in the mirror told me in no uncertain terms that I should not open the door. My skin was gray, my eyes were shot through with red, and my entire body was covered with an unattractive sheen of perspiration. I peeled my dress off, nose scrunching at the splatter of vomit on the skirt and beer stains on the chest, and tossed it in the corner. Trying to do the best I could do in the least possible time, I splashed water on my face, then soaked one of Britta's clean washcloths and ran it down my arms and across my torso.

Sweet relief.

"Lia! Come on! Open the door!"

Cursing under my breath, I yanked on the T-shirt—black with a skull-and-bones motif—and slid into the baggy jeans. Then I slapped my face a few times and headed for the front door.

When I opened it, Jasper barreled in, guitar case in one

hand, sheet music in the other, and didn't even look at me. He went right to the coffee table, plopped the case down, and opened it.

"You have to help me."

"I'm sorry?"

My head was slowly cracking open. Trying to look nonchalant, I moved to the coffeemaker and dumped stale coffee into a mug, then threw it into the microwave. Once that was churning, I started to search the cabinets for Tylenol, Motrin, Aleve, anything.

"I e-mailed the showcase people and they accepted my application. The audition is tomorrow, and I need your opinion on some songs."

My brow knit as the microwave beeped, sending a dart of pain through my eyeballs. Weird. "Wait. How did all of this happen already?"

He stood up straight, slinging his guitar strap around his back. "It's after one. I replied to the e-mail late last night and they called about an hour ago." His eyes flickered as he seemed to see me for the first time. "Did you just wake up? What kind of mischief did you get up to last night?"

My heart sank. All that time at Ruckus and he hadn't even noticed that I was there? Not once? Was Charlene that engrossing?

"Pretty much the same mischief as you," I said. *Except without the dry-humping on the dance floor*, I added silently. "I was at Ruckus too."

"Oh." At least he had the decency to look sheepish. "You saw me there?"

"Yep." I took the coffee out of the microwave and slammed the door, which brought forth a new wave of pain. "Which begs the question: Why are you looking for my opinion and not the opinion of the girl who has an intimate relationship with your . . . privates?" I said, my gaze flicking toward his belt buckle.

Adorably, Jasper looked down for a second, as if he didn't know what I was talking about. When he looked up again, his face was a blank. "Because you, darlin', are the one who got me into this mess," he said. Then he smiled a wolfish smile. "Are you jealous?"

The headache focused itself on my forehead, grinding away with no mercy. Was it so obvious I was jealous? The idea that he thought I was made the pain even worse. I closed my eyes, breathed in, breathed out.

"How did you even get in here?" I snapped.

He looked confused. "You let me in."

"Noooo, into the building. There *is* a lock on the entry door, right?"

He tugged a key out of his pocket and held it up, where it glinted in the sunlight. "I have a key." He shuffled from foot to foot. Clearly, my annoyance was starting to make him uncomfortable. "Do you . . . uh, want me to go?"

The jury was still out on that one, so I ignored the question and asked the one that was on the tip of my own tongue.

"Why do you have a key?"

Jasper blushed. "I may have kind of used to date that Jen girl. You know, the one who lived here before you?"

I swallowed hard. "And by date you mean . . ."

His blush deepened. Ugh. I was so gonna hurl.

"Could you excuse me for just a second?" I said through my teeth.

Before Jasper could answer, I walked to the bathroom, turned on the water in the sink full blast, and screamed as loud as I could into a towel. It didn't help my headache, but it got out a little bit of my embarrassment, frustration, and residual anger. And yes, jealousy. For the first time I recognized the fact that the mirror was also a medicine cabinet. I popped it open and, eureka, painkillers! I downed a few pills, drank water from my palm, and straightened my posture.

"You are Cecilia Montgomery," I whispered to myself. "Poise is in your nature."

I'd never been one for embracing my family legacy, but

this was an emergency situation. Lifting my chin, I walked out into the living room and sat on the couch next to the spot where Jasper had settled himself and his guitar. My posture was straight, my head centered, every movement elegant. I was my mother sitting on Diane Sawyer's couch. Just without the severe fake smile. Or the evil, black heart.

"Are you okay?" Jasper asked, almost timidly.

"I'm fine. What you do, or have done, in your spare time is none of my business."

I'm not sure either one of us believed that I truly meant that, but it felt good to say it.

"Okay." I peeled a bit of a magazine page off the sole of my foot, crushed it between my thumb and forefinger, and flicked it across the room. "Let's hear what you've got."

I sat in a state of breathlessness as the final chords of Jasper's ballad faded, reverberating inside my chest. Jasper had finished the song looking down at the strings and the pick in his hand, and for this I was overwhelmingly grateful. If he'd seen the look on my face right about then, I would have been in serious trouble.

Note to self: When trying not to fall for a player, it's not a good idea to let him sing you love songs.

"Well?" he asked finally.

I cleared my throat, staring at his hands. I couldn't seem to stop staring at his hands. When I wasn't staring at his eyes. "That's the one."

"Really?" he asked excitedly. "I think so too. But why do *you* think so?"

"Why?" I was starting to feel like it was oral-finals day back at the Worthington School. Nothing made my nerves jump and my brain freeze up like oral-finals day. "Because . . . um, I like it?"

Jasper laughed, crooking his arms to rest them on top of his guitar. "No, I mean, *why* do you like it?"

I scratched my forehead and squeezed my eyes closed, trying to think and giving myself a break from all the staring. "Because it's romantic and heartfelt and all that, but then it picks up tempo in the bridge . . . so you get to see that you can get into a fast song, but it also shows your . . . soulful side?"

I bit my lip. Jasper smiled.

"Wow. Lia Washington thinks I have a soulful side."

"I'm sorry. I don't really know much about writing love songs. I mostly studied classical. You really should have gone to someone else."

I started to get up from the couch, embarrassed, but Jasper's hand came down over mine atop the back cushion. I froze, my heart all caught up in his touch.

"No, really," he said. "This was great. You were perfect."

I blinked. "*I* was perfect?"

"Well, no. Yeah. I mean . . . what you said was perfect," he told me, a blush creeping up his chiseled cheekbones. He cleared his throat and looked me in the eye. "Point is, I'm glad I came over here."

My entire body throbbed with anticipation. Suddenly all I was thinking about was how to get his guitar out of the way so we could kiss.

"I'm glad you came over here too."

I heard the rattle of keys at the door, and suddenly Britta shoved into the room, carrying three heavy-looking boxes and followed by Fiona and Duncan. The twins were laughing about something, until they saw me and Jasper. Then the laughter died.

Suddenly I felt like I'd just been caught naked under the covers with the wrong boy. I quickly slipped my hand out from underneath Jasper's.

"What's this about?" Britta asked, dropping the boxes on the floor next to the kitchen island.

"Shouldn't you be getting ready for your shift?" Fiona asked. She tucked her hands under her arms, looking almost petulant.

"Crap. What time is it?" I stood up and my head went

weightless. When I reached back for the arm of the couch to steady myself, Jasper jumped up to catch me by the elbow. Every single person in the room focused on his hand.

"Have you eaten anything today?" he asked me.

My pulse fluttered weakly. "No, actually. I didn't think to."

Britta was already taking a bowl down from the cabinet for herself. "Want some cereal?"

"Sure."

She removed another bowl, and I walked slowly past Fiona and Duncan to the kitchen. Why were they looking at me like I'd just offended them? Yes, Duncan and I had flirted a little the other night, but it wasn't like we were together. And it also wasn't like Jasper and I had actually been doing anything. Had we?

"Thanks for last night, Fiona," I said tentatively, trying to break the ice. "I don't think I would have found the bathroom in time if it wasn't for you."

"No problem," she said with a tight smile. "Where did you disappear to? I was worried until Britta got home and found you passed out in your room."

"Right. Sorry about that. I took a wrong turn, and when I found myself outside, I just kind of staggered home," I lied.

"You've really gotta get yourself a cell phone," Britta said as she placed a full bowl of cereal in front of me.

"Yeah. Soon as I get paid." Though I wasn't entirely sure a phone would be my first priority. I had to buy some food. And do some laundry. How did people do laundry around here, anyway? Actually, how did people do laundry, period? I'd never had to take care of my own clothes.

"When *do* we get paid?" I asked.

"Every Friday," Duncan told me. "But since you started Thursday, Dad figured he'd roll it all into one big payday this coming Friday. I'm sure you can get an advance if you need it, though. I could talk to him if you—"

"No. That's okay. But thanks." I managed a wan smile. I could make it till Friday. Hopefully.

I dropped down on one of the island stools. Aside from my sudden ravenous hunger, my heart was pounding thanks to Jasper, and my mouth was completely dry and fuzzy thanks to the hangover. I almost felt faint. There was also a vague memory tugging at the corners of my mind. Duncan with his arm around me. Duncan's face, concerned. Then it hit me.

"Did you . . . walk me home last night?" I asked, blinking at him.

"Um, yeah. Kind of. We bumped into each other," he said, sheepish.

"Where?" I asked. "You weren't at the club, right?"

"No. Just out," he said. "For a run. I run sometimes. At night."

A dish clattered, and Britta muttered an apology.

"Well, thank you," I said, still unclear on the details, which was monumentally disturbing. "That was really nice of you."

"Anytime. So . . . what were you guys doing?" Duncan asked, eyeing Jasper.

"I've got an audition tomorrow night." Jasper placed his guitar into its case and flipped it shut. "Lia was just helping me pick out a song."

I took a tentative bite, and my stomach turned, then settled and screamed for more.

"Thank you," I said to Britta.

"No problem." Britta's shrewd eyes traveled from me to Jasper to Fiona to Duncan, taking in the tension.

"What're *you* doing here?" I asked Duncan, though it came out more accusatory than I meant it to sound.

He hesitated before answering. The look on his face was utterly betrayed. But all we'd done was flirt a little. In front of his sister and her best friend, no less. Of course, I'd felt betrayed by Jasper when he'd gone out with Charlene, and all *we'd* done was flirt.

So yeah, on top of everything else I was possibly a humongous hypocrite.

"I was going to offer to walk you to work," Duncan told me. "We have the same shift."

"Oh, yeah? Cool," I said, trying to sound enthusiastic. "That'll be fun."

Though the very thought of leaving the apartment made me want to curl up and cry. My shift was three p.m. to midnight. There was no way I was going to make it. But I had to. I needed the money. And the dragging hours would be a lot more tolerable with Duncan there. If he stopped looking at me like I'd just kicked the walker out from under his grandmother.

"Don't work too hard. We're taking you out to Lake Pleasant in the morning," Britta said through a mouthful of cereal flakes.

"You are?"

"It's the only block of time in the next week when none of us are working," Fiona explained. She hadn't moved an inch since she'd walked through the door. I could sort of assume why Duncan looked so bereft, but why Fiona? Was she mad at me about last night? Irritated on her brother's behalf? Her eyes flicked to the living room. "Jasper, do you want to come?"

Duncan visibly tensed. Britta, I could have sworn, choked a little bit, but she covered it with a cough. And just like that it hit me. Fiona had a crush on Jasper. Of course she did. She always went a little bit awkward around him, always seemed to blush a little in his presence. I hadn't really processed it, or had chosen not to notice it, maybe. But now, as she eyed him hopefully, toying with the hem of her hoodie, it was completely obvious to the world.

I was competing with one of three possible friends I had in the world for the same guy.

"Really? Sure," Jasper said with a big grin. "I've gotta be in Nashville for this thing tomorrow night, but it could be good to do something distracting in the morning. You know, kill the nerves."

"Oh, please. You're gonna be great."

I froze. Fiona and I had just said the exact same thing at the exact same time in the exact same tone. We stared at each other. Jasper scratched the back of his neck.

"Awesome," Britta said, standing up straight. "This won't be awkward at all."

She picked up her cereal bowl, grabbed a magazine from the countertop, and disappeared into her room, leaving me, Fiona, Jasper, and Duncan to sort out our quadrangle for ourselves.

Chapter Eleven

"So . . . do you want to come with me tonight?"

I looked at Jasper, shading my eyes with one hand. His convertible zipped along a two-lane road packed in on both sides by trees. Every once in a while a space would open up between evergreens, and I'd see a sliver of Lake Pleasant shimmering in the early morning sun. The air was warm and thick with the sweet and sometimes tangy scent of wild-flowers, which grew in random patches alongside the asphalt. It was so early in the morning there were hardly any cars on the road, and I stifled a yawn. After my long shift, I'd barely gotten five hours of sleep before Britta had shaken me awake, telling me Jasper was downstairs.

"Sorry if the idea bores you," Jasper joked.

"No. Sorry. Long night," I said. "You mean to Nashville?"

"Yeah." He downshifted and paused at a stop sign. "I could use the moral support."

He hooked a left, and I pressed my palm against the door as the tires squealed. Even after yesterday, after sitting so close to him while he poured his heart into his music, after being the one he'd chosen to share that with, I was surprised. Didn't he have a dozen girls lined up to go with him?

"Do you have to work or something?"

"No. I'm off all day, actually. I just . . ." The wind bounced my curls around, tickling my scalp. "Are you sure you want me to be there?"

"Wouldn't be asking if I wasn't," he replied.

"Why?" I asked.

He glanced sideways at me and slowed the Jeep as we approached a speed bump. Up ahead I could see a wide parking lot, already dotted with cars, and a dock a few yards off where a group of guys were directing their friend as he backed his boat trailer toward the water.

"Hey, you got me into this thing. The least you could do is be there to back me up," he said with an edge in his voice.

Okay, ouch. "Look, if you don't want to go to the audition, don't go to the audition."

"No, it's not that. I just . . ." He blew out a sigh. "I'm sorry. I didn't mean to snap. I'm just really nervous, and honestly? I guess I'm hoping some of your bravery will rub off on me or something."

There he went, calling me brave again. We popped over the speed bump and my butt lifted off the seat.

"Honestly, Jasper, I don't think you give yourself enough credit," I told him. "You can do this."

"Ya think?" he asked, his fingers curling and uncurling on the steering wheel.

"Yes! Look at you!" I said as he pulled into a parking spot and killed the engine. "You project this total confidence at all times. You never fidget; you never second-guess yourself; you don't even care when people call you out on stuff. You're, like, Mr. Cocky."

"There's an attractive nickname."

He released his seat belt and hoisted himself up, resting his butt on the door frame and his hands at his sides. His tanned muscles flexed in the sun. I climbed up to sit opposite him, the two of us with our legs dangling down into the car.

"Can I tell ya a secret?" he asked, squinting an eye as he looked off at the water.

Please do, I thought. "Sure."

"That Mr. Cocky thing? That's just what I want y'all to believe," he said. "Half the time I feel like I don't know what the hell I'm doing."

He looked me full in the face. I was about to laugh at his joke, but then I saw that he was telling the truth. I was still trying to figure out how to respond when Fiona and Duncan pulled up next to us.

"Beautiful day to be on the lake," Duncan said loudly as he climbed out of the car.

"You know it," Jasper replied, giving me a wink.

Interrupted in the middle of a fairly deep conversation, I felt the meaning of what he'd just shared with me full force. That wasn't something he'd admit to just anyone. And the wink was him telling me that. Him telling me that for now, at least, that topic was closed. I just hoped we could pick it up again later.

"Where's Britta?" I asked.

"She was a couple minutes behind us."

Fiona got out of the car wearing cutoffs and a blue T-shirt, the strap of a deeply purple bathing suit peeking out of the collar.

"It took her and her mom a little while to get the boat hitched up to her truck," Duncan added. He clapped his hands and grinned at me. "You ready for your first water-skiing lesson?"

The sight of the water skis when he pulled them out of the trunk sent my heart palpitating. I was all for being brave and trying new things until the prospect of face-planting and being dragged behind a speeding boat became an actual reality. Were skis always that skinny?

"You ever skied before?" Jasper asked, opening his trunk to pull out a sizable cooler. "On water or snow?"

"Nope," I replied. Skiing was strictly verboten in my family after my uncle Max died in a random accident on the slopes when I was four. Not that I could tell them that.

Jasper frowned, holding the heavy cooler in front of him. "Maybe she should just do the tube."

"She wants to ski," Duncan snapped.

"Maybe we should let the lady speak for herself." Jasper put the cooler down and crossed his arms over his chest.

"She did speak for herself. When we talked about it at the diner, she said she was going to try it," Duncan said. "Right, Lia?"

Suddenly I found myself as the object of a two-boy staredown. There was no good way to answer them. Luckily, an engine roared, and Britta's bright-blue pickup careened into the parking lot, a sleek, white boat bobbing behind it. She pulled up alongside us and leaned out the window.

"I'm really sorry," she said.

"For what?" Fiona asked.

Then the passenger-side door opened and closed. All I

saw were a pair of heeled sandals, until the wearer of said sandals strode around the front of the idling truck.

"Hi, kids!"

Shelby. Awesome.

She was wearing a pin-striped 1950s-style halter bikini top and a flouncy white skirt, her hair done up in an elaborate topknot. She looked like a pinup poster out of some old war movie.

"What a beautiful day!" she trilled, looking out across the lake. By the grin on her face it was clear that she knew she'd just spoiled the party, and she was loving every minute of it. "You ready for this?"

Jasper looked at Duncan. Duncan looked at me. I looked at Fiona.

Suddenly I wasn't sure I was ready for anything.

Half an hour later I was seriously considering jumping off a moving boat and swimming for shore. I figured I had about a twenty percent chance of making it without cramping up and drowning. But even that would have been preferable to the mood on the boat.

Britta was driving, while Jasper sat on the rear bench with Shelby's legs draped over his. Fiona and Duncan were perched on the starboard side, each of them with arms and legs crossed so tightly they looked liked they'd been cemented that way, and I sat opposite them, trying not to glare at Shelby or make eye contact with anyone.

"You're going to do so great tonight, hon," Shelby said to Jasper, propping her chin on his shoulder and batting her eyes at his profile. "Before you know it, you're gonna be a superstar."

Duncan grunted. Jasper stood up so suddenly he almost lost his balance, and Shelby somehow managed not to hit the floor.

"Hey, Brit! I think this is good!" Jasper shouted.

Britta slowed the engine, and we puttered to a stop. She turned around and pushed her dark sunglasses up on top of her head. "So no one's thrown anyone overboard yet? That's a good sign."

Fiona snorted a laugh.

"Who's going first?" Duncan asked, standing up.

Now that the boat wasn't moving forward, every time someone shifted their weight it leaned and bobbed. I'd never been seasick before, but my stomach was feeling a bit iffy. Was it possible I was still hungover from two nights ago? Or was it just the tense company making me ill?

"I'm gonna take Lia out on the tube," Jasper announced.

"What?" Shelby snapped, as Fiona sank lower in her seat.

"Yeah, what?" I echoed. "What tube?"

Jasper untied a rather large inflated yellow-and-blue tube from the back of the boat. I'd noticed it latched there but had thought it was some sort of life raft. It didn't have a hole in the middle, and the perimeter was dotted with thick blue straps. He stood it up in the center of the boat, and I dimly recalled seeing some kids at the Vineyard being towed behind a boat on something similar. This was a far better idea than trying to ski.

"Are you in?" Jasper asked, grinning.

"Oh, I'm in."

I got up and tugged my T-shirt off over my head, then wrapped my glasses inside it. I was so excited I had to chew on the inside of my cheek to keep from laughing. Not only was Jasper offering to go out there with me, but going out there would mean getting off this boat, away from the silent, snorting twins and Shelby "Sexy's My Middle Name" Tanaka.

"So you're really not gonna try skiing?" Duncan asked.

"I don't think so," I said, refusing to look him in the eye. "Don't hate me, but I didn't really think that one through."

"Why would I hate you?" Duncan said. "You gotta do what you gotta do."

"Okay, so how does this thing work?" I asked Jasper, trying to get past the awkward.

"I'll show ya."

Jasper put the tube in the water behind the boat, where it bobbed innocently, then climbed over the back of the boat onto his knees on the tube and held out a hand.

"Come on over."

I joined him, doing my best to keep my balance, but still ended up on all fours. Luckily, my butt was facing away from Jasper when that happened.

"Now what?" I said with a laugh.

"Lie down on your stomach next to me," he said, flattening out across the tube's surface. I did as I was told. "Now grab on."

Jasper reached for one handle to his left and another directly in front of him. I grabbed one handle to my right and another directly in front of me. My left arm grazed his right, and Jasper smiled.

"All set!" he shouted to Britta.

I glanced up and saw Shelby scowling over the back of the boat. Then the engine sputtered to life, and the vessel moved farther away from us. On the surface of the water a long tether spooled out, gradually straightening.

"You're gonna want to hold on tight," Jasper told me.

"I'm ready," I replied, though my pulse was hammering.

Suddenly the rope went taut and we lurched forward. I instantly lost my grip on the strap in front of me and started to slide backward, screaming. In a flash Jasper grabbed me around the waist.

"I gotcha!"

He laughed, but I had to gulp for breath. The wind dried my eyes out and water pelted me in the face.

My right hand shouted from holding on so tightly. Somehow I freed my left arm from beneath my weight and Jasper's and slid it up to grab the handle again.

"Is she going to slow down?" I demanded, as the tube caught someone's wake and we jumped into the air.

"Nope! I have a feeling she's just gonna keep going faster!" Jasper shouted in reply.

We jumped again, and when the tube came down, my chin slammed against the top. It was much more solid than it looked.

"I'm not sure if I like this," I said unsteadily.

"Here," Jasper said. "Allow me."

With that he somehow inched over on the speeding tube and pulled me so close that the right side of his torso was overlapping the left side of mine. He lifted his right leg over my left as well, and reached his arm around me, basically pinning me to the tube. I was still able to lift my head, but when I did, our wet cheeks grazed each other.

My terrified body was now also on fire.

"Okay?" he asked in my ear, his voice hovering between amused and aroused.

"Um, yeah. Much better," I replied.

I did feel a lot more secure, even as my mind made a mental checklist of all the many bits of our skin that were touching. Within a few minutes, though, I got used to it and started to look around. Trees whipped by, a dock, a couple of small, secluded homes. The wind tossed the curls atop my head, and I breathed in the fresh air. The sky above us was like a vast bowl of endless blue, and I realized, suddenly, that no one I'd known before one week ago knew where I was. That I was out in the world, on my own, having fun, and that I was okay.

A guy on a Jet Ski racing in the opposite direction waved at us, and Jasper lifted his hand from my back in acknowledgment. I felt a swoop of uncertainty and yelped, but then Jasper grabbed me again and we both laughed.

"That was a close one," I said.

"Don't worry, Red Sox." Jasper's lips grazed my ear. "There's no way I'm letting you go."

Cuddled under a towel on a picnic table bench, eating fresh biscuits and fruit and sipping coffee from Duncan's thermos, I had never felt so content. It might have also had something to do with the fact that Jasper had chosen to sit next to me rather than Shelby or Fiona. Every time he reached for something on the table, his arm brushed mine, and every time his arm brushed mine, I shivered.

"So where is this audition, exactly?" Shelby asked him, without looking up from her biscuit. She was cutting it into wedges with a plastic knife and fork and eating it bite by bite like it was steak. Her posture was so straight you could have hung a flag off her.

"At the Fairfax. I heard there are more than fifty acts trying out. It's gonna be a crazy scene," Jasper said with that old confidence I now knew was not 100 percent real. He glanced at his phone, then popped a piece of watermelon into his mouth. "Actually, I should go. I want to get some rehearsal time in before I have to leave."

As soon as he got up from the table, I missed his warmth. He swiped his hands across the front of his still-damp bathing suit and turned to me. "Pick you up around five?"

There was so much tension at the table it would have made a tone if you'd plucked at it, just like one of Jasper's guitar strings.

"I'll be ready," I told him.

Then I concentrated really hard on my coffee.

"All right." He grinned and squeezed my shoulder. "See y'all later, then."

As he backed off toward his car, Shelby jumped up from her seat across the table. "Actually, I'm supposed to be at work in half an hour. Can I catch a ride?"

"Sure thing, darlin'." Jasper lifted his cowboy hat out of the back seat and settled it in over his ears, fanning his blond hair out behind them. My stomach twisted with jealousy as Shelby flounced off after him, casting a smirk over her shoulder at me as she went.

"That's fine! We'll clean up after you!" Britta shouted sarcastically.

Shelby answered with a finger-twiddling wave, and two seconds later they peeled out. At the speed bump Jasper lifted a long, tanned arm up in a good-bye gesture.

"I think I'm gonna go for a walk," Fiona said, her voice flat.

When I looked up, she was glaring at me so hard that I flinched. Duncan's wrists rested at the edge of the table, his fingers curled into loose fists. When Fiona got up, Britta slid off the bench to follow. She had to jog to catch Fiona, who speed-walked away with her hands shoved under her arms.

"What was that about?" I asked.

Duncan didn't move. "Are you really going with him down to Nashville tonight?"

I swallowed a too-large gulp of coffee. Maybe it was time Duncan and I had it out about this. I knew Duncan was maybe sort of crushing on me, and he was cute and sweet, but I liked Jasper. There was no more getting around it. And as long as I liked Jasper, there was no way I could have feelings for Duncan.

"Why do you hate him so much?" I asked. "Fiona clearly likes him."

"Every person in this town with a bra likes him."

Duncan got up and gathered a whole mess of paper plates into his arms, turning to dump them into the garbage can between our picnic table and the next. Out on the water a girl shrieked as she and her friends zipped by on water skis. Duncan turned to me, hands on his hips.

"My dislike for Jasper is a very long story," he said, exhaling a loud breath.

"Well, you're my ride, so consider me a captive audience." I set my coffee aside, curious, but also feeling a tiny bit disloyal over the fact that I was basically digging for dirt on Jasper. But it was hard hanging out with this new group of people who had all this backstory and not knowing what the hell was going on half the time.

"Fine." He shook his head once, then sat down across from me. His gray T-shirt clung to him with wet patches here and there, and his brown hair stuck up on top, still damp from water-skiing.

"Shelby was my first love."

I sat up straight. I didn't know what I'd been expecting, but it wasn't that.

"Go on."

"We started going out in seventh grade and were together on and off all the way through tenth. That was when Jasper swooped in and asked her to the senior prom." He looked up at me then, the hurt plain in his brown eyes. "He asked her to the senior prom—my girlfriend—right in front of me."

"No," I said.

"Yeah. And even better? She said yes." Duncan scoffed and ran his hands over his face and through his hair. "But then she didn't even break up with me until the day of the prom."

"Oh my God. Why didn't you break up with *her*?"

"Because I kept thinking it was a joke. That she'd, I don't know, wake up and realize how insane she was being. But she didn't. She called me the morning of the prom and said she'd made a decision. She wanted to be with Jasper. And that was it."

"Oh, Duncan, I'm so sorry."

But even though the story was horrible, it seemed like Shelby was the real villain, not Jasper. What he'd done was a little immature and stupid, but everyone was a little immature and stupid in high school. And Shelby could have easily said no.

"It gets better," Duncan warned me.

"What?"

"A whole year goes by. They walk around town acting like they're the lead couple in some romantic comedy. Like they're so in love. Like nothing could ever break them up. Meanwhile, he's cheating on her all over the place, making her look like a fool, and everyone knows it. People try to tell her, but she ignores them, tells them it's not true. But she's not stupid. I'm sure she knew what was going on. She just didn't want to let him go."

"So what happened?" I asked.

"He finally met a girl who didn't like playing second fiddle to Shelby, so he dumped her," Duncan said flatly. "Two days after Shelby's dad bailed on her family without so much as a note, he broke her heart. Via text."

Okay. That was not cool.

"I swear she hasn't been the same since."

"Duncan, I'm so . . . I don't know what to say."

But even though the story was horrible, even though it painted Jasper in a pretty awful light, my brain was already making excuses. It was more than a year ago, at least. Maybe he'd matured since then. Maybe he knew he was wrong.

But did he? I'd seen the way he messed around with girls, with other guys' girls. And Shelby clearly still thought she had a shot with him. Did I really want to be with a guy who acted that way? Could a person like him change?

Duncan got up again, clearing away the cups and the plastic cutlery, jamming tops down on containers like he was mad at them. Then, suddenly, he paused, his fingers resting lightly on his hips. When he looked up at me, his expression was pained.

"Look, Lia, I know we haven't known each other very long, but I just don't want you to get hurt."

My heart responded, touched.

"Why are you so sure I'm gonna get hurt?" I asked.

"Because Jasper . . . he has an MO," Duncan said, crossing his arms over his chest. "You're not the first new girl in town that he immediately took an interest in."

I swallowed hard. Suddenly the picnic bench felt a lot less comfortable. "What do you mean?"

"It's like it's a game to him," Duncan said, stepping closer to the table. "I was pretty good friends with Jen, the one who left to sing backup? She told me all about it after she compared notes with a bunch of his other conquests. It's always the same. Like it's tactical or something."

"Duncan," I said shaking my head. "C'mon."

"No! It's true!" Duncan's voice actually cracked, he was so adamant. "He starts with the flirtatious 'I'm a totally hot musician' thing, and then, once he has you hooked, he shows you his vulnerable side or whatever. Has he done that with you?"

I blinked, the sun searing my face. "Well, yeah, but . . ." The other night in the garage wasn't a setup. I'd walked in on a fight. He couldn't have known that I'd be there. Right?

"Uh-huh. I thought so. And after that, he finds something to compliment you on. Something big. Not, like, your hair or whatever, but something personal about you. Makes you think he really *sees* you."

Oh, God. My chest felt tight. The thing about me being so brave. Was that a line? Suddenly I started to really and truly sweat.

"And then he turns it around to make you think he really needs you. Like he can't live without you. And that's how he gets you in bed."

"He hasn't gotten me in bed," I snapped, standing up.

Duncan's face paled. "Sorry. I didn't mean *you*, per se. I meant girls. In general. He's done it to dozens of girls, Lia."

He approached me slowly, pushing his hands into the pockets of the jeans he'd changed into before lunch.

"If I were you, I'd reconsider going to Nashville with him tonight," he said, his chin tucked.

"Why?" My mouth was completely dry.

"Because I can totally see him using this to seal the deal," he said apologetically. "You see him up there on that big stage, girls screaming for him like he's some superstar—they always have a small audience at these things to gauge reaction. He probably figures you'll be swooning so hard afterward he'll be able to do whatever he wants with you. That's why he didn't ask Shelby to go with him, which is what he'd do otherwise. He thinks he can score. Half the girls he's been with, he's been with after one of his gigs, trust me."

He started to step around me, but paused before passing me by, his shoulder nearly grazing mine, like he wanted to be close to me but couldn't look me in the eye. He must have thought I was so stupid. The humiliation coursing through my veins threatened to incinerate me from the inside out.

"I'm sorry," he said quietly. "I just thought you should know."

Chapter Twelve

I had never felt so sick in my life without actually throwing up. Every five seconds I changed my mind and was totally sure of my decision . . . until the next five minutes passed. I lay on my bed, staring at the ceiling, my stomach in knots and my heart not faring much better.

Was everything Duncan had said true? Was Jasper really using me? It seemed true. I mean, Duncan knew too much. He knew everything. How could he know the trajectory of my and Jasper's relationship unless this Jen girl had actually told him? Which meant that it really was a ploy.

I blew out a breath and turned over onto my right side, staring at the Johnny Cash curtain.

But then . . . Duncan did have a motivation for lying to me about Jasper. He liked me. That was pretty obvious.

Maybe he'd made the whole thing up—made an educated guess. Maybe he was just trying to undermine whatever it was Jasper and I had so he could swoop in and win my heart.

Stranger things had happened.

But what if he was right? I sat up straight, wanting to scream. I wanted more than anything to be with Jasper, but the Jasper I knew, not this calculating person Duncan had painted for me. If I went to Nashville with him tonight, was he going to break my heart? If he did what Duncan said he would do and tried to take me back to his place tonight, that's what would happen. My heart would completely shatter.

Brakes squealed outside the window, and I jumped up to look out. Jasper was just opening the door of his convertible, cowboy hat in place. In twenty-five seconds he'd be at my door.

It was go time. I had to make a decision, and I had to do it now. I didn't want fear to run my new life, but I also didn't want to look back on my first dating experience with a guy as something to be ashamed of, which is how I would feel if this all turned out to be some game. I didn't want to spend the next five or six hours wondering what he was thinking, whether he was playing me, whether he had been lying to me all along.

I needed more time to think, but there wasn't any.

A knock sounded at the door. My hands were clasped in front of me, sweat coating my palms. My heart pounded. I went to the door, still no clue what I was going to do.

I was just reaching for the doorknob when I heard him talking. He was on the phone. I leaned my ear as close to the crack between the door and the doorjamb as I could.

"No . . . I know. Next time, babe, I swear."

My heart turned to stone.

"Of course! Yes, I'll call you as soon as I wake up tomorrow." There was a pause. "You too. Good night."

I held my breath to keep from crying. Who was he talking to? Shelby? Or some other random girl? Was he standing outside my door lining up his next conquest? Because he knew this particular mission was almost complete? Duncan was right. He was completely, totally right.

Jasper knocked again. I slapped my hand over my mouth and caught my breath through my nose. A couple of tears had escaped, so I quickly swiped them away with my fingertips and opened the door.

"Hey," Jasper said uncertainly. "Are you okay?"

I opened the door a touch wider. "Actually, no. I'm sorry, but I can't go with you tonight."

I was shocked at how steady my voice sounded. Jasper's face fell.

"Why? Are you sick?"

I probably looked ill after hours of flopping around in my bed, stressing out over him. That and the fact that this very conversation was making me squirm.

Tell him, a little voice in my head shouted. *Tell him you overheard him.*

But I couldn't.

"No, but I have to work," I lied. "Hal called and one of the other waitresses can't make her shift."

Jasper looked confused. Disappointed. "Can't they find someone else?"

So sorry you won't be having sex tonight. At least not with me.

"Apparently not," I told him. "And besides, I need the money."

"Lia, come on," Jasper begged. "You can't bail on me now. I need you."

There was that word: "need." Just like Duncan had said. I couldn't take this anymore. I turned sideways and grabbed my backpack off the floor. "I really have to go," I said, shoving past him.

"Wait," he said.

"I can't." I turned and rushed for the stairs.

"Lia, did I do something wrong?" he asked.

I stopped, my keys cutting into the flesh of my palm.

Suddenly I felt like a coward. I couldn't just run away and not explain. That wasn't me. At least, I didn't want it to be me.

"I just can't do this, Jasper," I said. "I can't be another in your long line of random girls."

His face went slack. "Lia, you're not—"

"I'm better than that," I said firmly, cutting him off before he could say some practiced line to make me believe him. "I don't know what I was thinking. It's not like you were ever discreet about who you really are."

Now his eyes darkened. I saw his jaw working as he took a step toward me. "And who am I?" he asked, irritated.

"You're the town slut, Jasper," I said. "And I'm not gonna let you break my heart."

With that I turned around and raced down the stairs. It wasn't until the cool evening air hit me in the face that I choked out a sob.

When I stepped into the diner on Tuesday morning, exhausted after a sleepless night of wondering if I'd done the right thing, the first person I saw was Fiona. She was smiling as she handed over a check to a couple of middle-aged women, but her eyes darkened when I walked by. Her posture went rigid.

"Fiona. We really need to talk," I whispered.

"You can just bring that up to the register when you're done!" she said to her customers. "About what?" she asked me, all wide-eyed. "Is something wrong?"

I hesitated. What if I'd misread her yesterday? What if I'd imagined that she was mad at me and she was only in a bad mood or something? But no. I had to trust my gut. I couldn't be friends with someone if I was always wondering what they were thinking.

"It seems like there is. I mean, at the lake yesterday . . . were you avoiding me? Because it seemed like you were. And then Duncan said—"

"What?" she interrupted, wary. "What did Duncan tell you?"

"Nothing!" I said quickly. "I mean, nothing I didn't already know."

Fiona crossed her arms over her chest and held herself tightly, looking like she wanted to disappear. This conversation was making her as uncomfortable as it was making me.

"And what do you think you know?" she asked, her gaze resting somewhere in the vicinity of my pinkie finger.

"That you like Jasper," I whispered.

Fiona basically froze. The only part of her that was moving was one wayward hair that trembled in the direct line of the air-conditioning vent.

"And you also like Jasper," she said eventually.

"I . . . don't really know how to respond to that right now," I said honestly.

"Oh, come on! You were all over him yesterday!" Fiona exclaimed in a very un-Fiona-like way. The outburst drew curious glances from a pair of elderly men who were nursing their coffees at the counter.

"So you *are* mad at me!" I replied.

She turned her back to me, then quickly turned around again, her cheeks pink. "You know what? I was here first!"

The declaration clearly took some effort for her to make. My jaw dropped. Were we in first grade now?

"Actually, from what I understand, Shelby was 'here first,'" I said, throwing in some air quotes.

Her lips went tight. "Fine, but I've liked Jasper forever," she said, lowering her voice. "You can't just swoop in here and steal him away."

"Well, you're in luck, because after last night I don't think he's going to want to have anything to do with me anymore. And that's if I even decide I want to have anything to do with him."

Something seemed to hitch inside Fiona's eyes. Like a little hope springing to life. "What?"

"Lia Washington!"

Someone behind me said my name, and not in a nice

way. I turned around to find Ryan Fitzsimmons strolling over to me. He was wearing a plaid, short-sleeved button-down open over a white tank top and paused in front of me with his hands on his skinny hips. His eyes were narrowed as he looked me up and down.

"You, my friend, have one big mouth."

My spirits sank. Clearly, he had spoken to Jasper.

"We'll talk about this later," I said to Fiona.

"Ooookay."

I grabbed Ryan's arm and pulled him toward the back of the restaurant, away from Fiona and the perked ears of the diners around us. My pulse thrummed quickly in my wrists as I tried to gear myself up to talk to him. What was with all the confrontation lately?

"What did he tell you?" I asked under my breath.

"Oh, only that you called him the town slut. To his face. I gotta tell you, Lia, you completely broke the boy's heart," Ryan said, pressing his palms together. "He tanked that audition last night thanks to you."

Now I felt like I had whiplash. I pressed my hand to my forehead to try to stop the dizzy sensation taking hold of my brain. Broke his heart? Tanked?

"No, he couldn't have," I said. "He was totally ready for that."

"Well, what do you expect when the girl who's supposed to come cheer you on tells you to step off two hours before the audition?" Ryan asked.

"I'm sorry, I don't understand. *I* couldn't have broken *his* heart," I said, trying to maintain some scrap of dignity. "When he came to pick me up, he was standing outside calling someone 'babe' on the phone and saying he'd call her first thing."

Ryan rolled his eyes in a fed-up way. "Shelby. That girl has latched her talons in to him even tighter since you got to town," Ryan said. "You know why? Because she's threatened. For the first time, he's showing more than a physical interest in someone else."

I leaned back against the wall, next to an empty booth, barely resisting the urge to sink into the soft vinyl. I felt drained, suddenly. Any adrenaline I had left over from yesterday had been sucked right out of me.

"Well, if he doesn't want to be with her, why does he still call her 'babe'?" I asked. "Why do they still go out on dates?"

"Because he knows he screwed up with her," Ryan said, lifting his shoulders. "He feels bad."

"She should really get over it," I muttered.

"He should really stop leading her on," Ryan said.

"So . . . he really does like me?" I asked, shooting a concerned glance at Fiona. She was busy making a milkshake, the roar of the machine's engine drowning out everything we were saying. Hopefully.

"It's no joke, Lia. The dude is bumming. Hard." Ryan shook his head.

I tilted my chin up to stare at the ceiling, my insides torn to shreds. Five minutes ago, at least I'd been able to talk myself into believing I'd done the right thing, blowing Jasper off. But now . . . now I had an awful suspicion that I'd screwed up the best thing I'd had going for me.

Permanently.

"What're you up to after this?" Fiona asked, turning to lean back against the counter. She glanced at the clock, a round white face surrounded by a glowing pink trim, and crossed her feet at the ankles. It was almost five p.m. Quittin' time, as I had come to fondly call it inside my mind. Although I wasn't so fond of this one, because I knew that all I was going to do when I left here was sit around and brood.

Fiona and I had been working together for almost eight hours, but since our conversation about Jasper, we hadn't spoken to each other much. Just the occasional "Can you refill the sugar?" or "Is that damn order up yet?"

"I don't know." I pressed my chest forward, arching my back in an attempt to work out the kinks I'd acquired from being on my feet all day. "All I can think about right now is a shower."

Lie. All I could think about was Jasper.

From the corner of my eye, I saw my mother appear on the TV screen in the corner. The sound was muted, but the closed-captioning quickly spelled out what the voice-over was saying. SENATOR MONTGOMERY MET WITH LOCAL LAW OFFICIALS TODAY, STILL CONCERNED OVER THE LACK OF INFORMATION COMING OUT OF THE DADE COUNTY POLICE DEPARTMENT IN REGARDS TO HER MISSING DAUGHTER.

"Can we change the channel?" I asked wearily, turning my back to it. I was so sick of my old life invading this one. If only I could somehow do away with all the TVs in town, this place would truly be nirvana.

"Sure. I hate the news too."

Fiona grabbed the remote and changed it to ESPN. I was just trying to figure out a way to break our latest uncomfortable silence when Jasper's car pulled into one of the spaces out front. The windshield faced the diner, and he pulled up so close, I could see him clear as day. My heart began to pound. I could also see, as clear as day, the person getting out of the passenger seat. Shelby Tanaka.

"Oh, God," I muttered.

"What?" Fiona turned around and followed Shelby with

her eyes as she sauntered toward the door in high heels, a pencil skirt, and an off-the-shoulder top. "Well. Both of us are gonna need a shower after *this*."

"Hi, ladies!" Shelby stopped at the counter and placed a vintage box purse with rhinestone clasps up on the Formica. Her nails were lacquered red, and her hair was in a high ponytail. "Two sweet teas to go, please."

"Coming right up."

Fiona plucked a couple of paper cups from the dispenser. I stared out the window, trying to catch Jasper's eye, but he was wearing a pair of reflective sunglasses. His focus was trained straight ahead. I had no way of knowing if he was looking at me, or if he'd even seen me. My toes twitched to walk outside and talk to him, but I couldn't seem to make myself move. How could I apologize for what I'd said last night? And besides, he'd had twenty-four hours to come up with a response. Whatever *he* was going to say to *me*, I didn't want him to say it in front of Shelby.

"What's up?" Fiona asked, as she placed the full cups on the counter in front of Shelby and added two plastic tops. "Where're you two headed?"

"Oh, us?" Shelby flipped her ponytail to the side to grin out at Jasper and gave him a wave. He lifted his fingers off the steering wheel in acknowledgement, not bothering to uncurl his thumb. "We're going down to Nashville. Jasper made that showcase he auditioned for last night."

"He did?" I asked, surprised. At the same time Fiona said, "That's great!"

Shelby's eyes cut right through me. "Why? Did you think he wouldn't?" Then she looked at Fiona. "It *is* great, isn't it?" She leaned across the counter toward Fiona, pulling her in to whisper, like they were the oldest of friends, "This could really be his big break, Fiona!" Then she stood up straight and turned a snarky smile my way. "Told you he'd always come back to me."

She dropped a ten-dollar bill on the counter.

"Keep the change."

It was all I could do not to throw a fork at her back as she strode out on her crazy heels.

"That girl *needs* to fall on her face right now," I said quietly.

Seconds later, as she reached for the car door, Shelby's ankle wobbled. I held my breath and Fiona held hers as we watched her flail, grab the door handle, and catch herself before she could go down. She did spill half her tea. Though, sadly, it hit the ground and not her pristine outfit. Finally she managed to open the door and lift herself into the car. I couldn't help noticing that, through all of this, Jasper never got out to offer her any of his gentlemanly assistance. At least that was something.

I had to find a way to get him alone so I could apologize. I had to.

"Lia, what did you mean before when you said you weren't sure you wanted to have anything to do with Jasper?" Fiona asked tentatively.

"I don't know," I said honestly.

She swirled a towel atop the counter. "Because I was thinking . . . I kind of want to go to his show tonight."

I glanced at her out of the corner of my eye. "I kind of want to too."

Then maybe I could corner him and make him hear me out. Somehow.

"Would it be totally insane if we went together?" I asked, wanting to put the awkwardness behind us.

"No," she said thoughtfully. "But I think we should make a deal first. A truce, kind of."

I stood up straight, intrigued. "What kind of deal?"

Fiona turned toward me, leaning one hip into the counter. "We promise that neither one of us will make a move on Jasper without telling the other first."

"That sounds fair," I said, and offered my hand.

After all, I wasn't planning to go there and throw myself

at him. What I wanted to do was talk to him. See if he'd forgive me for what I'd said and for almost spoiling this chance for him. All I wanted from Jasper Case right now was forgiveness.

"Deal?" Fiona asked, shaking my hand.

I smiled. "Deal."

Chapter Thirteen

The last-minute tickets we ordered online turned out to be aisle seats in the very last row of a jam-packed auditorium. The theater was maybe double the size of the theater at my school, which had about five hundred seats. I'd never in my six years there seen it more than half filled.

"This is intense," Fiona commented, looking down at the well-worn stage and the lights flashing across the orchestra seats. "I don't think Jasper's ever played to more than a couple hundred people."

"He's probably freaking out," I mused.

"Jasper? Nah. Nothing bothers him."

I decided to keep my insider knowledge on that particular theory to myself. Though the fact that Jasper had shared it with me and no one else gave me a warm, fuzzy feeling around my heart. Too bad he hated me now. Hit with a sudden inspiration, I turned to Fiona just as her butt was about to meet the blue velvet seat.

"I'm gonna go try to find him."

On the long car ride up to Nashville, I'd told Fiona all about what I'd said to Jasper last night. She totally agreed that I had to apologize. But apparently she'd figured I'd wait until after the show.

"What? Lia, you can't. He's probably backstage. They're never gonna let you through."

There were three aisles in the auditorium, one cutting the rows of seats in half up the middle, the other two along the sides. I was currently standing in the one to the left of the stage. All the way at the very end, next to a set of stairs that led directly up to the stage itself, was a door covered by a blue curtain. A constipated-looking security guard with round shoulders and a small waist stood next to the entrance, glowering at every person who so much as glanced in his direction.

"What about Britta?" I asked.

"What about her?"

"She's here somewhere, and you said she has a press pass." Who knew bloggers could reap such perks? But I was glad they did. "Can you text her for me?"

Fiona looked at me like I should have my brain examined.

Clearly, she was not the rule-breaking type. Except when it came to underage drinking. But Lia Washington was all about breaking the rules. I'd spent way too many years doing exactly what I was supposed to. Now I was going to do exactly what I wanted to. And that included tracking down Jasper and apologizing to him before he took the stage.

"Okay. She says she'll get you at the door off the right wing," Fiona said, holding up her phone.

I started down the aisle. "You coming?"

Fiona chewed her lip, clearly torn between wanting to see Jasper and her total fear of facing down authority. "I'll just wait here."

She took her seat, and I ended up in the corner, two feet away from constipated security dude and trying not to squirm under his glare, which felt like a physical entity made up of a million tiny swords. Finally the curtain flicked aside, and there was Britta, waving me in.

"She's with me," she told the scary dude, as if this explained everything. He grunted threateningly, she lifted the laminated pass that hung around her neck with the big word PRESS stamped across it, and he grunted again. Fortunately, this grunt was more like a shrug. I was in.

"I have to get back to my interview with Carey Stilts," Britta said as we hustled backstage together. As if I knew who Carey Stilts was. The skinny hallway was crammed with musical equipment, spotlights on stands, creeping wires, and people. People everywhere. "Can you find Jasper on your own?"

"Yeah," I said. "I'm okay. Thanks, Britta."

She shrugged. "I like to occasionally use my powers for good."

She turned and disappeared into the crowd. Slowly, ducking behind the back of one security guard and somehow avoiding being nailed in the head by a falling microphone, I made my way down the hall until I came to a corner. To go straight, or to turn? That was the question. The adjoining hallway was just slightly wider, with lots of doors that I assumed were dressing rooms and a few other corridors leading toward the back of the building. Two larger openings facing opposite led up stairs toward the stage. The scene was complete chaos. I immediately regretted letting Britta get away from me. How was I ever supposed to find Jasper in this mess?

Taking a stab in the dark, I turned the corner. A group of harmonizing singers moved past me, and there he was, sitting on a folding chair with his back to the wall. His black cowboy hat was drawn low over his forehead, his forearms rested on his thighs, and his knee bounced beneath him as he kneaded his hands together. I could tell he was muttering something under his breath, probably a preperformance pep talk. I approached very carefully. I had a feeling any sudden movement might make him bolt for the hills.

"Jasper."

He looked up and, with one finger, pushed the brim of his cowboy hat up enough so that I could see his eyes. His beautiful, blue, terrified eyes.

"Are you okay?" I asked.

"What're you doing here?" he said. He didn't seem angry. Just baffled.

"I came to say I'm sorry," I said firmly. "I said some awful things to you last night, and then I bailed on you, and I'm sorry."

A couple of guys with guitars tromped past us, followed by two security guards in tight black polo shirts. I reached down to adjust Jasper's collar and brush his shoulder as if clearing away dandruff.

"Um, what're you doing?" he asked.

"Pretending I'm your stylist. Just go with it."

He smirked, which I took as a good sign, and I let out a breath.

"Look, I know I'm not exactly a monogamist," he said, facing forward as I smoothed the back of his shirt. "But a guy can change, can't he?"

My stomach was in so many knots I wasn't sure I'd ever be able to untangle them. This was the closest he'd come to some kind of declaration. Also, his shoulders were so perfect I almost wanted to bend over and lean my cheek against the back of the closest one.

"Sure . . . I guess," I said. I crouched to the floor in front of him, and we looked into each other's eyes. My heart caught. "If he really wants to."

"Yeah, well." He exhaled, turning his face away. "For me, I think it's about time."

"Why now?" I asked quietly.

He looked me in the eye. "You really gotta ask that question?"

For a moment I couldn't breathe. His words hung between us, waiting to be either acknowledged or laughed off. Then a guy toting a silver bass drum angled to get by me, and I fell forward attempting to get out of his way. Jasper grabbed me by the shoulders to keep me from face-planting into his crotch, and my hand ended up gripping the metal seat between his legs.

"Maybe we should stand up," Jasper suggested, amused.

"Yeah. That sounds like a plan."

He helped me to my feet, and we leaned back against the wall, our arms brushing. But still, the moment had passed. The spell was effectively broken.

"I should probably get back," I said.

I glanced at his profile. He was staring down at his beat-up brown cowboy boots.

"Thank you," he said finally. "Thank you for coming here and for saying all that." He looked at me out of the corner of his eye. "All's forgiven."

"Just like that?" I asked.

"Well, I happen to like you," he told me. "And I also happen to be wicked nervous, so at this very moment I can hardly even remember last night. You?"

I narrowed my eyes, pretending to think. "Can't hardly recall."

His grin widened at the hint of a Southern drawl I put on. "Perfect." He stood up straight and clapped his hands, then rubbed them together. "So you got any cures for stage fright on ya? 'Cause I could surely use one about now."

On impulse I reached out and grabbed his hands. He was so stunned he actually stopped his kinetic movement.

"You are going to do great," I told him, looking him directly in the eye. "You are *so* much better than those crappy loser bands you were in, and you are about to prove it."

Jasper searched my face, like he was waiting for the punch line. When it didn't come, he nodded. "Good. Okay. That's working. I like that."

"Now I have to go find Fiona and our seats before her head explodes." I didn't want to let go of his hands, but I did, giving them one last squeeze first.

"Fiona's here?" he asked.

"Yep. We both drove all this way to support you. See? You even come with a built-in fan club."

At this, Jasper smiled for real. "Oh, so now you're a fan, huh, Red Sox? You gonna be throwing your bra up onstage next?"

I rolled my eyes, even as my cheeks darkened. "You're gonna be just fine." I reached out and, in a gesture of patronizing reassurance, patted his chest. Big mistake. It was seriously firm, and now I was blushing even harder. "Break a leg out there!"

With that I turned away quickly before he could see the effect his physique was having on me. The last thing I wanted to do was walk back into the overcrowded auditorium. I felt more like taking a cold shower.

Down, girl, I told myself, glancing back over my shoulder. Jasper was still smiling at me. Snagged. When I turned around again, I nearly collided with Shelby.

"What're *you* doing here?" she sneered.

"People keep asking me that," I said, sidestepping her without answer.

Unfortunately, that maneuver brought me within two

steps of an extremely tall security guard. I froze.

"You don't have a pass, do you?" Shelby asked bitchily. I noticed with chagrin that she did have one, and hers was stamped TALENT. Clearly, Jasper had been given one extra badge, and it had gone to Shelby. That badge should have been mine. If only I hadn't jumped to conclusions yesterday, it *would* have been mine. Shelby raised her arm like she was in science class. "Security!"

The guard began to turn, and I did the only thing I could think to do. I ran. I ducked my head and bolted past his blind side so fast I was sure all he saw was a blur of red dress.

"Hey, you!" he shouted after me.

I dodged a pile of electrical equipment, then ducked under the beefy arms of a roadie lifting some sort of scaffolding piece high over his head. At the end of the hall, inexplicably, a bike was parked against the wall, I tossed it to the floor to impede the guard's progress and vaulted over some seated hipster's outstretched legs. When I came to the corner, I hazarded a glance back, and my pursuer was stuck behind the roadie. Still, there was really nowhere for me to go but back to my seat.

Far in the background, Shelby smirked and twiddled her fingers in a wave. She figured she'd gotten rid of me. And she had. For now. But hopefully not for long.

* * *

Jasper was a superstar. From the moment he took the stage, I couldn't tear my eyes off him, and neither could anyone else in the crowd. The girls down front were essentially whipped into a frenzy the second he launched into his up-tempo bridge; then they almost fainted as a group when the last romantic strains of his song drifted toward the vaulted ceiling.

The response was the loudest of the night. Fiona and I and half the people in the auditorium were on our feet. Jasper thanked the crowd, then slung his guitar behind his back and leaned in toward the mic.

"Now y'all keep your seats for me for a sec, 'cause there's someone special I gotta see."

He turned and, instead of striding off into the wings like the other acts had, jogged down the outer stairs I'd noticed earlier and into the auditorium. The girls in the first couple of rows grabbed at him, but he just kept right on walking, down the aisle, toward the back of the theater, toward me. I looked at Fiona, whose expression was unreadable, and by the time I looked back again, Jasper was there. How had he even found out where we were sitting?

"Lia," he said, his chest rising and falling with each ragged breath, "I've got something to tell ya."

"Really? Right now?" I asked, stunned. "Because I don't

know if you've noticed, but you're kinda in the middle of something."

He placed his hand over my mouth gently, but firmly. "Shut up, will ya? I'm trying to talk here."

"Okay," I said, as thousands of people stared. "What did you want to tell me? Go on. Talk."

He grinned. "You're the someone special."

Then he grabbed me around the waist with both strong, warm hands, pulled me against him, and kissed me.

That kiss. That kiss, that kiss, that kiss. It was still humming on my lips an hour later when the show was over and Jasper and I were backstage, his hand on the small of my back while he greeted a never-ending line of new fans, record label executives, and promoters. Everyone seemed to want to shake hands with Jasper Case, but Jasper Case couldn't seem to take his hands off me.

"So, where were we?" he asked, the second he had a break from all the schmoozing. He moved his hands to my hips and slowly backed me up against the poster-covered wall. I slid my arms around his neck and smiled. It turned out that Britta had told him where our seats were, and I was going to have to thank her later.

"Right about here, I believe."

I saw the grin spread across his face as my eyes fluttered closed. And then we were kissing again, and everything else faded—the champagne popping, the beer bottles clinking, the random strums of guitars and bursts of song. Jasper was all there was.

I couldn't believe this was happening. I couldn't believe I was here, backstage, at a Nashville music house, surrounded by musicians and publicists and groupies and roadies. Right now I should have been trapped in my dorm room, studying for finals, listening to the muffled murmur of Sarah Chin's voice as she recited her Latin verb conjugations next door. I should have been doing what was expected of me, like I'd always done. But instead I was here. I was free. And I was kissing the hottest guy on Earth.

Until he flinched. My eyes popped open as Jasper turned around. A man with slick black hair and a bolero tie over a white shirt stood behind him.

"Jasper," he said, offering his hand for a shake. "That song was gold. Gold! I'm so glad we took a chance and invited you back."

"Well, thanks, Jeff, I'm glad you did too." Jasper shook hands with the man, then put his arm around me. "Jeff Crandle, I'd like you to meet my . . . this . . . Lia. This is Lia Washington."

Jeff and I both laughed over Jasper's clear discomfort. He

seemed like a nice man. It was all in the eyes. They were kind and bright and crinkled around the edges. When he offered his hand, I shook it happily.

"Apparently, Jasper here isn't quite sure what you are," Jeff teased, making Jasper blush.

"It's okay. He can have a pass for tonight. This is all kinds of overwhelming," I replied.

"Well, it's about to get even more overwhelming." Jeff reached his thumbs inside the waistband of his jeans and hiked them up. "There's someone who wants to meet you, Jasper. Someone who only takes private meetings."

He gave Jasper this look like he should know who he was talking about, and suddenly Jasper's jaw dropped. "What? No. He's here?"

"Yep."

"And he wants to meet *me*?"

Clearly, this was super exciting. On par with the five-year-old me being told I was about to meet Dora the Explorer.

"Who's *he* and why are we so psyched?" I asked.

"*He* is Gary Benson, this incredibly reclusive record exec who is notoriously difficult to score a meeting with," Jeff explained, since Jasper was apparently too beside himself to form words. "You ready?" Jeff asked, turning to Jasper. "You don't want to keep him waiting."

"Um, yeah," Jasper said, repositioning his hat atop his head. "Are you gonna be okay here for a bit?"

I was honestly impressed he even remembered I was there, in his distracted state. "Yeah, of course. I'll just go track down Britta and Fiona. Do you think we should go? I mean . . . will this meeting be long, or—"

"No. Don't go," Jasper said firmly. He grasped my hand and squeezed it. "Please? I want you to be the first person to hear whatever happens."

My heart did a giddy twirling dance. He wanted me to be the first. Not Shelby, not Charlene, not window girl. Me. "Okay, then. I'll meet you back here."

He leaned in for another quick, firm kiss, then rolled his shoulders back and followed Jeff out the door and into the hall. I sighed and composed myself before trailing after them, determined to find Fiona and Britta, who would definitely know everything there was to know about this mysterious exec. Out in the hall I caught a couple of jealous scowls from overly made-up groupie types, but I ignored them. I was not going to think about all the girls who wanted Jasper. Not tonight. The only thing that mattered was that I wanted him. And clearly, he wanted me right back.

I moseyed down the rapidly emptying hallway, glancing into open doors as I went, and finally found Britta and Fiona, sitting on one of the two sets of stairs that led up to the stage. Fiona's face was in her hands, and Britta's arm was around her shoulders. My spirits instantly plummeted.

"Hey. Is everything okay?"

Fiona stood at the sound of my voice. "Let's get out of here," she muttered to the floor. Britta jumped up, shouldering her bag.

"What's going on?" I asked.

"We made a deal! You know I've liked him forever. How could you kiss him like that in front of everybody?" Fiona was so angry she was shaking. "In front of *me*?"

My throat was closing up so quickly, I couldn't find my voice.

"How could you?" she demanded.

"But Fiona, *he* kissed *me*!" I blurted.

Her face completely shut down. "Unbelievable."

Then she brushed past me and was gone.

"Britta," I stammered. "What just happened?"

"She said something about a pact?" Britta said, pushing her fake glasses up on her nose.

"Well . . . yeah. We said neither one of us would make a move on Jasper without telling the other first," I said, squirming. "But I didn't! You saw what happened, right? That was all him!"

Britta sighed. "Yeah, but he's basically the love of her life, Lia. Seeing a declaration like that in person . . . it might take her a while to adjust."

With an apologetic shrug, Britta chased after Fiona. I stood there for a long moment, wondering what I could have done differently. Should I not have gone backstage with him when he pulled me out of the crowd after the kiss? Should I have stayed to make sure Fiona was okay?

Oh, God. *Clearly*, I should have stayed to make sure Fiona was okay. But I'd been so wrapped up in the romance of the moment, in the kiss, in *Jasper*, that it hadn't even occurred to me until now.

There were many things I needed to learn about being in the real world. Apparently I could add friendship skills to the list.

Chapter Fourteen

"One southern fried chicken special and one burger deluxe, hold the pickles." I placed the food down on the tabletop with a broad smile. "Anything else I can get you folks?"

"You're sure happy," the woman who'd ordered the chicken said, looking me up and down with a smile. She had hair that was grayish purple, and she wore her pink-framed glasses around her neck, held by a beaded chain. "What's your secret?"

My secret? My secret was driving from Nashville to Sweetbriar in a classic convertible with the top down under the stars. My secret was spending two hours making out on a park bench in the middle of the night with a soon-to-be-superstar, handsome-as-all-get-out cowboy who shared his personal secrets with only me. My secret was that I was falling in love.

Jasper's meeting with Gary Benson had gone well. Right now he was meeting with an agent who might be able to negotiate some kind of deal for him. I knew zip about the music business, but it all sounded good to me, and this morning, when Jasper had stopped by my apartment, he'd been practically beside himself with excitement.

"Just having a good day, I guess," I told her, raising my shoulders and my palms.

She and her friend laughed as I twirled away. But then my smile died. Fiona stood behind the counter, scowling. The second our eyes met, she turned her back on me and went to check on some customers.

It had been like this all afternoon. Fiona hadn't said one word to me. Not "hello," not "hand me the sugar," not even "you suck." Every time I looked at her, I felt this distinct *thunk* inside my chest, like a door slamming closed. I hadn't meant to hurt her. I still wasn't entirely sure I'd done anything wrong. But she'd been so nice to me when I'd first arrived here, and ever since. I didn't want her to hate me.

But if she wouldn't even talk to me, what was I supposed to do?

I made the rounds of my various tables, refilling a coffee here, grabbing extra napkins there, then found myself with nowhere to go but behind the counter. Fiona turned around, her arms loaded down with half-empty, used dishes, and one of them bumped my hip. It crashed to the floor, shattering, and spewed tomato soup all over our shoes.

"Damn it, Lia!" Fiona shouted.

"I've got it! I've got it!" I said, grabbing a rag from under the sink.

I bent and quickly wiped off her sneaker, but it didn't help much. The tomato stain had already seeped into the white canvas. Fiona groaned, stepped over my hand and the shards of ceramic, and headed to the kitchen with the other dishes. I shakily cleaned up the mess, depositing the pieces of bowl in the garbage and mopping up the rest of the soup. At least it wiped right off my cowboy boots.

Which, I realized with a start, I still hadn't paid for.

"Way to be a klutz," Fiona muttered upon her return.

I stood up too fast, and all the blood rushed to my head. "That wasn't my fault."

"Well, it wasn't mine," she shot back.

The diner went quiet. Clearly, we were being way too loud. I grabbed Fiona's arm and dragged her toward the kitchen door, which was blocked from most of the diners' views.

"Are you going to hate me forever?" I asked under my breath.

Fiona's shoulders slumped. I sensed the hint of an opening. But before I could say anything, the front door of the diner swung wide and someone let out a loud, joyous, whoop.

"I got a record deal! I *have* a *record* deal!"

It was Jasper. He stood just inside the door, his arms outstretched, his face pink with joy and apparently exertion. Beads of sweat sluiced down his forehead, and he was heaving for breath, as if he'd just run a mile to get here.

"What?" I screeched.

A few of the diners applauded as I rounded the end of the counter and flung myself into Jasper's arms. He picked me up and twirled me around.

"I can't believe it! Can you believe it?" he asked me.

"Of course I can," I said, laughing. "I'm so happy for you."

"We have to go out to celebrate," he said, replacing my feet on the floor.

I looked over at Fiona. The scowl was back on. "Oh, I . . . I can't. I still have an hour left in my shift."

"Oh, please. Fiona won't mind—right, Fi?" Jasper said, so wrapped up in his own excitement that he was oblivious to the venom seeping from the corners of Fiona's mouth. "I mean, this is huge!"

Fiona stared at Jasper and, finally, her eyes softened. "Whatever."

With an air of defeat she pushed through the swinging door to the kitchen and disappeared.

"I really should probably stay," I said, feeling monumentally guilty. Though the pull to be with him, to share in his big moment, was overwhelming.

"Are you kidding? Come on. She just said you could go. And what's one hour when someone's lifelong dream just came true?"

"He's right, girlie. Go!" called out the woman with the fried chicken special.

A few of the other diners chimed in.

"Go!"

"Have fun!"

"Get out of here!"

"You only live once!"

It was that comment that finally convinced me. I'd escaped so I could live my life, right? I untied my apron from around my waist, tossed it across the counter, and went.

When I'd agreed to go back to Jasper's house, I'd been drunk on the romance of the evening and hadn't totally registered what I was agreeing to. We'd just finished the most delicious dinner at this adorable, candlelit restaurant where the staff waited on Jasper like he was a king, and treated me like his newly crowned queen. I hadn't eaten like that in days, hadn't felt this completely unstressed in years. So when he'd paid the check and leaned across the table and said, "Let's go hang out at my place," I'd immediately said, "Sure."

But now, there I was, on the porch of a tiny Victorian-style house, hoping it was too dark for him to notice my uncertainty as he unlocked the door. In the back of my mind I heard Duncan's voice, saying that this was exactly what he'd warned me would happen.

But things were different now. Jasper had kissed me in front of thousands of people, basically declaring that I was his one and only. He liked me. A lot. I knew this in my heart, no matter what Duncan's theories were.

"Well? What do you think?" Jasper asked as we stepped inside.

The first floor of the house had been converted into an open-concept apartment, with a modern kitchen at the back, a small dining area off to one side, and a living room right in front of us, which was dominated by a huge, leather couch and a flat-screen TV. Off to the right was a hallway, which I could only imagine led to the bedroom and bathroom. Which I did not want to think about.

"It's . . . nice," I said.

He closed the door behind us and stepped up next to me, surveying the room as if he was trying to see it through my eyes.

"You sound surprised."

"I guess I didn't . . . Do you have a job?" I asked, unable to stop myself. I'd only ever seen Jasper play onstage, and he seemed to wander the streets by day. He'd never mentioned any sort of job. And yet here he was with his own, very swank apartment.

Jasper laughed. "That's right, you don't know." He walked around the couch, the back of which faced the entry, and dropped down onto its comfy-looking cushions. "When I'm not taking classes at Freemont, I'm an assistant music teacher."

Now it was my turn to laugh. Jasper arched one eyebrow at me. "Wait. What?" I said.

"I teach music at the middle school and go to Freemont College," he said. "The year ended before you got here, so you caught me during my months of leisure."

"Oh. Wow."

I hovered behind the couch, toying with my own fingers as I tried to reconcile this new picture of Jasper as a responsible student and state employee with the picture I already had of a roguish singing cowboy. I didn't hate the combination.

"I'm working on getting my teaching certificate, but they

let me teach part-time in the meanwhile 'cause I'm just that good with a guitar," he said.

I nodded, and he turned in his seat, folding his arms on the back of the couch to look up at me. "So are you gonna join me over here, or what?"

"Oh. Sure."

I walked around the couch and sat next to him. Jasper let his arm fall around my shoulders, pulled me toward him with one hand, and kissed me, drawing my legs across his lap with his free hand. Suddenly I was very aware of every inch of my body. I was also very aware of how alone we were. How I'd never been this alone with a guy before. And how he'd been this alone with other girls. Many, many other girls.

As difficult as it was for my throbbing heart to understand, I pulled away.

"What's wrong?" Jasper asked.

"Nothing, I just . . ." I stared down at my lap, not wanting to ruin the moment, but unable to get the images out of my head. That girl leaning out the window the first day we met, Charlene waiting outside what was now clearly her apartment a couple of nights ago, Shelby warning me to stay away, Fiona's brokenhearted tears. And Duncan, Duncan, Duncan. I took a breath. "I just want to make sure that I'm the person you want to be here with."

"What?" he asked, leaning back. I noticed his lips were a bit swollen from the kiss. "Why would you say that?"

"Well, you could have anyone. Shelby, Charlene, all the girls at the concert last night, half the girls in town . . ."

You have *had them,* I thought but didn't say.

"Lia, you have to believe me. All that's over now," Jasper said, putting his hand on my knee. "I mean it. I know it might be fast, but you have this crazy effect on me. I can't explain it, I just . . . all I want is to be with you."

My heart swelled, but still I scoffed. Because how could this be possible? How could what he was saying really be true? He'd known me for less than a week—not counting those couple days when we were little—which he didn't technically know about.

"Hey? Who did I come to see the second I got the news today? Who did I kiss in front of all those people last night? You're the one I want to be with, and I don't care who knows it. I want *everyone* to know it."

My lips twitched into a smile. "Really?"

"Yes, really," he said. "You, Lia Washington, are the only girl I want."

He pulled me in for a hug, and I rested my head against his shoulder with a sigh. For a moment I felt perfectly content, but then the doubt began to creep in. I knew that

Jasper believed what he had said, but he didn't actually know what he was saying. I may have been the only one he wanted, but he didn't even know me. Not the real me.

Jasper held my face in his hands. "Why do you look like you're about to cry?"

I lifted my shoulders. "Happy, I guess."

He smiled and kissed me on the lips. "Good. Because I'm happy too. Everyone should be this happy."

Letting his hands fall to our laps, where they found and held mine, Jasper kissed me again, for real this time. The longer we kissed, the closer we moved to each other, the more the pounding of my heart intensified, and the easier it was to sweep my doubts to the furthest corners of my mind.

This was the real me now. Lia Washington was all I could be. Cecilia Montgomery was dead.

Or, at least, disappeared.

Spurred by a heady mix of freedom and desperation, I straddled Jasper on the couch, my knees pressing into the back cushions. He let out a surprised, but definitely pleased, sound and slid his hands around my back. I could feel him fumbling along the neckline of the dress, looking for a zipper or buttons, but it wasn't that kind of dress. It was more of a slip-on, slip-off kind of thing.

I imagined myself standing up and pulling the dress off

over my head, letting it pool on the floor, and standing in front of him in nothing but my lacy Target underwear. That was when I suddenly felt the need to come up for air. Again.

"Are you okay?" Jasper asked.

"Fine. Fine," I said, nodding. "I, um . . . I just . . . I've never done this before."

"Made out on a couch?" he asked, his brain clearly fogged over.

"I mean, I've never . . ." I cleared my throat.

"Really?" Every muscle in his body tensed, then suddenly slumped. "Oh. Okay, then." He sort of nudged me off his lap, and I ended up awkwardly sliding down his thigh until my butt hit the couch; then I had to extricate my legs from his. He drew a throw pillow into his lap and held it there tightly, like it was a life preserver. "So . . . we should talk about that."

"We don't have to." I was so unsure of what to do with my hands, I ended up sitting on them. "I mean, I just figured you should know."

"Well, we can, you know, go slow, if you want to," Jasper said.

He couldn't even look me in the eye. We'd gone from being closer than close to having a black hole yawn open between us.

"We don't have to do anything you don't want to do,"

Jasper told me, his voice clear, as if he was adjusting to the idea.

I tilted my head. All I knew was I was much happier five seconds ago when he was looking for a way to get my dress off.

"Well, I didn't say there weren't other things I wanted to do," I said flirtatiously.

He shot me a hopeful look and then smiled. "That sounds promising."

I grabbed his protective pillow, tossed it away, and settled myself back onto his lap. Jasper pulled me into the deepest but somehow gentlest kiss imaginable. After that, everything was a hazy, sweet, romantic blur.

I woke up cuddled back into Jasper's arms on Thursday morning, one week after my arrival in Sweetbriar, wearing one of his oversize white T-shirts. The sun slanted through the half-covered windows, and the birds outside were just beginning their morning song. I closed my eyes and tried to relax myself back to sleep, but I couldn't. What did people do in this situation? Should I get up? Wait for him to wake up? But now that I was fully awake, I realized his elbow was kind of digging into my side.

Finally I decided to roll over to face him. And when I

did, he stirred awake, squinting one eye open at me.

"I'm sorry. I didn't mean to wake you up. Go back to sleep," I whispered.

He smiled and kissed me with a closed mouth. "Best morning ever."

I smiled too. "Agreed."

Jasper rolled over onto his back, and I curled into the crook of his arm, resting my cheek on his bare chest. I couldn't believe that I'd spent the night at a guy's apartment. I couldn't believe all the things we'd done before we'd gone to sleep. I blushed now, just thinking about it, and my body gave an involuntary shiver.

"You okay?" he asked, reaching up a hand to toy with my curls.

"I'm great," I replied. I loved the way his chest rumbled against my ear when he talked.

"Good. Because I've been thinking. You helped make my dream come true, so as far as I can tell, now it's your turn."

I lifted my head. "My turn?"

"Yeah. You helped me, so now I'm gonna help you." Jasper lifted himself up onto his side, crooking his arm under him and resting his cheek on his hand. "So, what, exactly, do you want to do with your life?" he asked, nudging me in a teasing way with his knee.

I chewed on my bottom lip and mimicked his pose. "To . . . stay here with you all day and have you bring me breakfast in bed."

"That sounds perfect." He leaned in and kissed my nose, which just about killed me. "But that's what you want to do with your *day*. I'm talking about your life. Like, when you were a little kid, what did you want to be when you grew up? Or, I don't know, where do you see yourself in five years?"

"What is this, a college interview?" I asked.

He groaned. "Come on! Just humor me already."

He was so excited, it made me sad to admit the truth. "I don't . . . I don't really know."

I'd never allowed myself to dream of the future, of a career, of what I might actually want to do with my life, because I'd always known that my mother had every second of that life planned out for me. The only true dream I'd ever had was to get away from her. To escape the proverbial castle walls. To live life on my own terms. Jasper didn't know it, but I'd already achieved my dream, and he was a big part of it.

"You don't know?" His brow creased, like I'd just told him we were breaking up.

Of course. Jasper was a born dreamer. In his mind, being a person without something to strive for was like being a farmer without a field to hoe or a writer without a pen. Or a laptop.

A writer. I had always been good at that particular skill. It was the reason I'd had any money to speak of when I'd shown up in Sweetbriar. Writing term papers was my specialty. But it wasn't a dream.

"I guess I've never been much of a dreamer," I said, hoping he didn't think less of me for it.

Jasper reached out and ran his palm down my shoulder and along my arm. His touch sent my skin humming.

"All right," he said finally, then lifted my palm and kissed it. "I guess I'll just have to make that whole breakfast-in-bed thing come true."

He flung the covers off and got out of bed, hiking some jeans on over his boxer briefs.

"You don't have to do that."

"Oh, but you haven't eaten until you've tasted Jasper Case's scrambled-egg special," he replied with a wink. "I'll be right back."

In seconds I could hear him banging around in the kitchen, and I settled cozily into the pillows, sighing in complete and total happiness. The boy could sing, taught little kids for a living, and knew how to make eggs? No wonder everyone in town was in love with him.

Not wanting to think about that particular truth, I put my glasses on, picked up the TV remote from his bedside table, and turned on the small television atop his wide dresser. The second the screen lit up, I bolted up straight in bed, gulping for air. All sound was reduced to a loud buzzing in my ears. Behind a desk sat a female newscaster in a gray blazer, and emblazoned across the bottom of the screen in big red letters was the headline:

SEARCH IS ON FOR CECILIA MONTGOMERY, NOW PRESUMED A RUNAWAY.

Oh, holy disaster.

Shaking, I turned up the volume.

". . . though the senator has yet to release a recent photo. Sources close to the family say they prefer to handle the search on their own and not involve the public or the media. We now go to former FBI missing-persons expert Teresa Davidson for her opinion on this decision. Teresa?"

The screen split, and there sat a stern-looking woman with dark skin and a steel-gray helmet of hair. The greenscreens of the studio were badly reflected in her thick glasses, all but obliterating her pupils.

"Thank you for having me, Margot," Teresa said.

"Thank you for being here," the anchor replied. "We now know that the extra set of prints in the car belonged to a known associate of the car's driver, and that he has been cleared of all wrongdoing, which has led the authorities to shift their focus to Cecilia Montgomery herself, is that correct?"

"Yes. Without any other suspicious evidence, it seems clear that Miss Montgomery has fled on her own," the expert said.

I was going to be sick. I jumped out of bed and cracked the nearest window, but the air outside was hotter and thicker than the air in the bedroom, and it only brought on a new wave of nausea. I crawled back into bed, breathing deeply.

"All things considered, what do you think of this decision by the Montgomery family to continue to keep such a tight lid on their daughter's image?"

"It's idiotic, quite frankly," Teresa replied.

I groaned, holding both hands over my mouth. This wasn't happening. It was *not* happening.

"If this girl has run away and is out on some selfish joyride, then you can be sure someone out there has seen her," Teresa continued. "With the technology we have at our disposal today and the reach of social media, publishing her image increases the chances of finding their daughter exponentially. Senator Montgomery, wherever you are right now, I hope you're listening. If you want to find your daughter, you're going to have to show her *current* face."

I closed my eyes, but I could still see the expert's scowl as she stared down the camera. It was one thing if my mother thought someone had taken me. There would be leads to track down, suspects to interrogate, theories to hash out. The longer the investigation went on, the better the chance that they would one day give up and that I would be truly and utterly forever free.

But now that she believed I'd simply taken off, this whole thing would become personal to her. I had tarnished her image. I had made the world question what kind of mother she was, question her decision-making, question her character. For that she would hunt me down like a bloodhound. In one moment everything had changed. I knew my mother, and there would be no escaping her now.

I became dimly aware of Jasper's voice somewhere on the edges of my consciousness. Something moved in the corner of my vision, and I flinched. My finger automatically hit the off button on the remote.

"Lia? Are you in there? I only said your name ten times."

"I didn't hear you," I said.

Probably because my name isn't Lia. It's Cecilia. Which you're clearly going to know in the very near future, and then you're going to hate me for lying to you, and then you'll break up with me and run back to Shelby and my life will suck. Again.

"Okay . . . I just wanted to know if you like strawberries."

"Oh, no," I said absently. "I'm allergic."

He gave me an odd sort of look.

"What?" I asked, and it came out sharply.

"Nothing. I just had a weird déjà vu moment. When I was a kid, I gave this girl strawberries and almost killed her."

My stomach clenched. Yep. That was me. My throat had closed over until Gigi had stuck me with my EpiPen and saved my life. The allergy was less severe now—I'd just break out in hives and need an antihistamine—but it wasn't pleasant.

"Huh. Weird," I said, just to have something to say.

But Jasper was still looking at me. My insides began to squirm. Maybe we wouldn't have to wait until the media exposed me. Maybe he was realizing that I was, in fact, the girl he'd almost killed and was about to break up with me now.

Too good to be true. I should have known it was all too good to be true.

"Well, anyway. Grapes okay?" he asked.

"Sure."

He finally turned and walked away, though he did so very slowly, I noticed. As soon as he was out of sight, I lay flat on the bed and pulled the blue-and-white-striped sheets over me, letting them flutter down over my nose and forehead. I took deep breaths, trying to calm my nerves, trying to let the lingering scent of Jasper's warm body, mixed with the heady fabric softener, soothe me.

But they didn't. Because my mother was coming after me. And she wasn't going to stop until I was locked up in my tower again and she'd thrown away the key.

Chapter Fifteen

The sun blazed hot in the sky as I made my way across the park toward home. Jasper had offered to drive me, but I'd turned him down, telling him I wanted the fresh air and exercise. Which was true. I knew that if I didn't start moving soon, I was going to go insane.

But now that I was out in the open air, I was seriously regretting my decision. Every car held a team of reporters or an upstart private eye. Every slight movement was someone swooping down on me, ready to throw me into a waiting van. Was that man on that park bench watching me from behind those dark sunglasses?

As I passed by, he let out a snore, and I thought . . . maybe not.

Near the edge of the grass, the zydeco band played an upbeat tune while a group of men and women worked through a series of yoga poses, led by a lithe, dark-haired instructor. Was it just a few days ago that Fiona had been telling me how much she loathed this stuff? And now she basically hated me. As I hurried by, head down, the twanging of the banjo strings started to get under my skin. It didn't even make any sense—yoga was supposed to be relaxing, and this music was decidedly not. Maybe Fiona was right. Maybe this whole town was insane.

Or maybe I was just trying to find reasons not to like it because I knew that in the near future I was going to have to say good-bye to it.

I had almost made it to the sidewalk when I noticed a pair of joggers coming toward me. Duncan and Fiona.

"Oh, hey, guys!" I said brightly.

Maybe I could start to turn this thing around. Maybe Duncan would be able to broker some kind of peace between the two of us. "I was just heading back to—"

I stopped talking when Fiona and Duncan exchanged a glance, then parted to jog around me and kept right on going. I felt like one of them had hauled off and punched me in the gut. So now it wasn't just Fiona, but also Duncan giving me the silent treatment? Work was going to be a laugh riot this afternoon.

I turned in a brief, helpless circle, then sat down on the

nearest bench and hung my head in my hands. Maybe I should just give myself up. Someone was going to figure me out before long anyway. It wasn't as if everyone in Sweetbriar had their heads buried in the sand. At some point one of my mother's advisors would finally get through to her, she'd release the family picture from last Christmas, and the jig would be up. Maybe I should just go home and admit defeat. It wasn't like I was such a success story out here anyway. I had a low-paying job where the staff hated me and no friends to speak of.

But then there was Jasper. My body shivered, even as the sun beat down on my neck. I couldn't leave Jasper. That was not an option.

Suddenly a shadow fell across my face, cooling my skin. I squinted up to find Shelby standing over me in yoga pants and a blue crop top. The rest of the class was breaking up and moving off, and I realized that she had been, in fact, their instructor. I hadn't recognized her from behind.

"You teach yoga and zydeco?" I asked.

"It's Yoga *'n'* Zydeco," she said with a sneer. "And yes, I teach the *advanced* class, which meets every other Thursday. So. Getting the freeze-out from the Taylors, huh?" She tilted her head so that her heavy topknot shifted slightly from one side of her skull to the other. "That sucks. Those two are good people to know until they turn on you. Then they're like the New Jersey Mafia. Believe me. I should know."

I shoved myself to my feet, forcing Shelby back a few steps. "I don't remember asking your opinion."

"Wow. I thought you'd be in a better mood. After all, you officially snagged Jasper."

I narrowed my eyes at her. Had she just admitted defeat?

"For now," she added.

Of course not. Suddenly I remembered what Duncan had said about Shelby and Jasper, and how Ryan had described their relationship, and how he'd been talking to her right outside my door just a few nights ago. She was never going to give up. No matter what. Did I really want to live with that?

I shoved past her and headed for the sidewalk. A nice cold shower was seriously calling my name. Then I could take some time to myself and figure out my next move. Maybe I could ask Hal to pay me a day early and hit the road. But to where? If they could find me here, they could find me anywhere. And then, of course, there was Jasper.

"Where're you off to so fast?" Shelby asked.

"Is there a point to this conversation?" I demanded.

Her dark eyes narrowed. "You don't have to be such a—"

She stopped midsentence when I ducked behind the nearest tree, flattening my back against its trunk. I'd just spotted the black Town Car sliding ever so slowly past the park and had moved on instinct. I counted all the way to one hundred Mississippis before coming out of hiding. The car was nowhere to be seen, but Shelby still stood there, her gym bag on one shoulder and her rolled yoga mat hanging from a strap on the other.

"Is Jasper aware that you're a total freak?" she asked. "Because I think I'm going to call him right now."

Too overwhelmed to put together a comeback, I pushed past her and ran for Main Street. I emerged on the corner just across from the Book Nook, and the message on the side of the building nearly floored me.

IN A WORLD WHERE YOU CAN BE ANYTHING, BE YOURSELF.

"I can't believe we're actually doing this," I said, leaning in to take a sip through a red-striped straw.

"I know. We're just so cute, aren't we?" Jasper replied, sipping through his own. "I think I should write a song about us."

"You kids gonna order anything else?" Roy Hadley, my landlord and the man who'd tried to help me into his shop on my first morning in town, stood behind the counter, wiping his hands on a white towel.

Jasper was the first to lean back from our shared chocolate milkshake. It was so yum and so forbidden, I took an extra few draws on the straw while he wasn't looking. I'd spent half the morning locked in my room, trying to meditate but failing miserably to clear my mind. All I'd wanted to do was curl up under the covers for the rest of the day and will the world away, but that wasn't realistic. Not only because I didn't have superpowers, but because Jasper was leaving for Nashville this afternoon. He had to be there for the next few days to interview backup musicians and listen to demos at his new record label's offices. If anything was going to coax me out of my room and make me try to act normal, it was Jasper. Especially when I wasn't going to be seeing him for a while.

"I think we're good," Jasper said, sliding some cash across the counter. His phone beeped, and he checked the text, then quickly pocketed his phone.

"Who was that?" I asked, with a stomach-twisting feeling that I knew the answer.

"Shelby. Wishing me good luck." He forced a smile.

At least he wasn't lying. Or was he too oblivious to know that there was going to be tension about this?

"Jasper, about Shelby . . ."

His whole face tensed. "What about Shelby?"

I reached for his hand and held it lightly. "If we're going to do this . . . like, *really* do this . . . Be together," I clarified, when his expression didn't change. "I think you need to break up with Shelby."

I was going for a light tone, but Jasper didn't smile. "We did break up. Ages ago."

"Maybe, but I don't think she sees it that way," I said, my heart pounding. "She talks about the two of you like you're still together. And all the texts and the phone calls . . . And you call her 'babe.'"

Jasper finally let out a breath and his posture slumped. "I know. I know." He rubbed a hand over his face, then let it drop. "I've just never been able to say no to the girl, whether we were together or not."

I swallowed hard. What did that mean? If she called right now and asked him to come running, would he? And what would I do if he did?

"But for you, I will. I'll talk to her." He reached over and squeezed my hand. "I promise."

My relief could have inflated the entire store around us. "Thank you."

He checked his phone again. "It's almost time to go."

There was a hitch in my stomach that made me bend

slightly at the waist, but luckily, Jasper didn't notice. Roy rang us up and brought back the change, then moved down the counter toward the TV, where some football game was being replayed at a low volume. Roy was obsessed with Tennessee football, and always had some classic game cued up. Thank God. I wasn't sure I could handle another random appearance by my mother.

Jasper drew my hand onto his leg as my feet swung beneath me on the stool.

"Are you gonna be okay here without me?" he asked.

"This isn't really the nineteen fifties," I reminded him with a forced laugh, gesturing at the fluted milkshake glass. "I'm going to be fine."

I said it convincingly, even though I was lying through my teeth. Every time I thought about him not being here, I felt a tug on my heart so excruciating I wasn't sure I could survive it. I felt like if he left, this tiny little life I'd woven for myself was going to unravel. Like the moment he drove off, his space at the curb would be taken by that stupid Town Car, but this time, it would be full of FBI agents ready to squire me home.

Don't go, I wanted to say. *Don't leave me here all alone.*

But I couldn't. Because then I'd be the girl who was holding him back. The girl who was jeopardizing his dream.

I couldn't say it because then I'd be a pathetic loser, something I'd never thought I'd be. And above all, I couldn't say those words to him because if I did, then I might have to explain why.

"Make any headway with Fiona this morning?" Jasper asked.

"No. She still won't talk to me," I said, biting my lip. "I don't know how to fix it."

"I'm sorry if I made things worse between you when I stole you away last night," Jasper said, still holding my one hand with both of his. "I always knew she had a bit of a crush on me, but if I'd known it was going to get between you, I never would've—"

"Don't worry about it. Honestly," I said. "If anyone did something wrong, it was me. I just have to figure out how to make it up to her. I have to find a way to show her that her friendship matters just as much as you do."

"Really?" he asked, a joking lilt to his voice. "I don't matter just a scoch more?"

I wrinkled my nose. "Well, maybe just a scoch."

I leaned in to kiss him, and for that brief moment all my worries flew out the window.

"You should try to make up with her, though," Jasper said when we parted. "The Taylors are good people."

"Interesting how you say that when they all seem to dislike you so very much," I joked.

He chuckled and shook his head. "You have a point, but if they have any issues with me, that's my fault. You and Fi could be really good friends. See what you can do to work it out."

I sighed. Suddenly the weight of my many problems seemed to press down on me. Noticing my slumping body language, Jasper reached over to sling his arm around my shoulder, pulling me as close to his side as I could get without falling off my stool. I rested my head on his arm and smiled.

"I'll try," I said.

He turned his head to kiss my nose, which seemed to be his new favorite thing to do. "That's my girl. Come on. Let's head out."

He laced his fingers with mine, and we walked out into the sunshine, the bells over the door tinkling behind us. Half a second after we hit the sidewalk, the black Town Car slid into a spot right in front of us. Instantly my vision grayed, and my grip on Jasper's hand tightened even as my palm grew slick.

They'd found me. How the hell had they found me so fast?

The front door opened. A shiny black shoe hit the pavement, then another. I was opening my mouth, trying to find the words to explain to Jasper why I was about to be ripped away from him, when the man lifted his sunglasses from his eyes.

"Jasper Case?"

"That's me," Jasper said cheerily.

What? Why would the FBI know Jasper's name?

But then the driver went around to pop the trunk, and Jasper pulled a rolling suitcase away from the outer wall of Hadley's, and everything zipped into focus. This wasn't the FBI. It wasn't even the same Town Car I'd seen tooling around Sweetbriar. This was Jasper's ride to Nashville.

Jasper handed the luggage off to the driver, then faced me. "I figured I'd have them pick me up here so we could have a few more minutes together."

"That's so . . . sweet," I said, still recovering.

Jasper slipped his arms around me and drew me close. "I'll call Britta's phone when I get there and make her put you on the line," he said quietly.

"Sounds perfect," I replied.

We kissed, and I felt tears prickle at the corners of my eyes, as if I was sending him off to war or something. Idiotic. I knew it was. But at the same time, he was the only person here who cared about me. Possibly the only person in the world who cared about me. And after feeling so alone for so long, it was nice to feel needed, to feel seen, to feel like someone was looking forward to simply being with me. I didn't want to let that go.

Finally the driver cleared his throat. "Sorry, sir, but we should get going."

We parted, and Jasper gave me one last kiss. "Talk to you soon."

"Bye."

I waited until the car had pulled out and driven to the edge of the park before I turned away. My eyes fell on the gleaming sign for the Little Tree Diner, and I was suddenly infused with a fiery need to talk to Fiona. To make her talk to me. Maybe it was because I couldn't face my sadness or the idea of being alone, but I didn't care. What mattered was, I was feeling brave.

I stalked into the diner and walked right up to Fiona, who was chatting with one of the other waitresses. She tried to turn away when I approached, but I caught her arm.

"Fiona, come on. There has to be something we can do to get past this."

"Oh, really?" she fumed. "Does there? I've been trying to get Jasper to notice me forever, and then you just swoop in and steal him away. Thanks, but no thanks."

She turned and shoved open the swinging door to the kitchen, which almost hit me in the face when I went to follow. I caught it with the heel of my hand at the last second, sending sparks of pain up my arm and into my elbow. By the time I made it into the kitchen, she was slamming the door of the employee bathroom behind her. The lock clicked, and I deflated.

So much for the direct approach.

I was about to turn around and go when the small TV on the wall caught my attention. I knew I should look away before the news got any worse, but I couldn't. Because this time my dad was on the screen.

He wasn't front and center. That was my mom's natural position. But he hovered just behind her shoulder, and he looked haunted. There were bags under his eyes that I'd never seen before, and his hair seemed grayer around his ears. He stared directly into the camera as my mother spoke, but there was a distance in his gaze, like he wasn't really there. My mom had about fifty microphones shoved into her face.

I'd never seen my father look so distressed. So . . . shattered. Not even at Gigi's funeral.

But it was an act. It was all for the cameras, just like everything else in my parents' lives. It had to be . . . right?

"Honey, if you're out there and you can hear me, just come home," my mother said, her voice cracking at the perfect moment. "We love you, no matter what. We just want to know you're safe."

"That poor woman," one of the line cooks said. "To have an ungrateful daughter like that."

My heart twisted. She was such a fake. Such an awful, horrible liar. I was sure everyone watching that broadcast saw a heartbroken mother, issuing an emotional promise. But all I heard was a threat.

Chapter Sixteen

Sometime during my meditation the next morning—which was really not supposed to be spent thinking about such things—I realized I still hadn't paid for the boots Shelby had thrust upon me, and that fact didn't sit well with me. She'd basically handed them over as if they were some kind of payoff for staying away from Jasper, which I clearly hadn't done, and I needed to fix it. Plus, in all the chaos that my mind had become—worrying about my mother, about Jasper, about Fiona and Duncan—it was nice to have a clear-cut task to focus on. Something I could actually accomplish and put to rest. I got up, got dressed, and walked right over to Second Chances.

I glared at the stark black-and-white painting on the Book Nook's wall as I passed it.

THE TRUTH WILL SET YOU FREE.

I had started to sort of love the painter of these daily missives, but today he or she could suck it. The truth, in my case, would put me right back into solitary confinement.

My hand was on the door handle at Second Chances when I saw the HELP WANTED sign in the window. It was hand-drawn in big bubble letters decorated with glittery flowers. My pulse skipped ahead as I gazed through the glass at the racks of pretty clothes, the rhinestone jewelry twinkling in the sunlight. It all seemed so peaceful compared to the diner.

But then, did I really want to trade Fiona and Duncan's hostility for Shelby's? How had I made so many enemies when I hadn't even been here ten days?

I yanked open the door and stepped inside to the sound of tinkling bells. Tammy was behind the counter, placing a plate of lemon muffins atop the glass.

"Hey there, Fiddler!" she said brightly. "In the market for more sundresses?"

"Actually, I'm in the market for a job," I said, gesturing over my shoulder at the window. "Can I fill out an application, or—"

Tammy's dark eyes widened. "No. You can't."

"Oh." My heart sank. "Thanks anyway. Forget I asked. I'll just—"

"No! I mean, you're hired," Tammy said, waving her hands in a gesture of apology. "Can you start right away? Because old Mrs. Shilling just cleaned out her closets again and I have a whole mess of new stock to organize."

"Really?" I could barely contain my excitement. "Yes! That would be awesome."

"Well, then, awesome!" Tammy exclaimed. "Come on back and I'll show you the stockroom."

I walked around the counter and into a long, tight closet that was filled to overflowing with clothes. There were shelves marked HOLD FOR CUSTOMER, TO BE STEAMED, TO BE DRY CLEANED, and DONATE! Shoe boxes were shoved in every available corner, and a pile of hats teetered precariously on an old chintz chair.

"Wow. This is—"

"Wait a minute." Tammy's voice turned stern as she stared down at my feet. I was wearing the cowboy boots I had come here to pay for. The moment I'd seen the HELP WANTED sign, I'd completely spaced on my mission. "Did you pay for those?"

Her eyes narrowed shrewdly. How could she have possibly known I didn't pay for these boots? There was no computer in the store. No discernable security system.

"Um, no," I said, reaching into my pocket for some cash. "That's actually what I came over here to—"

"Good," Tammy said. "Consider them a signing bonus. Now let me show you what I need you to do."

I felt such a rush of relief I thought I might pass out. Tammy steered me toward the back corner of the room, where brown bags filled with rumpled clothes had been tossed on the floor. As she explained about checking for stains and wrinkles, how to sort what needed cleaning and what just needed to be pressed, I realized how blissfully quiet it was. Aside from my new boss's voice, there was nothing but the faint rustle of fabric when she pulled out a skirt, or a click of button to button as she lifted a blouse.

There were no order-up bells, no shouting diners, no plates crashing to the floor. And best of all, there wasn't a TV in sight.

The clothes! The clothes Tammy had stashed in her stockroom were divine. Every other garment I picked up and unfolded just begged to come home with me. Going through the bags was like taking part in a treasure hunt. And hanging the clothes just right, feeling the soft fabrics slip through my fingers, doing up the tiny pearl buttons or straightening a collar . . . it was all so satisfying. After years of being forced into pleated skirts, button-down shirts, conservative turtlenecks, and straight-legged jeans, this was like a dream come true. I even found myself arranging some of them into outfits on the racks. A plaid bolero jacket with a graphic T-shirt, a pair of chic crop pants, and a funky taxi-driver cap. A little black dress with a fuzzy white cardigan and a chunky faux-pearl necklace. A silk jumpsuit with stiletto heels and a glittery clutch. It was such fun I didn't even notice the time passing.

I wished Jasper was there so I could show him what I'd done. Maybe my dream was to be a stylist, or a buyer, or a designer. All I knew for sure was that in that tiny room surrounded by those beautiful things I felt at peace for the first time in two days.

"Wow, Fiddler! These are stunning!"

Tammy's voice startled me. I turned away from the jeans I was folding and saw her checking out my lineup of outfits.

"You think so?" I asked, my face warm. "I was just messing around."

"No! This is fabulous. You have a great eye," she said, touching the sleeve of the cardigan. "I think I'm going to put this one up in the window."

"Really?" I said, grinning. "I'm so flattered."

"Don't be," she said. "Be proud. You have a real talent."

As she lifted the outfit from the rack, I felt an almost overwhelming urge to throw my arms around her. Proud. When was the last time anyone had told me to be proud of anything I'd done? My eyes actually prickled, even as I realized how idiotic I was being. I'd put together an outfit. No big accomplishment. But somehow Tammy made it feel better than getting a big, fat A.

She came back from the front of the shop carrying the green dress that had been in the window.

"I think that'll do it for your first shift," she said. "So what did you think?"

"I had so much fun," I said, placing the jeans I was still clutching on the shelf behind me. "Thank you so much for hiring me!"

"No, thank you. Really, Lia. I think you're going to be a great fit here," Tammy said with a confident look around the stock room. "If you're free, you can come back on Monday, same time."

"Sounds great," I replied, though in the back of my mind I knew I had a shift at the diner on Monday. I decided right then and there to walk over and tell Hal I was moving on to another job. It had been in the back of my mind all day, but now I was officially sure. I couldn't keep working with people who hated me, and I was much more comfortable at Second Chances.

"Take a muffin on your way out!" Tammy called after me.

So I did, gratefully, carefully tearing little bits off and

popping them in my mouth as I walked down the street. I wondered what Jasper was doing right then and wished I could call him. But it was probably better that I couldn't. I didn't want to be too clingy. And besides, I was feeling better somehow. More secure. There was no way my mother was going to find me in the back room of a tiny consignment shop in the middle of nowhere Tennessee. I was safe in Sweetbriar. This was my home.

I walked into the diner through the back door and found Hal at his desk to the side of the kitchen. He was writing tiny numbers on tiny lines inside a huge ledger.

"Hal?" I began.

He looked up, his normally bright eyes tired. "Hello, Lia. Are you on today?"

"No. I actually came to . . . tender my resignation," I said. It sounded so much better than "quit."

"Oh. That's too bad." He turned a page in the ledger and ran his finger down a column of numbers that had my name printed at the top. Then he opened the bottom drawer of his desk and took out the lockbox where he kept petty cash. He counted out a wad of bills and handed them to me. "Good luck, wherever you're headed."

That was it? He wasn't upset with me? He wasn't going to beg me to stay?

"I'm not headed anywhere," I said. "I just got another job."

His thick eyebrows rose in surprise. "Huh. I figured you for a pit-stopper. Figured you were off to New York or California or something."

I shook my head, clutching my money in one hand and what was left of my muffin in the other. "Nope. I'm staying right here in Sweetbriar."

Hal nodded, and I wasn't sure if he was impressed or disappointed. His gaze trailed over his desk and he stopped to stare at something. I couldn't tell what.

"Is everything okay?" I asked him.

"What? Yeah. Yes. It's just, have you noticed anything wrong with Fiona lately?" he asked. "You two are friends. Maybe she told you something? She won't talk to me about whatever it is, but she seems so depressed."

My whole rib cage caved in on me. Little did he know that I was the reason she was depressed. "No," I replied, feeling seriously crappy. "I don't know what's going on."

"Well, I'm glad you're staying," he said, forcing a smile. "The more friends a girl has that she can trust, the better."

On my walk back to the apartment, the muffin sat in the pit of my stomach like a brick, but I tried to give myself a pep talk and reclaim my positivity. Fiona wasn't any angrier at me than she had been this morning when I was feeling better about things. All that had changed was that I now knew it was affecting her father. But somehow I couldn't get him out of my mind. The concerned expression on his face. He really cared about his daughter. About how she was feeling. And then I saw my own father's face. The way he'd looked on the TV yesterday. Was he really worried about me—or was he worried about what this was doing to my mom and their public image?

But what if he was *really* hurting? Because of me?

I didn't want to think about this. For years I had hoped and wished for a real relationship with my father, but every conversation cut short, every dismissive glance, every formal reply to an e-mail had crushed those hopes a little bit more until I'd finally closed myself off to the possibility. If only to protect myself. I couldn't start believing in him now. Not now.

I shoved open the door to my apartment and froze. On the front page of *OK!* magazine, which was right in the middle of the kitchen counter, was a picture of me and my parents. It was a photo that had hung, framed, on the wall of my bedroom at home my entire life. Originally published in the *New York Times*, it was an image of my mother and father sitting on a couch, holding a bundled-up baby with a pink cap on her head—me. My parents were glowing. My mother looked genuinely happy and for once was looking at me and not the camera.

It was my favorite picture of us, and of course I couldn't even remember where or when it was taken. And suddenly I couldn't look at it for one second longer. Britta's cell phone had been tossed onto the nearest couch, and I could hear her banging around in her bedroom.

"Hey, Britta! Can I borrow your phone for a sec?" I called out.

"Go crazy," she replied.

Inside my room I locked the door behind me and clutched the phone in both hands so tightly I was surprised it didn't shatter into a million tiny pieces. As sure as I'd been that Sweetbriar was my new home, I suddenly felt a burning need to get the hell out of here. To start running and never look back. Luckily, the one person who was keeping me here was not, in fact, here. At least not at the moment.

I perched on the edge of the bed and lifted the phone. Luckily, Britta had Jasper's number in her contacts list. My fingertips left tiny sweat prints on the screen. Jasper picked up on the first ring.

"Britta?"

"No. It's me."

"Oh. Hey, you," he said, his voice warm. "I was hoping you'd call."

"Yeah? Good. Want some company down in Nashville?"

There was a pause. "Are you kidding? Of course. Get your sweet butt down here."

That was all I needed to hear. "I'm on the next bus."

Chapter Seventeen

I'd been off the bus from Sweetbriar maybe thirteen seconds when Jasper had started talking, and he hadn't come up for breath once in the last hour. He was so excited about his publicist and his stylist and his meetings and just being in Nashville, it was like listening to a little kid describe his first ride on a horse. No, on a space shuttle. He was that beside himself.

Not that I was complaining. As we toured the streets of Nashville, the sun sinking low over the gleaming buildings, I was perfectly happy just relaxing into his excitement. I didn't have to worry. I didn't have to think. I could just be.

"Check this out!" Jasper grabbed my hand and pulled me toward a shop window surrounded by fluorescent orange lights. "They have every guitar known to man in this place, and a whole wall of 'em signed by every country act you've ever heard of—Emmylou Harris, Blake Shelton, the Dixie Chicks, Brad Paisley—everyone!"

"Maybe one day you'll have your guitar on the wall of fame," I suggested.

Jasper laughed, an incredulous laugh. His eyes were bright as stars. "Can you even imagine?"

"God, you're so cute. Just like the time when you—"

I paused, coughing on my own words. I had been seconds from giving myself away, from bringing up a memory I had of Jasper executing his first backflip off the monkey bars when we were little. He'd run around the playground with his arms raised in the air as if he'd just won a gold medal.

"The time when I what?" he asked, tilting his head quizzically.

"When I first saw you perform," I improvised. "I mean, you were all excited. Like a little kid."

Not really, but I couldn't think of anything else to say. Jasper eyed me in a suspicious sort of way, and I was sure I was toast. He was just about to figure it all out. But then he cracked a smile. "You're never gonna let me live that down, are you?"

I shook my head once. "Wasn't planning on it."

We turned and strolled in silence, hand in hand all the way down to the river, where the colorful lights of the city were reflected in the lazily moving water. Jasper paused and leaned in to the railing, looking up toward an illuminated bridge connecting the city to the far banks.

"I can't believe I'm actually here," he said, wide-eyed.

"You've been to Nashville before."

He lifted a shoulder as he turned around to look back at the downtown area. "Yeah, of course, I've been here a lot, but that's not really what I mean. I mean *here*, as a real musician, living the dream. It's insane."

My heart rate quickened on his behalf as I leaned back next to him.

"I guess I just never really thought it would happen. I mean, after my father bailed, I didn't think *anything* good could happen. Not for a really long time," he said. "Daria's great, don't get me wrong, but I always sort of felt like I was just waiting for the next tragedy . . . for the next person to up and leave. I think I knew she'd never do that to me, but I still woke up in a cold sweat more than once, terrified about it."

On impulse I reached out and took his hand. He let me, and I held it between us, gently rubbing his skin with the pad of my thumb.

"That's actually why I started writing music," Jasper told me. "To try to find a way to sort of deal with the loss. To deal with the fear. Ya know?"

"I can see that," I said.

"But I feel good now," he said, giving my hand a squeeze. "I feel sort of . . . solid, if that makes any sense. Like I can actually do this. Have a life and a future and live my dream."

I sighed and leaned over to rest my head against the side of his arm. It must have been so nice to feel that certainty. To know where you were headed and to feel secure in the fact that you were the one who'd chosen your path. I'd never chosen anything for myself. At least not until I met Jasper.

"You're not gonna up and leave, are ya?" Jasper asked. His tone was light, but I could hear the worry behind it, and it broke my heart. Because I might have to leave. I might have to leave in the very, very near future.

But when I looked up into his eyes, I knew I couldn't tell him that. Not now. Not when his whole life was about to change.

"No," I said. "I'm not going anywhere."

And in that moment I meant it. Because while someone might swoop in here and force me to go, I was never going to *choose* to leave him. Of that I was one hundred percent sure. And that had to mean something. It had to.

"Room service!"

I pushed myself up in bed as Jasper rolled the silver cart

into the room on Saturday morning. So far this trip had been an absolute dream. On Friday, whenever Jasper wasn't working, we'd spent our time cozied up in his posh, all-expenses-paid hotel room, and I felt completely detached from the outside world. Occupied as we were with each other, neither one of us had felt the need to turn on the television or look at his laptop or phone, and I was loving every minute of it. I'd spent my life locked away in a proverbial cell, resenting my isolation, but if I could have been locked in this room with Jasper forever, I wouldn't have minded it at all.

"What's your pleasure? Pancakes or waffles?" Jasper asked, lifting the silver domes off the plates with a flourish.

"One of each," I said.

"Indecisive, I like it," Jasper joked.

"Not indecisive. Adventurous," I corrected.

Jasper's grin widened. "Even better."

He handed me a wineglass full of orange juice, then grabbed the two plates and plopped down next to me on the bed, making me bounce. OJ sloshed over the rim onto the thick white hotel robe I was wearing.

"Oops. Sorry." He grimaced, then held out a piece of sausage. "Peace offering?"

I took a bite of the sausage. "What, no silverware?"

"You need silverware?" he asked, rolling up a pancake and taking a bite out of it like it was a burrito.

"No. I guess I don't." I snagged a waffle, dunked the corner in the tiny pitcher of syrup, then bit it off. Yum. I really did love this no-rules-having existence. My mother would have been appalled.

"So, tell me a little bit more about your dad," Jasper said out of nowhere.

He munched on a piece of bacon, an open, totally interested look on his face. Meanwhile my guts had twisted themselves up so tightly that the hunger I'd felt moments before was obliterated.

"My dad?" I repeated, stalling. The waffle found its way back to the plate, and I gripped the sheet at my sides. Suddenly all I could see was that image of my father from the press conference. His sad, staring eyes.

"Yeah. Or your family. I know you don't want to talk about your mom, but do you have any brothers or sisters?"

"No."

"Cousins?"

"Not really," I replied.

"Well, what about school? Did you like the school you went to? I bet you were adorable as a kid."

"Can we please talk about something else?" I blurted.

"Have you talked to Shelby yet?" I asked, hoping to change the subject.

Jasper's expression darkened. I knew I'd done something seriously wrong when he picked up his plate and put it on the bedside table. He leaned back against the headboard, crossing his arms over his perfect and bare chest. "No. I haven't. I figured I'd do it in person when I got home. And nice maneuver, trying to turn this around on me. I told you some pretty personal stuff last night, you know. I thought maybe you'd be in the mood to share."

I was at a loss for words. I hadn't meant to "turn it around on him." I'd simply panicked. And I had loved the fact that he'd opened up to me the night before, but there was no way I could do the same. I chewed on my lip, trying to figure out what to say. When I took too long to answer, Jasper reached for the TV remote.

"Forget it."

"No! Don't." I put my hand over his and he looked at me, startled. "I'm sorry, okay? I just didn't have the greatest childhood. The whole reason I came to Sweetbriar was to put it all behind me, so that's where I'd like it to stay. Behind me."

Please just leave it alone, I hoped. *Please, please, please.*

Finally Jasper lowered the remote into his lap. The look he gave me was so sympathetic it made me feel like a tremendous jerk. He thought I was some kind of victim. Like I needed to be handled with kid gloves. And maybe I was, on some level. Maybe the way my mother had treated me was wrong enough to call me a victim. But I certainly had it four hundred times better than a lot of other kids with negligent parents. At least I was always fed and clothed. I'd had a great education. I'd been protected, for what it was worth. And here I was, letting this awesome guy think I was needy and vulnerable and hurt.

"I just want you to know that you can trust me," Jasper said finally.

"I know," I told him. God, I sucked.

"Okay then. I hope one day you'll decide to tell me, but in the meantime I can wait."

"Thanks, Jasper," I said weakly, cuddling into the crook of his arm.

He kissed the top of my head, and I felt like the worst person alive. He was going to hate me when he found out who I really was, when he found out I'd been lying about everything. And I knew in that moment that it could never happen. I could never let him find out. I'd do everything in my power to keep my past a secret.

The photo shoot was in a long white room with lots of windows. Sunlight cut across the floor in big trapezoidal shapes as the photographer rearranged his screens to block it out. I sat on a wide, soft suede couch near the craft services table—which no one other than the photographer and Jasper had seemed to notice—and watched while Jasper was pawed by a half dozen models.

Not my favorite way to spend a Saturday morning, but Jasper was loving every minute of it.

"All right, Jasper, give me that closed-mouth smile the girls seem to love," the photographer directed.

A few of the leggy stick figures murmured their approval of this plan. One of them ran her hand through Jasper's thick blond hair, and then the stylist had to rush in and fix it. I tried not to turn entirely green.

"What is this for again?" I asked Evan Meyer, Jasper's new publicist.

There were about a dozen random people milling around, and only a few of them had been introduced to me. Micah, an A&R rep; Jasmine, the stylist; and Evan, who was permanently attached to his phone.

"Publicity stills," Evan answered, glancing up from the screen and through his thick glasses. He was wearing a wool scarf and a fedora, even though we were inside and it was ninety degrees out. "And possibly the album cover."

"Oh. Okay." So someday soon Jasper was going to be all

over iTunes being assaulted by six hot chicks in barely there dresses. Cool.

"Rebecca! Get in a little closer!" the photographer instructed. "Pretend he's a chocolate bar and you haven't eaten in two weeks."

"I haven't!" Rebecca joked, flipping her thick black hair over her shoulder. Everyone laughed. She had the darkest skin I'd ever seen and very full, very wide lips. She and Jasper made a dazzling couple, which was probably why she'd been chosen to stand right next to him for the photos.

Rebecca draped her arms around Jasper's chest and brought her leg up to his waist, where he was forced to hold it by the crook of her knee. She leaned so close her breasts flattened, and she made this fierce face, like she was actually about to bite a chunk out of his neck.

Jasper grinned.

"No, no. Give me the serious face for this one," the photographer ordered.

Jasper's eyes went smoldering. He was so good in front of the camera, while I couldn't even imagine being in his position. I absolutely hated having my picture taken. Always had, probably always would.

After snapping off about a hundred shots, the photographer told the girls to take a break. He wanted to get some pics of Jasper solo. Thank God. I was shocked when the model contingent raced for the craft services table. Every one of them grabbed a bottle of water, a coffee, and some sort of vegetable—dry.

"So, you're Jasper's girlfriend?" Rebecca asked, standing in front of me while she gnawed on some celery.

"Yes," I replied, rising to my feet. I tried to channel my mom's confidence, but they were all half a foot taller than me—which was weird, because I was used to being the tallest girl in any room—and a zillion times prettier. I shook my hair back, but of course my hair wasn't there anymore. "I'm Lia Washington."

"I'm Becks," she replied. "This is Sonia, Martika, Jen, Tonya, and Free."

"Hi," I said in a friendly way. None of the others replied.

"So tell us about him," Becks said, perching on the arm of the couch and sipping her water. "He is soooo hot. Where did he come from?"

"He's from Sweetbriar, Tennessee," I said. "A little less than an hour south of here."

They all laughed, but it wasn't a happy sound. It was quiet and snickery, as if no one had ever taught them how to properly feel or express joy.

"No, she means what's his deal? How was he discovered?

Is he actually going to be someone?" the girl named Sonia asked. She was wearing a white tank dress that was nearly the same color as her skin, and her shoulder blades stuck out of her back like shark fins. Her white-blond hair was cut short and styled so that it hid one of her eyes.

"He already is someone," I said defensively, and a few of them rolled their eyes. "He's a talented songwriter and an amazing singer." When these declarations seemed to bore them, I threw in, "Gary Benson signed him himself."

This got their attention. Every last one of them turned to look Jasper up and down covetously.

"Really?" Becks dragged the word out for the ultimate dramatic effect. "That's interesting."

I could practically see the scenario playing out in her mind's eye. How the second I went back to Sweetbriar she'd show up at his hotel, ask him out for drinks, maybe convince him to walk some red carpet with her somewhere. It would probably be great for her, or for any one of them, to snag the hot new prospect in town. My stomach turned at the thought.

"Okay, let's take five!" the photographer announced, popping a flash off his camera.

Jasper's shoulders relaxed, and he walked over to join us. "Ladies," he said, with his practiced, flirtatious grin. "How's it going over here?"

"Actually, I think I could use some fresh air."

I picked up my bag and headed for the hallway. I could feel the girls watching as I went, and I heard someone titter that awful laugh. Then Jasper caught up to me.

"Hey. You okay?" he asked, as the door swung closed behind us.

"I'm fine," I lied, feeling like I wanted to crawl out of my skin. "You should go back in there."

He smiled a knowing smile. "Lia, come on, you're not jealous of those girls, are you?"

"The Amazonian goddesses? Why would I be?" I shot back.

Jasper reached up to touch my cheek, his hand warm and familiar. "You are prettier than all of those girls put together."

"You mean like if you chopped them up and then Frankensteined them back together?" I commented. "Yes, then I could see how I might be prettier."

Jasper laughed, a real, hearty laugh. "Don't go," he said. "You're only here for a couple of days, and I don't want to be without you."

I took a deep breath, letting his words work their magic to uncoil my heartstrings.

"I know, but—"

"I told you, I only have eyes for one girl now," Jasper said, lowering his voice.

I smiled, and he leaned down and kissed me, pressing me back against the wall next to the door. I pulled him to me, holding him close, trying to make an impression for him to take back in there for the next two hours of being clawed by supermodels.

Then the elevator pinged and we broke apart. A short woman with purple bangs scurried over to us, a photographer right on her heels.

"You're Jasper Case, right?" she said, breathless. "I'm Virginia Daly from the music blog *Nashville Today*. Evan Meyer said he'd set aside some time for an interview."

Without warning the photographer lifted his camera and snapped a picture. I quickly turned away. Sweat prickled my upper lip. Had he gotten my face in that shot? What if it was published?

"Right. Yeah. He told me you'd be here," Jasper said.

"And is this your girlfriend? I'd love to talk to you, too," Virginia said hungrily. "Get the inside scoop on what Jasper's really like."

I heard the camera reel off another few shots. If I was in them, it was only the back of my head, which looked entirely different than it had a couple of weeks ago.

"What do you think, Lia?" Jasper asked.

"Actually, I really have to use the bathroom," I said,

making an awkward circle around them, trying to keep my back to the photographer. "You should get back in there. I'll just be a few minutes."

I rushed down the hallway and ducked around the corner, waiting for their voices to fade. When they did, I glanced over and saw the door to the studio swinging closed. I heard Jasper's laugh, muted by the door, and felt one horrible pang of regret before I changed into my sunglasses and bolted for the stairs.

Chapter Eighteen

"You sure you have to go back so early?" Jasper asked the next morning, stifling a yawn.

I slung my bag over my shoulder, wishing like hell I could stay. But I had a brand-new job and was expected to be there first thing tomorrow. I couldn't let Tammy down. Not if I wanted to stay in my apartment.

"I'm sorry. The Sunday bus schedule sucks." I leaned in to the bed to kiss him good-bye. He draped his heavy arm around me and almost succeeded in dragging me back down into the rumpled covers. Almost. I regained my balance and stood up straight.

"What're you doing today?" I asked.

"More meetings," Jasper said, reaching for the room-service

menu. "But I may actually get to listen to some demos. Apparently the label has a dozen songwriters who want to work with me. I'm cool like that."

"That's awesome. But they *are* going to let you record your own songs too, right?" I asked. "Because your songs are great and you need to get them out there."

"Yep. It's in the contract," Jasper replied, then gave me a slow smile. "Look at you, looking out for me."

"Hey, if I don't, who will?" I joked back.

Jasper laughed, then snapped his fingers and got out of bed. "Speaking of which, I bought you a present! Well, two presents. I mean, one's more for me and the other's more for you, but . . ."

Wearing only his boxers, he looked so completely gorgeous that I almost gave in to myself and crawled back into bed. Who needed a job? My boyfriend was about to be a superstar.

But I knew I couldn't think like that. Jasper (or his record company) had paid for every meal I'd eaten over the past couple of days, and it was starting to feel wrong. Like I was a kept woman. I wanted to rely on myself for a while, not go from relying on my mom to relying on some guy.

"Why do I get presents?" I asked.

He came back from the closet with his hands behind his

back and a serious grin on. "Which one do you want first? Yours, or mine?"

"Um . . . mine, I guess." What could he have possibly bought for me?

He brought his right hand out. It was clutching the neck of a cherry-red violin.

"What the—Jasper! You didn't!" I cried, my heart leaping.

"It's used, but refurbished," he said. "I got it at a little shop downtown. I had some free time when I first got here. They said it's perfectly tuned, so you can just have right at it."

He ran back to the closet for the bow and handed it to me.

"This is amazing!" I placed my chin in the chin rest and played a few notes of Tchaikovsky. The violin's sound was strong, its tones true. A shiver raced down my spine. Jasper watched me happily.

"I didn't think you should go another day without owning your own instrument," he said.

"Thank you so much!" I said, leaning in for a kiss. "It's perfect."

"You're welcome. The case is in the closet. But first, the second present."

I put the violin and bow down on the bed, and he handed me a clear plastic bag. "Sorry. I shoulda wrapped this one, but I hope you like it."

I pulled a small box out and gasped. It was an iPhone—the new one they'd introduced just last month. "Jasper, this is too much," I said.

"No, it's not. Like I said, it's not even for you, really; it's for me," he said, reaching for a T-shirt and pulling it on. "If I'm going to be here on occasion and you're going to be there, I need to have a way to get in touch with you."

I smiled. He really couldn't have been sweeter. "Thank you."

"It's all activated and whatever. You're on my friends and family plan."

I stood up on my toes and gave him a nice, long, grateful kiss. "Thank you. And now I have something to play with on the long ride home. I don't think the bus driver would want me messing around with the violin."

"I wish you were going to have me to mess around with," he replied. Moving his hips against mine, he pulled me to him.

I shoved him away with a laugh, and he waved me off like he was done with me. He went to the closet for the black violin case, put the instrument and bow away carefully, and then snapped the lid closed.

"Oh, and do me a solid, would ya?" he asked, crawling back onto the bed. I swear he was just rubbing it in. "Go by

Daria's and check in on her. She's not used to not having me around to bother her."

Like Daria was ever going to be anything other than strong, wise, independent Daria.

I smiled. "Will do."

After one last lingering kiss we said good-bye, and I found myself in the hallway, feeling heavy and sad and tired. Walking out of that room was a lot harder than I expected. When the elevator doors closed behind me, I leaned back against the wall and sighed. Then I heard a ping.

"What the—"

It took me way too long to realize it was my new phone. I dug it out of the box and checked the screen. There was a text from Jasper. It read:

MISS YOU ALREADY.

And I laughed, all alone, as the elevator zipped toward the ground.

When I stepped up onto Daria's porch that evening, uninvited, I was armed with a chocolate marble Bundt cake from Bake Me a Cake on Main Street. I had vivid memories of sitting around Daria's kitchen table, devouring one of these with her and Jasper and Gigi, laughing as we played Monopoly Junior and Jasper tried to buy up everyone's properties so he could be Lex Luthor. Which made sense at the time even if it didn't now. I couldn't believe Bake Me a Cake still sold these things, but then, if you managed to create cake perfection, I guess you didn't mess with it.

I took a deep breath and knocked on the door. I knew I was risking a lot, giving Daria some one-on-one face time. If she recognized me, I was in deep trouble. But I'd promised Jasper. And I'd only stay long enough to have dessert and a quick chat. Long enough to be able to assure him that Daria was just fine.

She opened the door. I put on my biggest smile, but it instantly fell. It was clear Daria had been crying.

"Oh," she said, with about one tenth of her usual enthusiasm. "Hello, sweet pea."

"Hi. I'm sorry . . . is this a bad time?" I asked.

Daria sniffled and straightened herself up, but her efforts did nothing to erase the redness around her eyes or the puffiness of her cheeks.

"No, no. I'm fine. Just an old woman being far too self-indulgent." She eyed my bakery bag. "Whatcha got there?"

"Chocolate marble cake," I replied meekly.

"Well, that's my favorite," she said, brightening a bit. "Weren't you sent from heaven at the exact right moment? Come on in."

Night was falling, and there wasn't a single light on inside the house. Everything felt dreary, even though nothing was out of place. Daria went right to the coffeemaker on her kitchen counter as I stood awkwardly in the doorway, wondering if I should turn on the light.

"I heard you went to see Jasper," she said, squinting back over her shoulder at me.

"Yeah. He sends his love." I placed the bakery bag on the small kitchen table and hung my bag on the back of the chair.

"Nashville's probably eating him alive by now." She reached for a tin of coffee and paused. "You mind turning on the light?" she asked. "When did this day get away from me?"

"Sure." I flicked the overhead light on, and the room was bathed in brightness so harsh I had to blink a few times to see. "And he's not being eaten alive, I promise. He seems very happy there, actually."

My heart turned a bit as I remembered Becks and the others, and my hand went to the phone in my back pocket. No new messages.

Daria scoffed. "He thinks he wants to be famous, but he doesn't know what it can do to a person."

I wondered if she was thinking about my dad. The way

he pulled away from her best friend, my Gigi, once the celebrated Montgomery family sucked him into their world of red carpets, state dinners, and summers at the Vineyard. But of course I couldn't ask.

She got everything measured the way she wanted it, then hit the on button and went for a knife, forks, and plates. I stood there feeling as if I should offer to help, but she moved so quickly she didn't even give me time. At the table she nodded toward the chair my bag was on, then sat down across from it. Obediently, I sat as well.

"Jasper may seem like he has it all together, like he's this confident adult person, but inside he's still a lost little boy."

Daria pulled the cake box out of the bag and popped it open. We both inhaled the thick, chocolatey scent of the cake, and my tongue prickled in anticipation.

"I don't know," I said, as she sliced into the cake. "He seems to be thinking a lot about his past and his future, and he even told me he feels solid right now. Like everything's coming together."

"That's great," she replied. "Until it all falls apart."

I chewed on my bottom lip. "I never knew you could be so negative."

Her eyes flashed a bit as she lifted a slice of cake onto a plate. "Well, you hardly know me at all, do you?"

My face burned. She handed me the plate, and I placed it in front of me but didn't feel like eating. "I just meant . . . from the way Jasper talks about you. . . ."

Really I was thinking about the way Gigi spoke about Daria back in the day. Like she was the be-all and end-all. Wise beyond her years. Solid and strong and always with her chin up. In Gigi's mind Daria was a cheerleader, the type of person who let the bad roll off her back. That was not the person staring back at me with watery eyes.

I wondered what had unsettled her so deeply, and then I thought of what Jasper had said. *She's not used to not having me around.*

I cleared my throat. "He's going to be fine, you know. And he's going to be back before you know it."

This was the mantra I'd been clinging to all day too. That soon Jasper would be back, and everything would return to normal. Sweetbriar felt empty without the possibility of bumping into him at every turn, of hearing his laugh just around the corner. But he'd be home again. Back before I knew it.

Daria took in a deep, broken breath, and her lips flicked quickly into a semblance of a smile. She took a bite of cake and closed her eyes, clearly savoring the taste. I felt proud of myself, suddenly. I'd said the right thing. I'd done the right thing.

But then she opened her eyes again and sighed. "Yeah, but not for long, honey. Not for long."

"New phone?"

I looked up from my lap, startled. Shelby stood in the doorway of the stockroom, her slim arms crossed over her chest. Her appearance was perfect, as usual, in a light yellow sundress with a white belt, her hair up in a high ponytail. If anyone ever popped in looking for extras for a movie that took place in the 1950s, Shelby was their girl.

"Yep. Bought it over the weekend. I lost my old one."

Wow. The lying was coming a lot easier these days. For some reason I didn't want to tell her that Jasper had given it to me. Jasper, whose radio silence was making me tense. Not that I thought something had happened to him, but what if he'd been distracted by something so huge that he couldn't check in? Or someone? I got up, shoved the phone into my back pocket, and went back to folding sweaters. Shelby just stood there.

"Oh."

Shelby leaned against the doorjamb, watching me. The longer she watched me, the hotter my skin burned.

"Did you need something?" I asked.

"You could have gotten a new one for free, you know.

Over at Teddy's? I mean, if you had the insurance. Did you have the insurance?" Shelby asked.

"No," I lied. Why were we talking about this? "It was a pretty cheap phone."

In fact Cecilia Montgomery's phone had been the most expensive phone on the market, complete with state-of-the-art GPS tracking system. Which was why it was now a wet pancake, probably sitting in a lab somewhere being analyzed by an expert CSI.

"Well, that one's not cheap." Shelby nodded at the bulge on my butt. "How'd you pay for that? I know you couldn't have been making much at the diner."

"How is it any of your business how I paid for my phone?" I asked incredulously. I grabbed a pair of jeans and whipped them in front of me to straighten them, but also to punctuate my point.

Shelby lifted her shoulders, unfazed. "I just think it's weird. You appear as if from nowhere, no phone, no clothes, no money. This is, what, your second shift here? Just wondering how you found the cash to buy a swanky phone."

"It was a gift from Jasper, okay?" I snapped. "Happy now?"

Shelby blinked, and I realized I'd hit her where it hurt. But my blood was up and I just wanted her to go away. And who knew? Maybe if she realized how serious Jasper and I were, she'd back off.

I pushed past her into the store, not really sure what I was doing. I just felt like I needed to move. But as soon as I stepped onto the floor, I saw the black Town Car again, through the plate-glass windows. It was pulling into a parking space right outside the door, and this time someone got out of the backseat. Not just anyone. This man was tall, no-nonsense, with square shoulders, gray hair, and a well-cut suit. His shoes shone in the morning sunlight as he buttoned his jacket closed. Then he adjusted the back placket, like he was trying to conceal something. Something like a holster.

I turned around again and bolted for the storeroom, slamming Shelby in the shoulder and knocking her sideways against the counter. The side door was completely barricaded with boxes, each one half dented and overflowing with clothes. Total fire hazard. Panic rose up in my throat. I had to get away. I had to get away.

"What are you doing, you freak?" Shelby demanded, clutching her shoulder.

The bells on the front door rang. I ducked behind a rack of winter coats.

"I'm not here, okay?" I whispered hoarsely. "I know

you hate me, Shelby, but please. Please! I'm not here."

Shelby was clearly baffled, but she reached over and pulled the door most of the way closed. I thanked her silently, though I wasn't convinced she was doing it for me. Maybe she was just trying to keep the crazy person away from her new client.

I heard her greet the man in the suit, but their voices were muffled by the coats and the door and the fact that they seemed to be speaking in unusually quiet tones. I could only make out a few words here and there.

". . . help you with . . . ?" Shelby said.

". . . looking for some . . . ," he replied.

Some*thing*? Some*one*? My heart pounded in my ears.

". . . right. No, no. Not necessary to . . ."

". . . that's it for now . . . be back. . . ."

Back? He was coming back? Why? When?

I heard the doorbells chime again and counted to twenty Mississippis. The door creaked open. I said a quick prayer. Then, with a sudden screech of metal against metal, the coats split and the air-conditioning rushed in on me.

"What. The hell. Are you *doing*?" Shelby demanded.

Crouched on the floor like a stowaway, I opened one eye.

"Is he gone?" I asked, cautiously standing.

"Who? Mr. Benson? Yes, he's gone!" Shelby said in a

huff. "Why are you hiding from Gary Benson?"

My jaw dropped slightly. "Wait. That was Gary Benson? The record producer?"

"Um, yeah!" Shelby raised one palm. "If you didn't even know who he was, then why the freak-out?"

"I don't . . . I thought . . . I thought he was someone else," I improvised, bringing a hand to my forehead. I stepped out of my hiding place, tripping on the top of an old hat box on my way. "Does he live around here?"

"Yeah. He lives up on Treemont," Shelby replied, gesturing vaguely. "He's Sweetbriar's most famous resident."

"So what's with the chauffeur? He doesn't drive?" I asked, trying to deflect attention from my odd behavior, stalling for time.

Shelby gave me this look, like I was asking the most irrelevant question ever. "No. He doesn't. So when he comes into town, he has a driver."

That explained it. That explained why I kept seeing that Town Car everywhere. It wasn't the government. They weren't tracking me somehow. It was Gary Benson. Jasper's new boss. I'd never felt so relieved in my life.

"Okay, *what* is your deal?" Shelby asked. "You are acting totally mentally unstable today."

"Back off, Shelby."

Her whole face fell. I couldn't believe I'd just said that. Apparently, I really was unstable. But between missing Jasper and not speaking to Fiona and knowing my mother was out there looking for me and the near miss with Gary Benson, I felt like I'd been pushed over the edge. Tears stung my eyes, and I realized I was shaking.

"Seriously. Stay out of my business," I said, somehow holding it together long enough to get my point across.

"I think you should go on your break," Shelby replied, her words clipped.

I felt this overwhelming need to apologize, but why? She was the one who was being nosy and rude. So instead I lifted my chin.

"Fine. I'll be back in fifteen minutes."

I slid past her into the store, then out the back door, behind the dressing rooms. The second the warm summer air hit my face, I started to cry. Big, loud, racking sobs of fear and relief and anger and sorrow. It was like every unshed tear from the last two weeks was coming out of me at the same time. It felt awful and cathartic all at once. Then my phone beeped with a text.

HAVING A GOOD DAY? IF NOT I'LL BE HOME IN EXACTLY SEVEN AND A HALF HOURS.

I laughed once through my tears and covered my face

with my hands. I really was losing it. And I was going to have to go back in there in fifteen minutes and work the rest of the day with Shelby. I was going to have to apologize and give her some kind of explanation for my behavior. I just hoped she stopped asking questions for which I didn't have any answers.

Chapter Nineteen

That night I found myself sitting at a center table at Sharky's, a midsize bar on the outskirts of Sweetbriar, with Duncan, Britta and Shelby. I'd come with Jasper, but Jasper was the talent (suddenly every venue in town wanted a piece of him), and by the time I'd come out from backstage to find a seat, nearly every seat had been taken. So even though Duncan was barely speaking to me and Shelby was my archnemesis, I'd decided to squeeze in with them. At least Britta didn't seem to be freezing me out on Fiona's behalf.

Now, about halfway through Jasper's set, I was seriously regretting my seating choice. Jasper was doing great, but the four of us had barely spoken in the twenty minutes we'd been sitting there. Aside from Shelby occasionally leaning over to whisper-shout something in Britta's ear, we were like four strangers.

"No laptop tonight?" I asked Britta during a break between songs.

"I've covered Jasper enough," she replied. "I'm going to wait until his first big show with the label. Which he'd better give me backstage access to."

"I'll make sure he does," I replied.

For some reason both Shelby and Duncan hit me with snide looks after that remark. What? What did I say?

Up onstage Jasper slung the strap of his black acoustic guitar over his shoulder and leaned toward the microphone. "This one goes out to that special girl in my life."

He winked at me and launched into an up-tempo song. Muttering something under her breath, Shelby left the table to get a drink. As she moved away, the crowd parted, and I caught a glimpse of Fiona down in front at a small table. She was leaning in to some guy, her hands folded on one of his shoulders as she whispered and giggled into his ear.

"Who's that guy Fiona's with?" I asked.

"Some dude she met at the diner today," Duncan replied flatly, the first words he'd spoken to me all night. "I think he goes to the college."

I rose up in my seat a bit to get a better angle. Fiona threw her head back in laughter and looked up at Jasper. He didn't notice, but it was obvious she was trying to get his attention. Maybe even trying to make him jealous. My butt hit the chair again, hard. I wasn't sure what to make of this. Should I be annoyed? Angry? Because the only thing I felt was sad. Fiona deserved better than to be crushing on a guy who had no interest in her. And if I hadn't been going out with that very same guy, I would have told her that. But as things stood, our situation was way too complicated. If I said anything to her about Jasper, she would take it the wrong way. In fact, when I'd stopped by Peach Street earlier today, the message on the wall had read:

WHEN IN DOUBT, SHUT UP.

So what was I supposed to do?

As Jasper launched into a guitar solo, Fiona and her guy got up from the table. He held her hand behind him as he navigated the crowd, headed for the back of the bar where the bathrooms were situated. Fiona glanced at Jasper one more time, but he still wasn't watching her. I saw her face fall, and almost wished he'd look over—give her the attention she wanted.

I kept an eye on the back of the room. Fiona and her man were nowhere to be seen. After five minutes I felt a tad concerned. After ten I was definitely worried. Finally I pushed my chair back and stood up.

"I'll be right back," I told Britta and Duncan.

Neither one of them replied or asked where I was going, which was fine by me. Hopefully, I was just going to find Fiona making out in the hallway with the new love of her life. But when I came around the corner, all I found was a long line of women waiting for the bathroom. Fiona and her man were nowhere. I edged along the wall, lined with photos of acts from days past, and came to the exit door. Before I even had a chance to look out the tiny window, I heard a shriek.

I shoved the door open. Pressed up against the wall was Fiona, and her date had his hand halfway up her skirt, pushing it up even higher. Fiona was trying to shove him away, but he kept her pinned to the wall with his hips and one hand against her shoulder. I glanced around, ripped the metal top off an old-school garbage can, and shouted as loud as I could.

"Hey!"

The guy instinctively turned around, and I whipped the garbage can lid across his face with a clang. The guy's head snapped to the side, and he hit the ground, out cold. Fiona stepped away from the wall, shaking.

"Omigod! Omigod, Lia, thank you!" she cried, throwing herself into my arms.

"Are you okay?" I asked, holding her at arm's length so I could check her over.

"I think so. I don't know."

Suddenly her face crumpled and she dissolved into tears. "I thought he really liked me."

I enveloped her into a hug and let her cry for half a second. "We should probably get out of here before he wakes up."

The guy let out a groan, and his knee started to bend.

"Go!" Fiona cried.

We raced around the corner and didn't look back until we'd made it to the sidewalk in front of the bar. Then we looked at each other and dissolved into nervous, adrenaline-fueled laughter.

"Truce? For real this time?" I asked.

Fiona nodded. "Let's go get some coffee."

"I feel so stupid."

Fiona sat at a booth at the diner, turning a white coffee mug around and around on the surface of the table. It was after midnight, and the skeleton shift was on, which was a good thing. If her father had seen how shaken and upset she was, he might have gone after the guy in the alley himself. Fiona didn't need any more drama. Not tonight.

"That's the last thing you should feel," I told her. I touched her wrist with my hand, and the cup stopped moving. "This was not your fault."

"Why are you being so nice to me?" Fiona asked. I could see her eyes fill with tears even though she was looking down at the table. It was like she was afraid to make eye contact. "I was so insane the other night at Jasper's show, and ever since . . ."

"You weren't insane. You just like the guy." I gave her wrist a squeeze before sitting back again. My own mug full of coffee sat untouched in front of me. I was too emotionally wound to drink it. "It's not like I can blame you."

"I know, but it's not your fault he likes you and not me," Fiona said, slumping back in her seat.

"Just so you know, Jasper does really care about you," I told her. "When he found out we weren't talking, he was all over me to find a way to make it up to you."

"Well, that's nice, I guess." Fiona started to spin her mug again. "Who wants one brother when you can have two?"

She managed another smile, but I could hear the regret in her voice. She really did like Jasper, and clearly it was going to take her a while to get over him. I just hoped that she would, and that we could find a way to be friends in the meantime.

A gaggle of girls walked by the diner window, dressed in tight jeans, leather jackets, and sky-high boots. One of them clutched a picture of Jasper, and I saw his signature scrawled across it.

"Honestly, you probably dodged a bullet with Jasper anyway," I said. "Everyone and their mother was in love with him already, but now that he's getting famous it's like everyone, their mother, their sister, and the house full of models next door."

Fiona laughed. It was a real laugh, which was very rare coming from her. That was when I knew for sure that she was going to be all right. That we were going to be all right.

"Wow. Fun!" She sat up a bit straighter in her seat and took a sip of her coffee. "Good luck with that one, Lia."

I laughed as well. "Thanks. I have a feeling I'm gonna need it."

When I glanced through the peephole early Tuesday morning and saw Shelby standing there in a blue-and-white seersucker dress, I recoiled. If there was one person I didn't want to deal with first thing in the morning, it was her.

"Britta went to work already," I said through the door.

"I'm not here to see Britta," she replied, looking directly at the peephole. The lens flattened her nose into a misshapen pancake. "I'm here to see you, *Cecilia*."

My whole body turned cold. I took a step back from the door. "What?"

"Let me in. We need to talk."

I glanced around the apartment. There was a fire escape out the front window, but I was wearing nothing but an oversize T-shirt and a pair of cotton shorts I'd stolen from Jasper. And where was I supposed to go? To Jasper's apartment? Like she couldn't find me there. Like she couldn't sic the police on me wherever I went in Sweetbriar.

Wait. Had she already told the police?

I lunged for the door and opened the lock. "Who did you tell?"

Shelby smirked, stepped into the room, and closed the door, her sleek ponytail swinging behind her.

"I haven't told anybody." She glanced at the stack of magazines on the kitchen island and snorted. Half of them were covered with pictures of me prior to second grade, or shots of my parents. "Oh. My. God. I can't believe Britta hasn't figured it out yet. She's *living* with you! But then again, I guess she's so busy trying to figure a way out of this town, she can't imagine anyone would ever actually run *to* here."

I locked the door but stayed close to it, just in case I had to bolt. What was I supposed to say here? Should I beg? Should I threaten her somehow? But with what?

"How did you figure it out?" I asked, both genuinely curious and stalling for time.

"One, you showed up here the day after Cecilia disappeared. Two, you had blood on your shirt when you dumped the tea all over me. Three, you 'lost' your phone, which is the only thing of Cecilia's they've recovered, and four, you go insane at the sight of a Town Car. Oh, and also? I heard on the news that Cecilia Montgomery was trained in three different martial arts, so when I saw you take out that guy last night? That was pretty much the clincher."

"You saw that?" I asked.

She nodded blithely as she flipped through the magazines. "You looked freaked when you breezed past the bar, so I followed you. I was watching through the back window."

"Well. Thanks for all the help."

"Clearly you don't need any, *Cecilia*."

She lifted up a copy of *Star* with my second-grade class photo on the cover and held it next to my face. Our eyes met. She looked way too satisfied with herself.

"What I don't get is why?" she said. "You had the perfect life. Famous parents, millions of dollars, everything you could ever possibly want. Why the hell would you run away?"

"Don't talk about my life," I said through my teeth. "You have no *clue* about my life."

Trembling, I stormed over to my room, where I started shoving the very few things I owned into my backpack.

"What're you doing?" Shelby asked, following me.

"Leaving. Isn't that what you want? You win. You want me gone so you can have Jasper all to yourself? He's yours."

Shelby leaned back against the doorjamb, eyes to the ceiling. "Cecilia," she said, drawing out my name in exasperation. Her voice had taken on this familiar tone, like we'd known one another our entire lives. It made me distinctly uncomfortable. "I'm not going to tell anyone."

I slapped my laptop closed and turned around slowly. "Somehow I hear an 'if' coming."

"That's because you're so well educated." She crossed the room very slowly. "I'm not going to tell anyone *if* you break up with Jasper. Today."

"Ha!" I picked up the laptop and shoved it into my backpack. "Why not just let me leave, then? You really need to torture me first?"

"Wow. You have a very low opinion of me," Shelby said. "I'm *letting* you stay because I know you need a place to hide out. Clearly there was something you liked about Sweetbriar, and I can't blame you, so why throw you out in the cold? You have a job, a place to live . . . friends, such as they are. I'm not totally callous."

"No. Not totally. All you're asking me to do is give up the guy I'm falling in love with." I blurted the words before I realized I was going to say them. Shelby's eyes widened slightly.

"Excuse me! *He's* in love with *me*. He always has been and he always will be." She sniffed. "He just needs to be reminded of that fact."

Her words still hung in the air when someone started pounding on the door.

"Now what?" I groused.

"Lia? It's me!" Jasper called out.

Shelby and I locked eyes. "Break up with him," Shelby said. "I mean it, Cecilia. Do it now or this whole adventure of yours is over. I'll have CNN, NBC, and MTV here before noon."

"Lia! Come on, open up! I have news!"

Feeling sick to my stomach, I rushed to unlock the door. Jasper barreled in, a bundle of excited energy. He wore a wrinkled gray T-shirt that showed off every one of his muscles, and his hair was mussed as if he'd just woken up.

"You are never gonna believe what my agent just told me!"

Shelby stepped out of the bedroom and Jasper stilled. He actually looked a little scared. "What're you doing here?"

"Just visiting. What did your agent tell you?" Shelby asked.

The smile returned full force. "Guess who's opening up for Luke Ralston at the arena *tomorrow night*!"

"No way!" I shouted.

"Jasper, that's amazing!" Shelby put in.

When Jasper grabbed me up in a hug and spun me around, I couldn't help feeling a rush of triumph. Take that, Shelby. The feeling died when he put me down again and I felt the sting of every last dagger she was staring at me. She wanted me to break up with him. She wanted me to break up with him now so she could take in every last, gory detail.

"They got me six seats down front with backstage passes," Jasper said, wiping his hands on the back of his jeans. "You'll be there, right? You know there's no way I can do this without you."

I glanced at Shelby. She looked quickly away. I couldn't believe she was really going to make me do this, but what choice did I have? It was either break up with Jasper or leave, which would mean being without Jasper anyway. As much as I hated Shelby in that moment, she had a point. I'd started to make a life here. I had a great apartment with a cool roommate, a job I loved, and as of last night Fiona and I were on the mend. Did I really want to press my luck and try again somewhere else?

But how could I possibly break the heart of the only person who cared about me?

Pressing my lips together to keep from crying, I looked up into Jasper's eyes. He was so happy. So very excited. I couldn't do it. I just couldn't.

"Jasper, I—"

"Lia? I need to talk to you a second," Shelby interjected.

"What?" I asked, baffled.

"Your room. Now."

Jasper looked about as confused as I felt when Shelby grabbed me by the wrist and dragged me into my bedroom. She turned around and clicked the door closed.

"You can't break up with him," she whispered.

My brain went weightless. "What? But you *just* said—"

"Not now," Shelby whispered through her teeth. "You saw how excited he is, and you know what almost happened when you didn't show up for that audition last week. If you don't go to this show, he's going to be devastated. We can't risk him getting up there and messing up. You can't break up with him. Not yet."

My brain was reeling. Was this how it was going to be now? Was Shelby Tanaka going to run my entire life?

But I decided not to look a gift horse in the mouth. I'd been granted a reprieve. I didn't have to crush Jasper's heart at the happiest moment of his life. I didn't have to crush my own heart.

"But after tomorrow night, as soon as this gig is over, you'll do it," Shelby said.

"Shelby . . ."

She leveled me with a glare. "You'll do it, or the entire

world will know exactly where Cecilia Montgomery's been hiding out."

"He's going to be shattered," I said, trying to make her hurt one tenth of the amount she was hurting me.

Oddly, Shelby smiled. "Well, that's just perfect, because then I'll be there to pick up the pieces."

She turned and yanked the door open, flouncing out of my room. "Good news, Jasper! I'm free tomorrow night too! Lia and I can *both* come."

Chapter Twenty

Sitting in the front row the following night with Britta, Fiona, Shelby, Daria, and Ryan, I was so nervous it might as well have been me going up on stage. The "arena" Jasper had so casually mentioned the day before had turned out to be Bridgestone Arena, where the Nashville Predators hockey team played and artists like Bruce Springsteen and Katy Perry had performed for sold-out crowds. The stage was huge and the audience was rowdy. We were so close, I could see the scuffs on the roadies' shoes as they placed the microphones on little x's of tape and made sure the drum set was perfectly positioned under the huge banner with the name JASPER CASE scrawled across it in red cursive.

"I can't believe he's playing the arena," Shelby said. For once there was not a hint of insincerity or judgment in her voice. She was as awed as the rest of us. "This is unreal."

"I hope they've set up their equipment right," Daria muttered, clutching her purse on her lap. "I've heard stories about people getting electrocuted on these stages just 'cause they plugged one wire in wrong."

"That's a happy thought," Shelby said.

Daria cut her a look that could have sliced through the heart of a raging bull. Shelby averted her eyes, and the lights went down. I didn't think anyone in the world could intimidate Shelby Tanaka, but clearly, Daria was the exception.

"Omigod." My hand automatically found Fiona's as the arena filled with cheers from the floor all the way up to the lofty ceilings miles above. "It's happening. It's really happening."

"He's gonna do fine," Fiona assured me, though her hand was sweating almost as much as mine. "He's gonna do great."

"Yes, he is," Shelby said, and looked at me. "You just remember what you have to do when he's done."

As if she was ever going to let me forget. I'd been trying not to think about it—trying to focus on sending only positive vibes Jasper's way—but every once in a while the reality of my tenuous situation would creep into my heart, shutting out everything else.

Break up with Jasper or get caught. Break up with Jasper

or go home. Break up with Jasper or face my mom. There was no choice really. Either way, after this concert Jasper and I were done.

"What's she talking about?" Fiona asked.

"Nothing. Don't worry about it."

I could tell Fiona was about to press the issue, but then Jasper walked out onstage and I automatically rose to my feet, dragging Fiona with me. The noise around us swelled once more. It was amazing how all those voices could blend into one bone-shaking shriek. How could Jasper look so comfortable up there? So confident? Clearly, he'd been blessed with natural stage presence. I couldn't imagine being in his shoes. Daria clutched her purse even tighter, while Shelby watched Jasper with covetous eyes. I looked down the row at Ryan, but he seemed to be busy telling all the girls around him that he knew Jasper personally. Smart guy.

Jasper and I had talked before the show about what he'd say when he came out and decided that he should keep it simple. "No one's really there to see me," Jasper had said. "They don't need to hear my life story. They just need to hear me sing."

Now he stepped up to the microphone and smiled. The arena's cameras projected his face up onto the jumbo screens surrounding the stage, and I could feel every girl in the room swoon. Or maybe that was just my heart flopping over.

"How y'all doin'? I'm Jasper Case," Jasper said. Then he looked down at me and winked.

The arena filled with more cheers, but Jasper had already launched into his first song, a quick, danceable tune that would definitely get the crowd in the mood to party. Fiona and I grinned at each other as his voice seemed to fill me from the inside out.

Jasper was doing it. He was living the dream, right here and now. I decided to let him take me along for the ride, to not think about what was going to happen later. This moment was all his.

Backstage was a total scene. We'd watched the entire concert, including the second opening act after Jasper, as well as Luke Ralston and his two encores. The moment the lights had gone up, the arena had started emptying out, and a bodyguard three times the size of the Tank had appeared to escort us to Jasper's dressing room. I had thought that having a backstage pass meant something, that only a few people would be allowed in this hallowed space, but as it turned out, the hallways were packed.

There were musicians, makeup artists, publicists, fans, and, of course, reporters. Every time I saw someone with a notepad, a recording device, or a camera, I turned my face away. By the time we got to Jasper's dressing room, I had whiplash. There was a line of girls waiting alongside the door, each of them clutching a T-shirt or a program and a Sharpie, and some of them bouncing on their toes like they had to pee.

Jasper's autograph. These girls were waiting to get my boyfriend's autograph.

"Wait here," the bodyguard ordered our little band. His voice was like an earthquake.

He rapped twice on the door, and Evan Meyer, Jasper's publicist, opened it. He smiled from behind his thick glasses when he saw me. "Lia! Come on in!"

The six of us walked inside to the groans of the waiting horde. Jasper was sitting on a red velvet couch answering questions into a smartphone for a reporter. His face lit up at the sight of us.

"Hey, y'all!"

He got up and hugged Daria, giving her a big kiss on one cheek. Then he grabbed me and bent me backward in a dramatic dip. I blushed and laughed as his hat tumbled off his head. He kissed me, and the rest of the world faded away, until I was back on my feet again.

"Can you believe this?" Jasper asked, widening his arms. The dressing room was large, with a flat-screen TV, a few couches, a well-lit mirror, and half a dozen people milling around.

"Jasper, you were amazing," Fiona told him, reaching out to squeeze his hand.

He leaned in to hug her. "Thank you. Thanks for coming."

He hugged Shelby, too, and slapped hands with Ryan. The second his back was turned, Shelby gave me a wide-eyed, prompting look. My heart thunked. Now? She wanted me to break up with him now? In front of everybody?

"Hey, you guys mind if I have a minute alone with Lia?" Jasper asked, holding my hand in his.

Now my heart really started to pound. He didn't know what he was asking for. If we were left alone, then I'd really have no excuse not to break up with him.

"No, that's okay, really," I said. "Don't throw them out. We just got here."

But Evan was already ushering everybody to and through the door. I heard the girls outside groan again when it started to close.

"C'mere."

Jasper pulled me to him by the belt loop on my jeans and kissed me in a way that made me forget about everything else. His hand cupped my neck, and I could practically feel the energy pulsating off of him. When he finally pulled back, he held me so close, all I could see was him. His deep blue eyes, his kiss-stung lips. I wanted to stay right there, forever.

"I love you," he said.

My heart exploded, and my smile nearly split my face. But in the next second it hit me, what I was supposed to be doing—what I *had* to do—and I took a step back.

"No . . . you don't mean that," I said, my insides twisting and contracting. "That's just the adrenaline talking."

"No, no. It's not." Jasper grabbed my hand and pulled me against him again. "I was going to tell you the other day, before you left Nashville, but I chickened out. If anything, the adrenaline's making me brave." He held his hands gently against the sides of my face and made me look him in the eye. "Lia, I know it's fast. I know it's crazy. But being with you . . . it's like coming home. I feel like with you is where I'm supposed to be. It's where I want to be."

My resolve crumbled. How could it not, hearing a speech like that? He'd just put into words exactly what I'd been feeling for days. "Jasper . . . I love you too."

His smile was heart-stopping. Our lips met, and we kissed and kissed like there was nothing else in the world to do.

Then there was a knock at the door, and it opened a crack. Evan stuck his head in.

"Hey, Jasper, you really should come out here and greet some of your fans," he said.

Jasper grinned at me. "Fans. You hear that? I got fans."

"Go. Meet your adoring public," I said, squeezing his hand.

Evan opened the door wider.

"Only if you come with me."

I laughed and Jasper tugged me over to the door. The second we were through it, the screaming started, and then I was blinded. Camera flashes popped and strobed as the girls waiting in line moved forward as one to mob Jasper. I threw my hand up to block my face from the wall of photographers. My heart pounded an erratic beat inside my throat as Jasper's hand was ripped out of mine. He was surrounded. I searched for an escape route and saw Fiona, Britta, and Daria shooting me concerned looks. Then Shelby grabbed me and flung me back into the dressing room, slamming the door behind us.

"That was not good," she said.

"Oh my God. Oh my God. Oh my God."

My brain could form no words other than those. I walked to the farthest wall and pressed my back up against it, sinking to the floor with my hands to my temples. Phantom flashes floated across my vision, and I knew Shelby was talking—could see her lips moving—but all I could hear were the screams and the sound of the blood rushing through my ears.

They'd gotten my picture. They must have. There were dozens of them. Dozens. And not just professional photographers. All those fans with camera phones and Facebook pages and Instagram accounts and blogs. Someone was going to post a picture with me in it.

I should have known this was going to happen. I'd gotten sloppy. Careless. Too wrapped up in Jasper. And now I was totally and utterly screwed.

Shelby knelt on the floor in front of me and brought her hands down on top of my boots as if she was holding my feet down to help me do sit ups in PE. Suddenly the room zipped into focus. I could hear again.

"Lia! Lia! Talk to me! Are you okay? Are you having a panic attack?"

"They're gonna out me," I said. "You won't have to do it because they're going to do it for you."

Someone pounded on the door, and I flinched.

"It's okay. I locked it," Shelby said.

"I can't go home, Shelby. I can't go back there. I can't."

She sat back on her heels. For the first time since I'd known her, I felt as if she actually saw me. "Wow. What did they do to you?"

I looked away, rubbing my chin on the side of my arm.

I couldn't have stopped shaking if I tried, so I didn't bother. I just sat there, trembling like a leaf, in front of my worst enemy.

"Listen, maybe it's okay," she said kindly. "Maybe none of them got a clear shot of you."

"You think?" I knew it was impossible, but if there was hope, my heart wanted to cling to it.

"It's possible. Phones take crappy pictures anyway, and the photogs will crop you out. They don't want Jasper's random girlfriend; they want Jasper."

I sat up a little straighter. She was making sense. I wasn't sure why she was helping me, but she was making sense.

"But you do realize now that you *have* to break up with him. Right?"

She didn't sound malicious or mean or condescending. Just matter-of-fact.

"After tonight, his life's only gonna get crazier. He's going to have photographers following him around everywhere. If they didn't get a picture of you now, they will eventually."

"Lia! What's going on in there? Are you guys all right?" Fiona called out from the other side of the door. The doorknob jiggled and Shelby got up.

"One second!" she shouted. Then she turned to look down at me. "This isn't just about me and Jasper anymore. If you want to stay missing, you can't be photographed. And if you can't be photographed . . ."

I swallowed back tears as the truth of what she was saying crept across my chest and froze my heart.

". . . then I can't be with Jasper."

"That was amazing. Jasper was *amazing*!" Fiona gushed from the front seat of Britta's truck.

"Yeah, Lia, how's it feel to be dating a superstar?" Britta asked.

I didn't answer. I couldn't have even if I wanted to. I could feel Shelby's eyes on me from across the bench in the backseat, but I didn't dare give her the satisfaction of returning her gaze. Instead I stared out the window, trying to distract my mind by counting the stars, but it was no use. My heart had been beaten to a bloody pulp, and every time I tried to take a deep breath, I nearly choked.

It didn't matter whether or not Shelby was holding my secret identity over my head. I was going to have to break up with Jasper anyway. I couldn't go anywhere near him if he was going to be hounded by photographers and fans. My mother would find me in a hot minute.

There was no getting out of it. Jasper and I were through.

"Lia? Are you okay?" Fiona asked, turning around in her seat.

"Fine. Just tired," I muttered.

"How can you be tired? I feel like I'm never gonna sleep again!" Fiona replied. "This is the coolest thing that's happened to one of our friends since . . . well, ever. And you're his girlfriend. You're going to get to go to red-carpet events and concerts and maybe even be in magazines! It's so cool!"

I clenched my jaw. There was no way she could have known how she was gnawing on every last one of my frayed nerves right then. How she was spelling out my worst nightmare.

My phone rang. I looked at the screen. Jasper. Of course it was Jasper. Who else would have been calling me?

"Is that him? Where is he? I bet he's at some awesome Luke Ralston after-party. We should go!"

I hit the ignore button.

Fiona's eyes narrowed. "Did you just ignore him?"

"Fiona, enough," Shelby snapped.

I saw Britta's eyes flick in the rearview to look back at us. I stared at Shelby.

"What?" Fiona asked. "I was just—"

"You're just driving everyone crazy with your nonstop commentary," Shelby said. "Leave Lia alone. She's clearly crashing. In fact, I think we could all use some peace and quiet for the rest of the drive."

As if to contradict her sister, Britta turned on the stereo full blast. Thankfully, she chose an alt-rock station and not a country one. But while it wasn't the peace and quiet Shelby had asked for, it did have the desired effect. Fiona sat back down in her seat in a huff and faced forward. There was no way anyone could talk over the din.

As grateful as I felt toward Shelby for getting Fiona to stop, I wasn't about to show it. Instead I curled into a ball, as far away from her as I could get, and leaned my head on the door. I had no clue why she'd gotten my back just then, why she'd been so nice to me earlier in the dressing room, but she was not my friend.

I closed my eyes and prayed for sleep and that somehow when I woke up, this would all turn out to be one big nightmare.

Chapter Twenty-One

I was up all night trying to figure out what to say to Jasper. How was I going to explain the fact that I was breaking up with him? He knew I loved him. He knew I was happy whenever I was with him. I couldn't walk in there and say, "Jasper, I have to break up with you because I can't be photographed with you," so . . . what?

As I approached Daria's garage, I could hear the strains of his guitar music. My insides were tied into intricate, inextricable knots. He was going to hate me. He was going to hate me forever. And the thought of that was worse than anything else I'd ever dealt with.

This morning the Peach Street wall had proclaimed, in big red letters:

COURAGE IS BEING SCARED TO DEATH AND SADDLING UP ANYWAY.

But did that mean I should be brave enough to break up with Jasper, or brave enough to come clean and deal with the consequences?

Maybe I should just tell him the truth, I thought, arriving at the exterior door. *Maybe he'll understand and we can run away together.*

But I knew that wasn't even a remote possibility. Even if Jasper did forgive all the lying I'd done, he'd never agree to go on the lam with me. We'd only known each other two weeks, and he was just now grasping his lifelong dream. There was no way I could ruin that for him. I loved him too much to do that.

Chin up, Cecilia. Just get in there and get this over with.

Hand shaking, I pushed open the door. Jasper immediately looked up, and his face broke out in a killer grin. He was standing in the middle of the room in front of a mic stand, his guitar strap slung over one shoulder, his blond hair still wet from his shower. He took the guitar off, placed it on a nearby stand, and threw his arms open.

"How's it feel to be the girlfriend of country's newly minted Next Big Thing?" he asked.

All I wanted to do was run into those arms and let him

hold me. I wanted to tell him everything and have him say that we'd figure it out. That everything would be all right. But that just wasn't possible. I hugged myself but otherwise couldn't seem to make myself move.

"What's wrong?" Jasper's arms fell along with his face.

"I can't do this," I croaked.

"Can't do what?" he asked.

"This. Us," I said. Somehow I managed to look him in the eye. I owed him that much, at least. Jasper looked stricken.

"What?" He closed the space between us in three long strides and reached for my hand. I angled away from him, still clutching my own arms, afraid of what I might do if he touched me. "Lia . . . why? What's this about? Is it about last night? All those girls? I told you, none of that means anything to me. You're the only girl I want."

I blinked. How had I not thought of this before? It was the perfect excuse for a breakup. Jealousy. Irrational, insane jealousy.

"Really?" I spat. "Have you talked to Shelby yet? Have you told her it's over?"

He groaned and covered his face with his hands. "It's complicated."

"How is it complicated?" His response had gotten right under my skin, and real anger bubbled to the surface. "You told me you'd talk to her. You promised me. If you won't even do that, then how do I know you *won't* hook up with some other girl on the road?" I demanded, infusing my voice with venom. "You're going to be spending more time in Nashville, going to all these swank events, meeting more models and singers and . . ."

My throat tightened at the thought, and I realized that all of that actually would suck, knowing he was out there surrounded by girls who wanted a piece of him. It made it that much easier to sound believable when I said, "How am I ever going to be able to trust you?"

Jasper took a step back. His hurt was written all over his face. "How will you be able to trust me? Because I'd never cheat on you, Lia. I told you I loved you. You know how many girls I've said that to?"

I shook my head ever so slightly, not trusting myself to speak.

"Zero. Zilch. Not one," he told me.

Not possible. Not. Possible. All that time he'd been with Shelby, all the faith she had in the fact that they were going to be together in the end, and he'd never said those three little words to her?

But when I looked into his eyes, I knew he was telling the truth, and my heart shattered all over again.

"It doesn't matter," I said.

"How?" His voice broke, and the look on his face nearly

killed me. "How can you say that to me? It does matter. It matters more than anything."

He grabbed me by my upper arms, gently but firmly, and pulled me as close as we could get with my elbows and wrists between us.

"I love you, Lia."

One tear spilled over onto my cheek. What I wouldn't have given to hear him say that and use my real name. But he wasn't talking to me. He was talking to a lie. And it was my fault. I'd done this to him. To us.

"I know you think that, but it's not true," I said. "Besides, your dream matters to you too. And you're right on the verge of living it."

I managed, somehow, to squirm my way out of his grip and turn my back on him.

"You should go live it, Jasper. Go start the life you were meant to have . . . without any strings attached."

My limbs felt heavy as I moved toward the door, as if uttering those words had added a hundred pounds to my frame.

"Lia." His voice was strained. "Lia, don't."

"Break a leg, Jasper," I said.

Then I yanked the door open, leaving my heart on the garage floor behind me, and ran.

* * *

IT'S DONE.

I texted a simple message to Shelby and hit send, just as I got to the top of the steps on the Taylors' front porch. The sky was overcast, a blanket of swirling shades of gray, and as I reached for the doorbell, a warm wind nearly knocked me sideways. I was barely holding it together, gasping in breaths and hugging my hoodie to my sides, and when Duncan opened the door, I just started crying.

"Lia, what happened?" he asked.

I took a step toward him, he took a step toward me, and before I knew it my face was pressed into his shoulder and his arms were around me. My whole body was racked with sobs, and try as I might, I couldn't seem to get out a coherent word other than "Jasper."

"Oh, man." Duncan reached up and placed his warm hand atop my head. "He broke your heart, didn't he?"

I looked up at him through my tears. "No," I managed to get out. "I think I broke his."

Duncan blinked. "Come on inside before you get blown away."

We walked into the house, through the foyer, and into the large living room. There was a NASCAR race on the large-screen TV. We sat down on the couch and Duncan handed me a box of tissues.

"It's gonna be okay," he told me. "Honestly, as crappy as you feel now, you're better off in the long run. Jasper is . . . he's not good enough for you."

I looked up at him, my eyes rimmed with wet. "Thanks, but don't do that. Don't talk bad about him. He didn't do anything wrong."

Duncan shoved his hands down his thighs. "Yeah, not yet," he said under his breath.

The front door slammed, and Fiona walked in, shaking out her denim jacket. "It just started to pour out there," she said, and froze in the doorway when she saw me.

"Lia! What's wrong?" she asked.

"She and Jasper broke up," Duncan informed her.

"What? No! Why?"

Fiona plopped down next to me and pulled me into a hug. As awful as I felt at that moment, this was kind of nice, having people to talk to, people to commiserate with. Maybe Jasper wasn't the only person who cared about me after all.

"I don't want to talk about it," I said.

In truth I couldn't talk about it. None of it would make sense without all the details. Details I could never, ever share.

"Okay, then you don't have to," Fiona said. "Duncan,

find us a stupid buddy comedy to watch. I'm going to go make the sickest ice cream sundaes you've ever seen."

"No, that's okay," I said, and blew my nose. "I'm sure you guys have stuff to do. You don't have to sit around and coddle me."

"Oh, but we want to," Duncan said, reaching for the remote.

Fiona paused halfway to the kitchen and looked back at me. "That's what friends are for."

By the time the sun began to creep through my windows, my eyes were so puffy and dry I wasn't sure I'd ever see straight again. Fiona, Duncan, and I had spent all day watching stupid movies and eating junk food, and by the time I'd left their house late the night before, I'd started to feel like maybe I could do this. Maybe I could lead a Jasper-free existence.

Then I'd been alone, for hours on end, and my brain and my heart had gone to war. And there is no sleeping in wartime.

The pounding on the door sent me vaulting to my feet. I grabbed my phone and checked the time. It was barely five a.m. This time it had to be the FBI. Who else would be here that early? Clearly, one of the pictures from the concert had gotten out. Someone who knew me had seen it and contacted the authorities. I stood there for a moment at the foot of my bed, frozen, my pulse racing a mile a minute and then, suddenly, I didn't care. I was too tired and too sad and too disappointed to care.

I walked to the door and opened it without even checking the peephole. Jasper took two steps into the room, grabbed me in his arms, and kissed me. He tasted of beer covered up by mint toothpaste, but it didn't matter. My whole body surrendered, until I heard Britta's footfall behind us.

"What's going on?" she asked.

Jasper pulled away and looked me in the eye. "What's going on is that I'm not going to let you break up with me," he said. "I love you, okay? I told Shelby last night that I love you. That whole thing? It's over. And I am going to show you exactly how much of a choirboy I can be. I'm going to *make* you trust me. You got it?"

My chest heaved. He'd talked to Shelby? Really? Now? Finally?

And then I went weightless. If he'd broken it off with her, she must have been pissed. What if she'd decided to take revenge? What if she'd outed me?

"Lia? Are you even listening to me?"

I focused on Jasper. His blue eyes. The desperation and hope in them. And I forgot about everything else. I just wanted him. He was the only thing in the entire world that I wanted. I leaned in to him and he wrapped his arms around me and sighed.

"Yes," I said. "Yes, I'm listening. And I love you, too."

"Thank the good Lord," he said into my hair.

This was going to work. It had to work. I'd tell Jasper the truth. If he really loved me, he would understand. Daria could back me up—tell him just how strict my mother was. He'd understand why I'd done what I'd done. And then he could help me talk to Shelby and convince her not to sell me out.

It was a thin hope, but it was hope.

Two hours later, at Jasper's house, I was curled up against his chest, content and half-clothed, while he gently combed his fingertips over my hair in a soothing, rhythmic way.

"What were you thinking yesterday?" he murmured, and kissed my forehead lightly.

"I don't know. Obviously I had some kind of psychotic break."

My tone was light, but my chest felt heavy and full. At some point I was going to have to tell him the truth.

About who I was. About why I was here. At some point I was going to have to deal with Shelby, too. Convince her to let us be.

But not now. Not right this second. So I decided to enjoy this while it lasted.

"I love you, you know," Jasper said, leaning back so he could look me in the eye. "No matter what."

His gaze was so intense that for a brief, crazy moment I wondered if he knew. If maybe he was prompting me to say something to reveal myself. It was on the tip of my tongue, but then my meager courage dissolved.

"I love you too." I took a breath. "No matter what."

The front door opened and slammed, and Jasper instantly sprang out of bed. "What the—"

Suddenly Shelby appeared in the bedroom doorway, totally out of breath and disheveled in pajama pants and a sweatshirt. Sitting up, I was about to explain what I was doing in Jasper's bed, but she didn't seem at all shocked. Just pale. Sweaty and very pale.

"Shelby?" Jasper exclaimed, grabbing a pair of shorts off the floor. "What the hell? Do you really think you can just waltz in here and—"

"You have to go," Shelby said to me, cutting him off. "They're here, Lia. You have to get out of here. Now."

My heart plummeted into my toes, even as I swung my legs over the side of the bed. Jeans. Where the hell were my jeans? I fumbled my glasses from the bedside table and shoved them on.

"What do you mean?" I demanded. "Who did you tell?"

"I didn't tell anyone. I swear."

She strode past me toward the window, and I heard the squealing of brakes. It was like a death knell. Shelby turned and looked me in the eye. "It's too late. They're here."

"What are you guys talking about?" Jasper said, his brow creased as he yanked his shorts up. "Who's they and why are they here?"

I didn't answer him. I couldn't. I ran out of the bedroom and headed for the back door, but I could see them through every window. Men in black, slowly approaching the house. I was surrounded. I stood in the kitchen, shaking, and brought my fists to my temples. Of course there was no escape. How had I ever thought I could get away with this? There was no possible way my mother would let me win. No way in hell.

There were heavy footsteps on the front porch. I slowly returned to the bedroom, where Jasper stood in his rumpled T-shirt and shorts, his hair matted on one side. I closed my eyes and braced myself for what was about to happen.

"Jasper," I said. "I'm sorry. I'm so, so sorry."

His eyes were concerned, scared. He reached for one of my hands with both of his and held it tightly. "Lia, what—?"

Outside the windows, voices began to shout. The press. "Cecilia! Cecilia, come to the window!"

I looked at Jasper guiltily, and his face flooded with understanding. In fact, he understood so quickly it was almost wrong.

"Oh my God, you *are* her!" he exclaimed. "I can't believe it. I thought it was you, but I—"

"You did?" I asked, panicked. "What? When?"

Someone pounded on the front door. Shelby yelped.

"At the lake that night. And then with the strawberries . . . and in Nashville the other night something you said kind of clinched it, but I didn't think it was possible." He said this in a rush, grasping onto my hand. I was so grateful that he was still grasping onto my hand. "Why didn't you tell me?"

"I couldn't," I said, terrified tears spilling over. I felt like my life was about to end.

"Why?" Jasper asked again, his eyes pleading.

"Because." My voice was a whisper. "I didn't want to go back."

I envisioned my mother standing on the front porch in one of her severe suits, her fingers clasped in front of her waist, her face fixed in a determined scowl. She'd come at last. Come to take every last thing away from me. My worst nightmare was coming true, right here and now.

"Jasper Case! We know you're in there!"

The three of us shared an alarmed glance. The oxygen was sucked out of the room. Why were they shouting Jasper's name and not mine?

"Miss Montgomery! If you can hear us, stay clear of the door. We're coming in!"

Jasper made a move for the living room, but before he took three steps, there was a bang, and a crack, and half a dozen men in riot gear were breaching the front doorway. They had guns. Big, ugly, terrifying guns. And they were all trained on Jasper.

"No!" I screamed. "Don't!"

"Hands up! Hands where we can see them!" they shouted.

Jasper flinched, a full-body convulsion, and backed up against the wall.

"What are you doing?" Shelby shouted.

One of the men whirled on her, gun at the ready. "You too! Hands up!"

Shelby complied, shooting me a terrified, shocked, and somehow also murderous glare.

"Down on the floor! Down on the floor!" the man in the lead shouted in Jasper's face. The barrel of his gun loomed ever closer to his chest.

"Stop it! He didn't do anything!" I cried. "He's just my—"

"Get her out of here," the lead man growled.

Someone stepped up from behind and grabbed me, his arms locked tight around my body, pinning my elbows to my sides.

"No!" I screamed. "You have to listen to me! He didn't do anything wrong!"

But the men ignored me. They converged on Jasper and Shelby, forcing them first to their knees and then flat to the floor. As I was carried through the door, I heard the sound of handcuffs snapping around Jasper's wrists.

"Jasper Case, you are under arrest for the kidnapping of Cecilia Montgomery . . ."

Outside, an army of press was being pushed back by local police. A crowd of neighbors had formed off to the side, everyone craning their necks to see what was going on. As I was hauled off toward a waiting FBI van, I saw Jasper and Shelby being led out of the house, their hands cuffed behind their backs, their heads down.

"No, please. You have to listen to me," I said to the officer manhandling me into the van. Tears spilled down my face, but I wiped them quickly away. “They didn’t do anything.”

Without replying, the man shoved me inside and slammed the door in my face. I whirled around. There my mother sat, against the far wall of the van. The suit was just as I’d imagined, the hands clasped in her lap. But she wasn’t scowling at all. In fact she was smiling.

“Hello, Cecilia.”

Acknowledgments

Thank you so much to Sara Sargent, who knows a good hook when she thinks of one, and to Sarah Burnes, who is such a great support in everything I do. Also, most humble thanks to Liesa Abrams, who swooped in like the Batgirl Editor she is and helped me find the right project when I needed it, and to Alyson Heller for bringing it all home. I love it when a great team comes together!